Charles M. Schulz

PEANUTS ™

Special thanks to the Schulz family, everyone at Charles M. Schulz Creative Associates, and Charles M. Schulz for his singular achievement in shaping these beloved characters.

Cover
Art by **Charles M. Schulz**
Color & Design by **Nomi Kane**

Trade Designer: **Kara Leoaprd**
Assistant Editor: **Alex Galer**
Editor: **Shannon Watters**

For Charles M. Schulz Creative Associates
Creative Director: **Paige Braddock**
Managing Editor: **Alexis E. Fajardo**

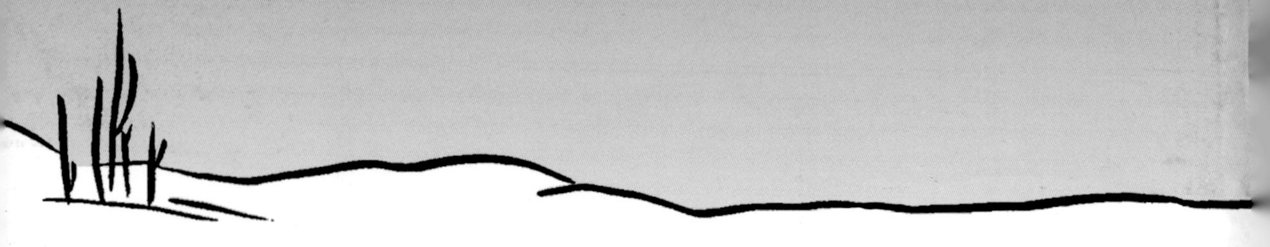

ROSS RICHIE CEO & Founder • MATT GAGNON Editor-in-Chief • FILIP SABLIK President of Publishing & Marketing • STEPHEN CHRISTY President of Development • LANCE KREITER VP of Licensing & Merchandising • PHIL BARBARO VP of Finance • BRYCE CARLSON Managing Editor • MEL CAYLO Marketing Manager • SCOTT NEWMAN Production Design Manager • IRENE BRADISH Operations Manager • CHRISTINE DINH Brand Communications Manager • SIERRA HAHN Senior Editor • DAFNA PLEBAN Editor • SHANNON WATTERS Editor • ERIC HARBURN Editor • WHITNEY LEOPARD Associate Editor • JASMINE AMIRI Associate Editor • CHRIS ROSA Associate Editor • ALEX GALER Assistant Editor • CAMERON CHITTOCK Assistant Editor • MARY GUMPORT Assistant Editor • KELSEY DIETERICH Production Designer • JILLIAN CRAB Production Designer • KARA LEOPARD Production Designer • MICHELLE ANKLEY Production Design Assistant • AARON FERRARA Operations Coordinator • ELIZABETH LOUGHRIDGE Accounting Coordinator • JOSÉ MEZA Sales Assistant • JAMES ARRIOLA Mailroom Assistant • STEPHANIE HOCUTT Marketing Assistant • SAM KUSEK Direct Market Representative • HILLARY LEVI Executive Assistant • KATE ALBIN Administrative Assistant

PEANUTS Volume Seven, April 2016. Published by KaBOOM!, a division of Boom Entertainment, Inc. Peanuts is ™ & © 2016 Peanuts Worldwide, LLC. Originally published in single magazine form as PEANUTS: Volume Two No. 21-24. ™ & © 2014, 2015 Peanuts Worldwide, LLC. All rights reserved. KaBOOM!™ and the KaBOOM! logo are trademarks of Boom Entertainment, Inc., registered in various countries and categories. All characters, events, and institutions depicted herein are fictional. Any similarity between any of the names, characters, persons, events, and/or institutions in this publication to actual names, characters, and persons, whether living or dead, events, and/or institutions is unintended and purely coincidental. KaBOOM! does not read or accept unsolicited submissions of ideas, stories, or artwork.

A catalog record of this book is available from OCLC and from the BOOM! Studios website, www.kaboom-studios.com, on the Librarians Page.

BOOM! Studios, 5670 Wilshire Boulevard, Suite 450, Los Angeles, CA 90036-5679. China. First Printing.

ISBN: 978-1-60886-790-5, eISBN: 978-1-61398-461-1

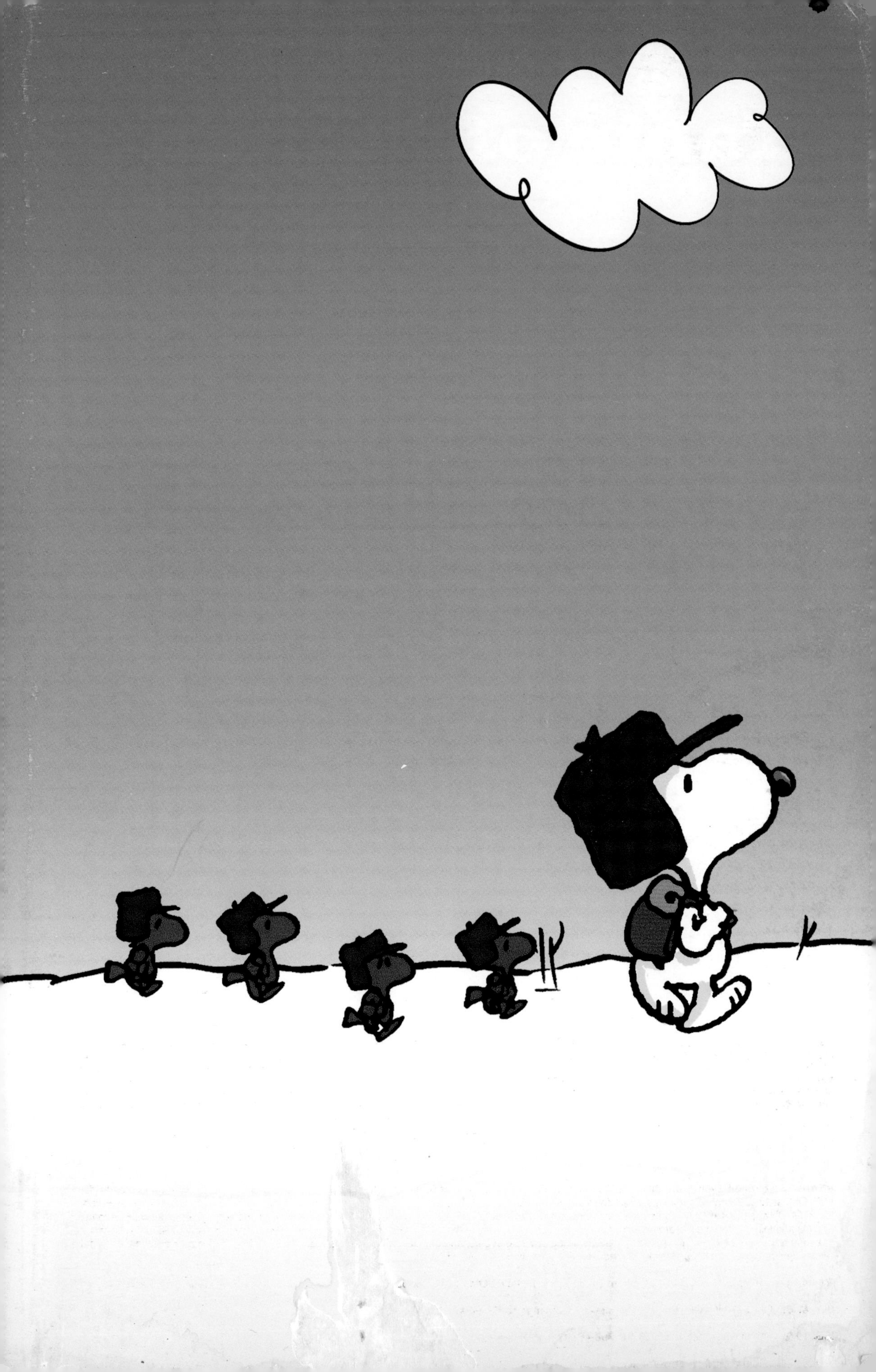

Table of Contents

Classic Peanuts Strips by
Charles M. Schulz
Colors by Justin Thompson & Katharine Efird

From the Drawing Board
Designed by Nomi Kane

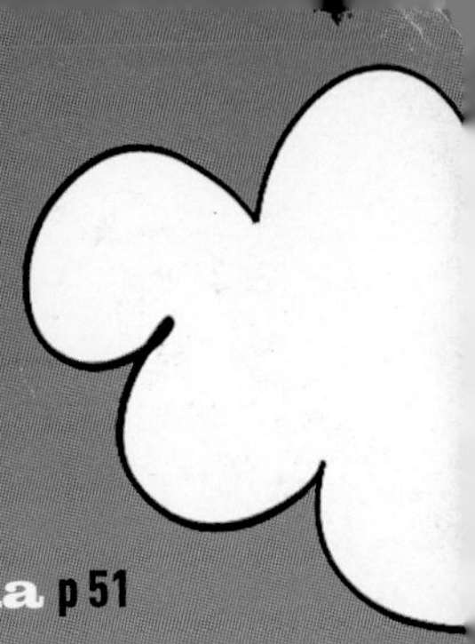

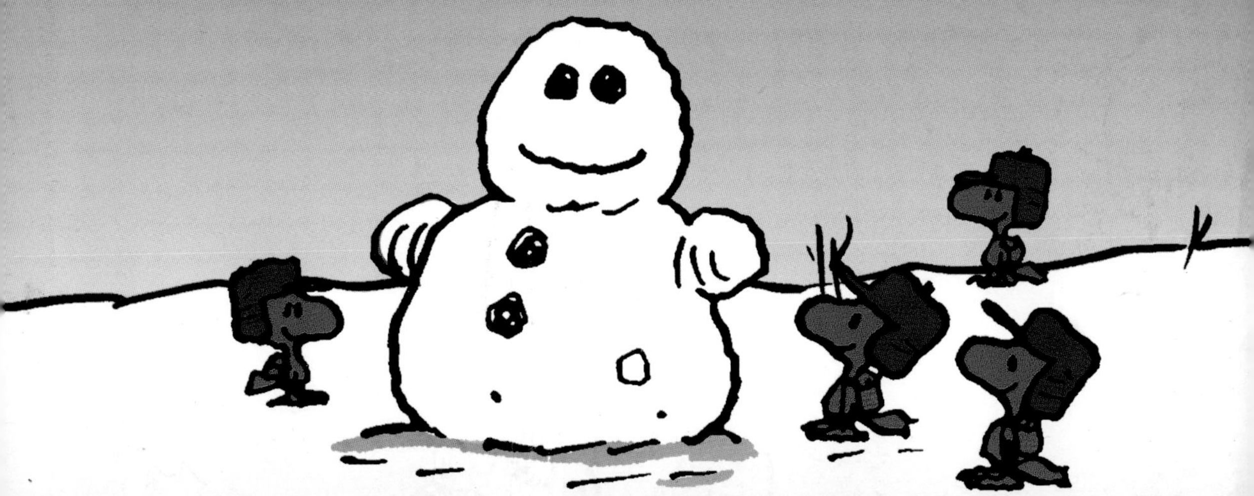

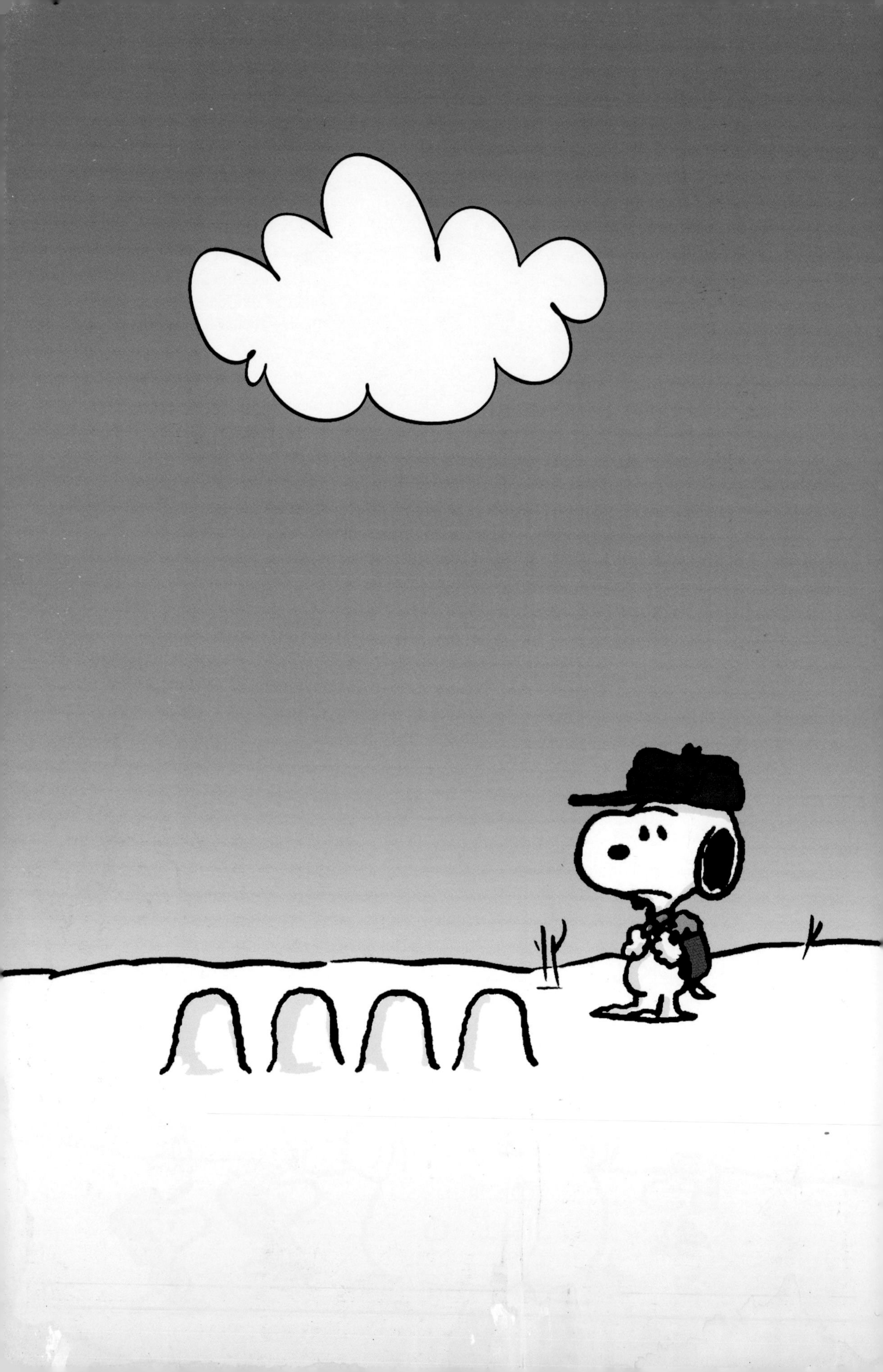

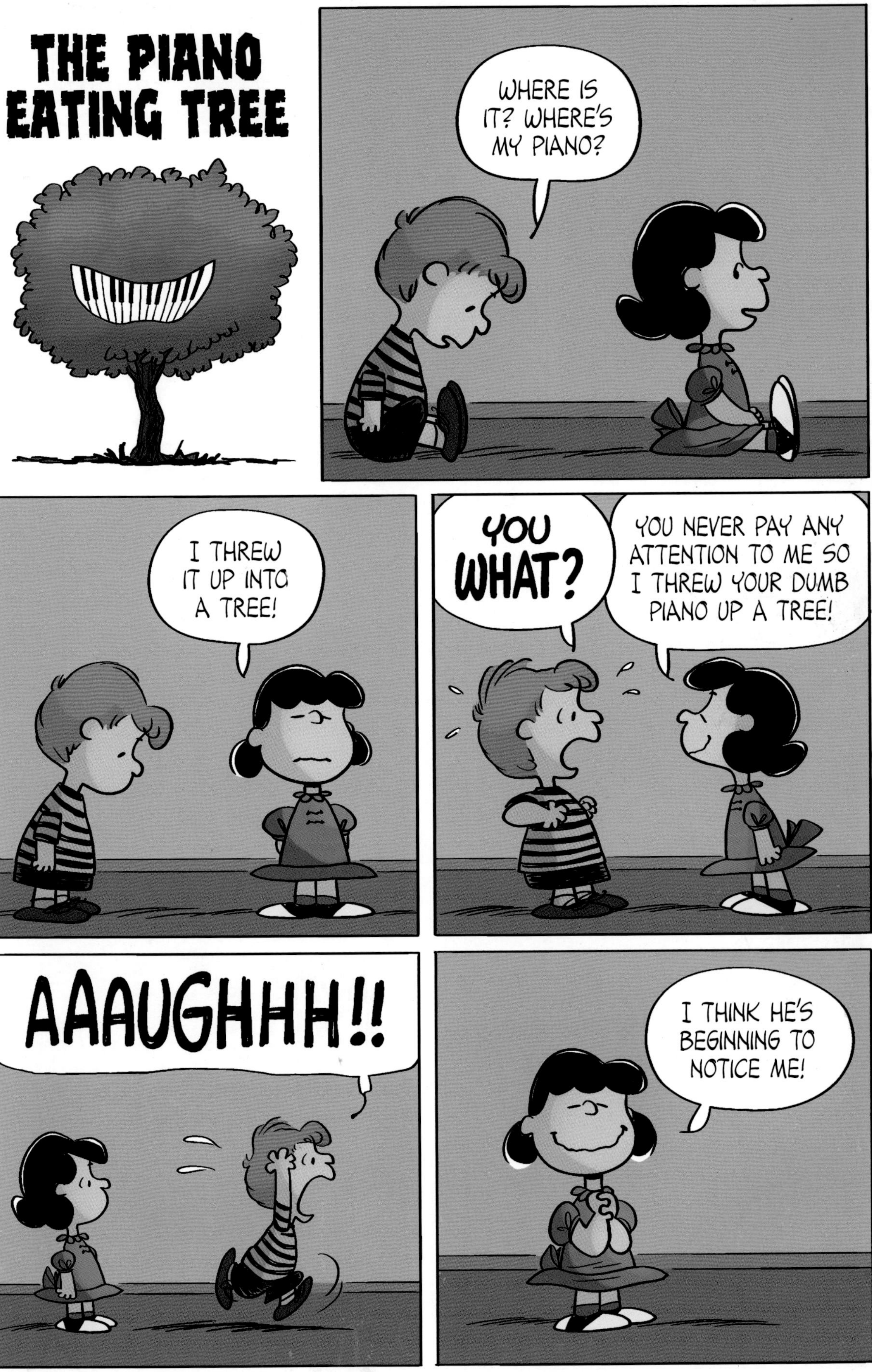
THE PIANO EATING TREE
WHERE IS IT? WHERE'S MY PIANO?
I THREW IT UP INTO A TREE!
YOU WHAT?
YOU NEVER PAY ANY ATTENTION TO ME SO I THREW YOUR DUMB PIANO UP A TREE!
AAAUGHHH!!
I THINK HE'S BEGINNING TO NOTICE ME!

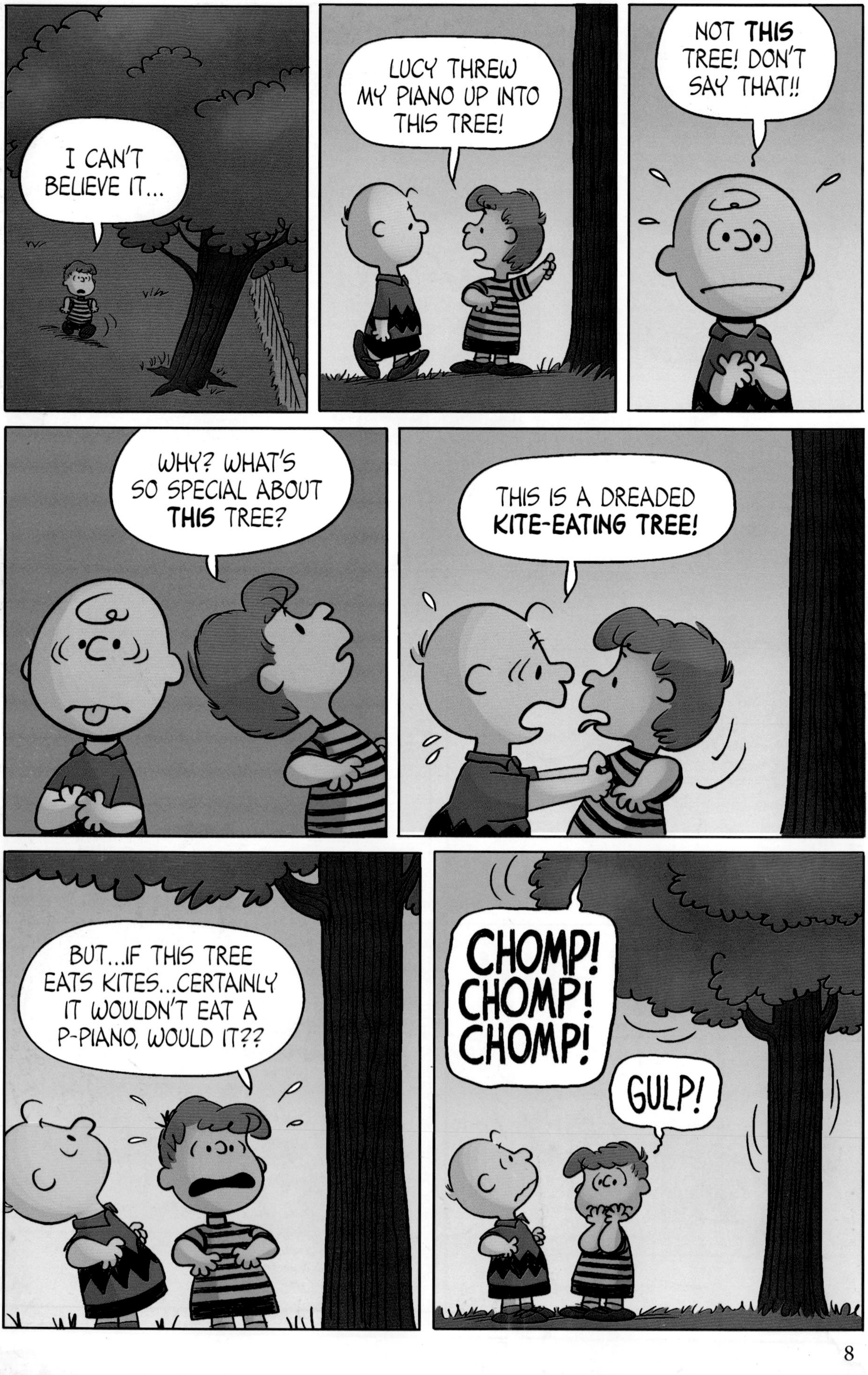
I CAN'T BELIEVE IT...
LUCY THREW MY PIANO UP INTO THIS TREE!
NOT **THIS** TREE! DON'T SAY THAT!!
WHY? WHAT'S SO SPECIAL ABOUT **THIS** TREE?
THIS IS A DREADED **KITE-EATING TREE!**
BUT...IF THIS TREE EATS KITES...CERTAINLY IT WOULDN'T EAT A P-PIANO, WOULD IT??
CHOMP! CHOMP! CHOMP!
GULP!

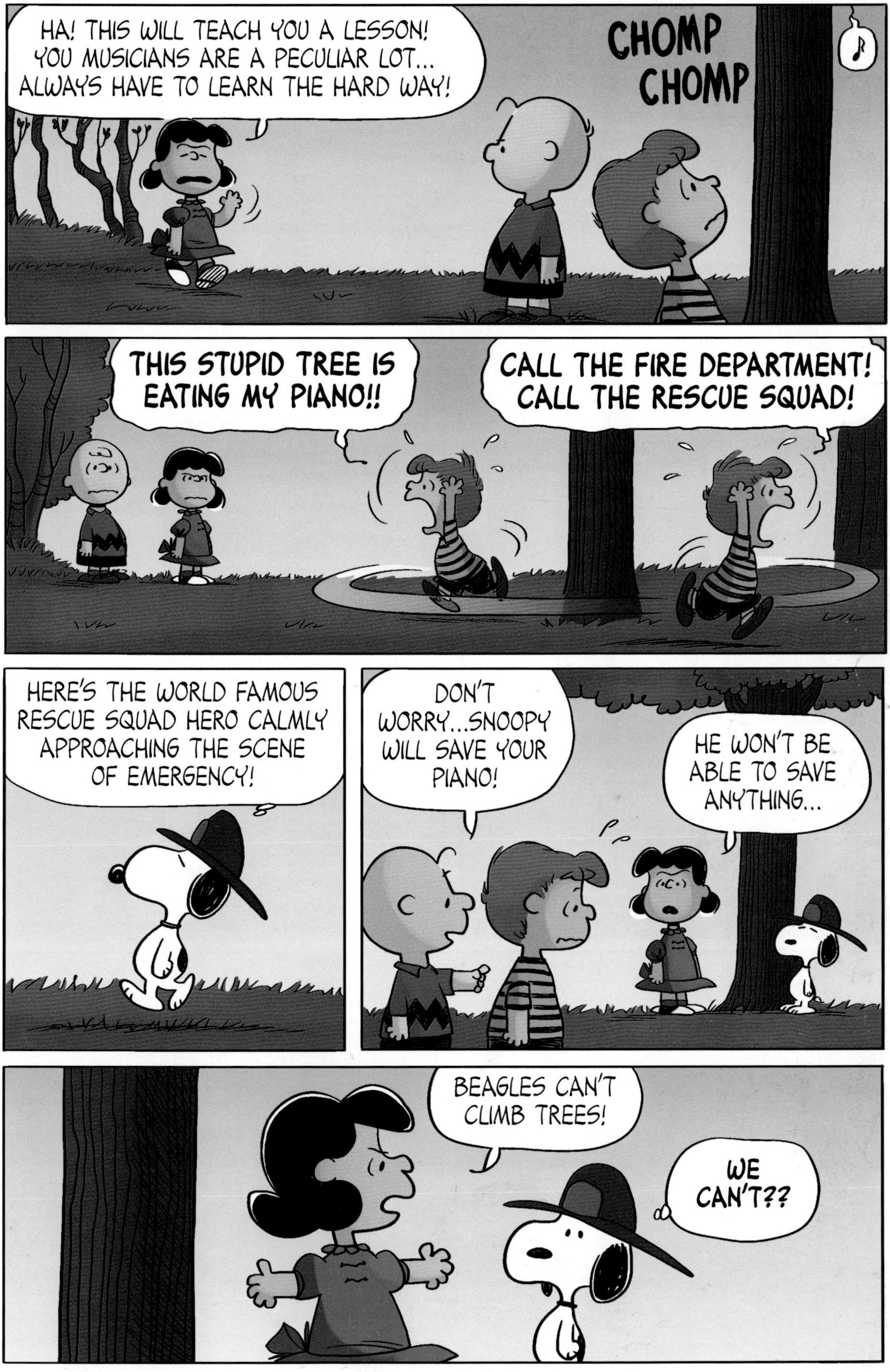
HA! THIS WILL TEACH YOU A LESSON! YOU MUSICIANS ARE A PECULIAR LOT... ALWAYS HAVE TO LEARN THE HARD WAY!
CHOMP
CHOMP
THIS STUPID TREE IS EATING MY PIANO!!
CALL THE FIRE DEPARTMENT! CALL THE RESCUE SQUAD!
HERE'S THE WORLD FAMOUS RESCUE SQUAD HERO CALMLY APPROACHING THE SCENE OF EMERGENCY!
DON'T WORRY...SNOOPY WILL SAVE YOUR PIANO!
HE WON'T BE ABLE TO SAVE ANYTHING...
BEAGLES CAN'T CLIMB TREES!
WE CAN'T??

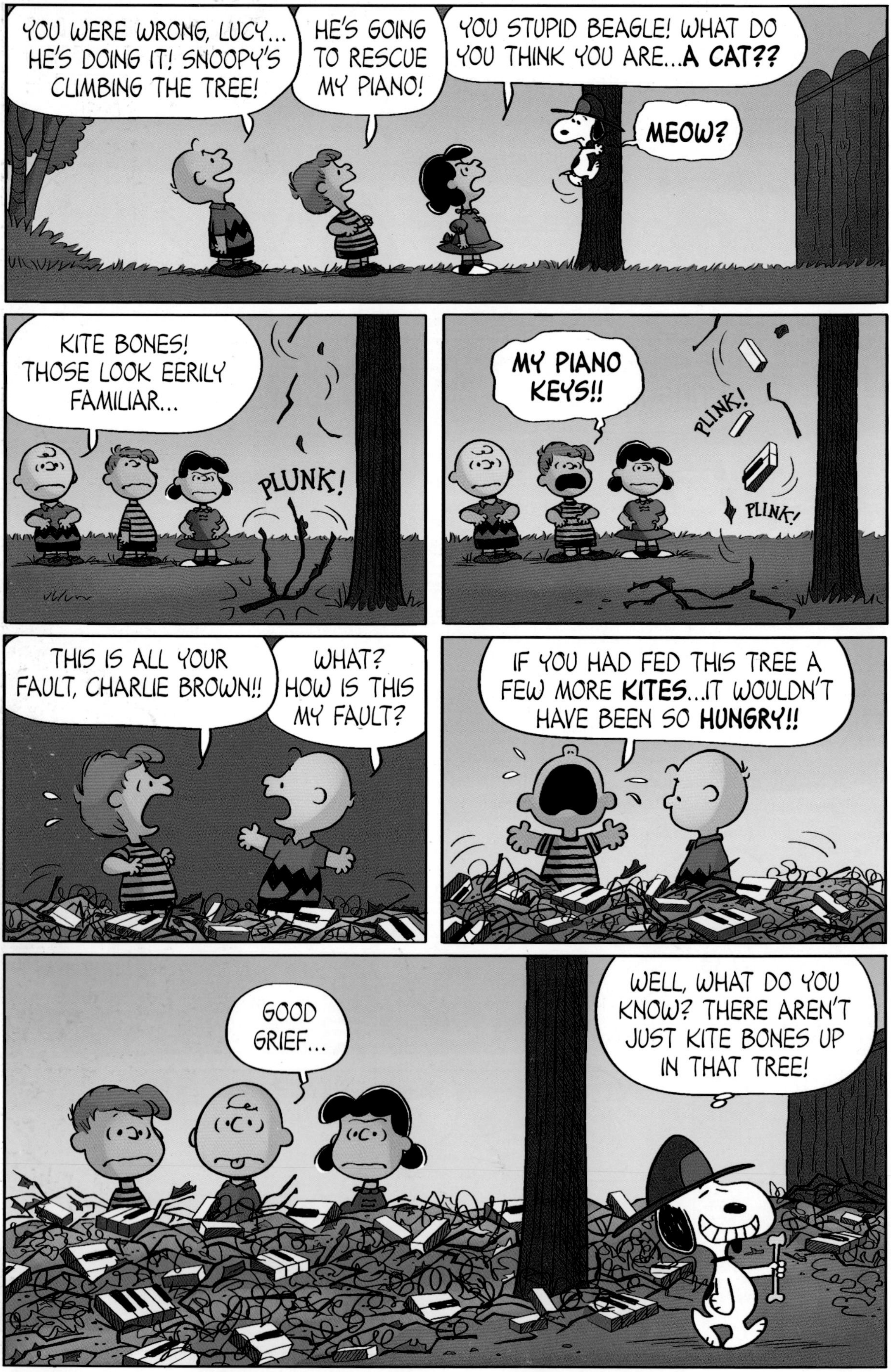
YOU WERE WRONG, LUCY... HE'S DOING IT! SNOOPY'S CLIMBING THE TREE!
HE'S GOING TO RESCUE MY PIANO!
YOU STUPID BEAGLE! WHAT DO YOU THINK YOU ARE...**A CAT??**
MEOW?
KITE BONES! THOSE LOOK EERILY FAMILIAR...
PLUNK!
MY PIANO KEYS!!
PLUNK!
PLUNK!
THIS IS ALL YOUR FAULT, CHARLIE BROWN!!
WHAT? HOW IS THIS MY FAULT?
IF YOU HAD FED THIS TREE A FEW MORE **KITES**...IT WOULDN'T HAVE BEEN SO **HUNGRY!!**
GOOD GRIEF...
WELL, WHAT DO YOU KNOW? THERE AREN'T JUST KITE BONES UP IN THAT TREE!

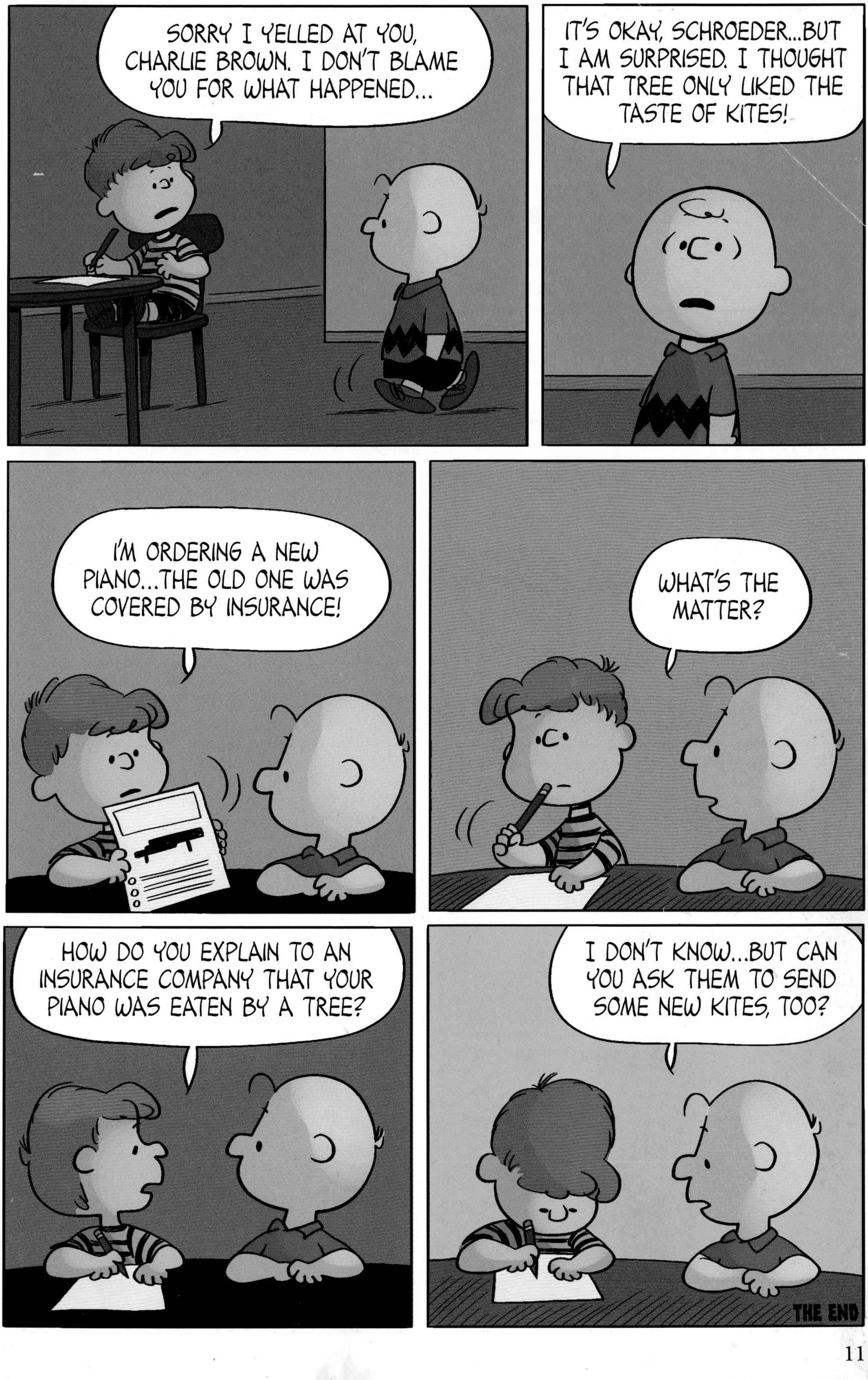
SORRY I YELLED AT YOU, CHARLIE BROWN. I DON'T BLAME YOU FOR WHAT HAPPENED...
IT'S OKAY, SCHROEDER...BUT I AM SURPRISED. I THOUGHT THAT TREE ONLY LIKED THE TASTE OF KITES!
I'M ORDERING A NEW PIANO...THE OLD ONE WAS COVERED BY INSURANCE!
WHAT'S THE MATTER?
HOW DO YOU EXPLAIN TO AN INSURANCE COMPANY THAT YOUR PIANO WAS EATEN BY A TREE?
I DON'T KNOW...BUT CAN YOU ASK THEM TO SEND SOME NEW KITES, TOO?
THE END

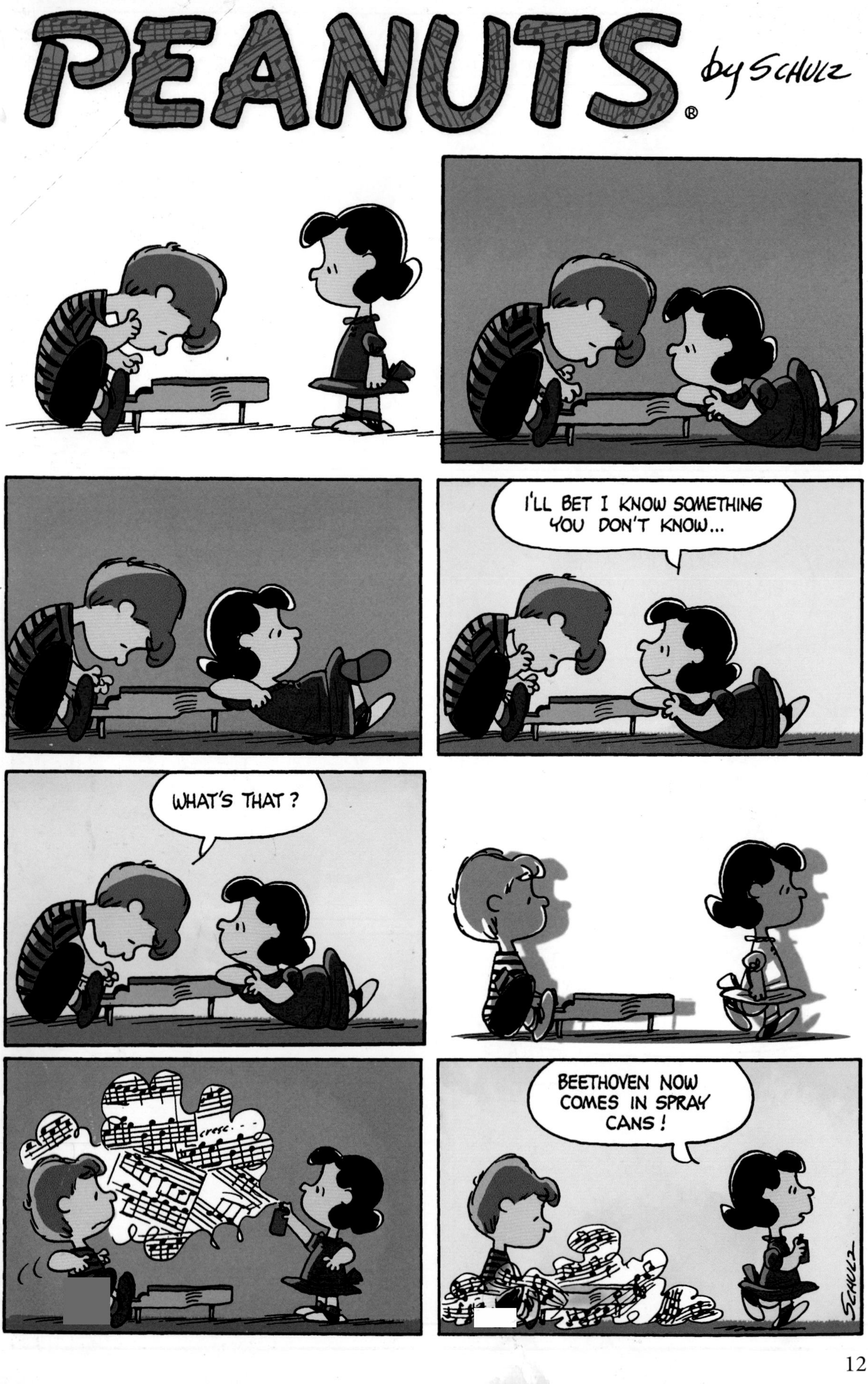
PEANUTS
by SCHULZ
I'LL BET I KNOW SOMETHING YOU DON'T KNOW...
WHAT'S THAT ?
cresc.
BEETHOVEN NOW COMES IN SPRAY CANS !
SCHULZ

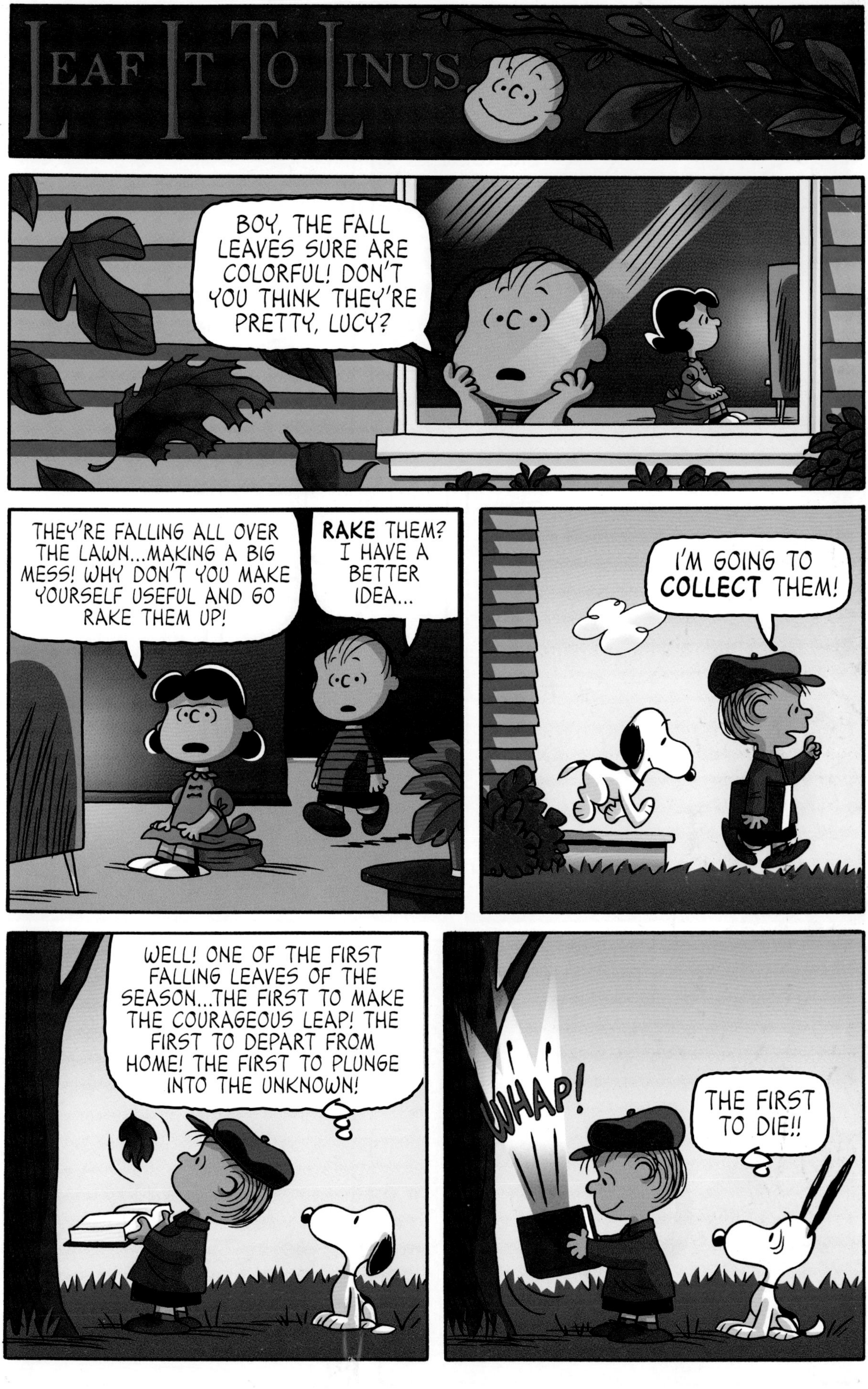
LEAF IT TO LINUS
BOY, THE FALL LEAVES SURE ARE COLORFUL! DON'T YOU THINK THEY'RE PRETTY, LUCY?
THEY'RE FALLING ALL OVER THE LAWN...MAKING A BIG MESS! WHY DON'T YOU MAKE YOURSELF USEFUL AND GO RAKE THEM UP!
RAKE THEM? I HAVE A BETTER IDEA...
I'M GOING TO COLLECT THEM!
WELL! ONE OF THE FIRST FALLING LEAVES OF THE SEASON...THE FIRST TO MAKE THE COURAGEOUS LEAP! THE FIRST TO DEPART FROM HOME! THE FIRST TO PLUNGE INTO THE UNKNOWN!
WHAP!
THE FIRST TO DIE!!

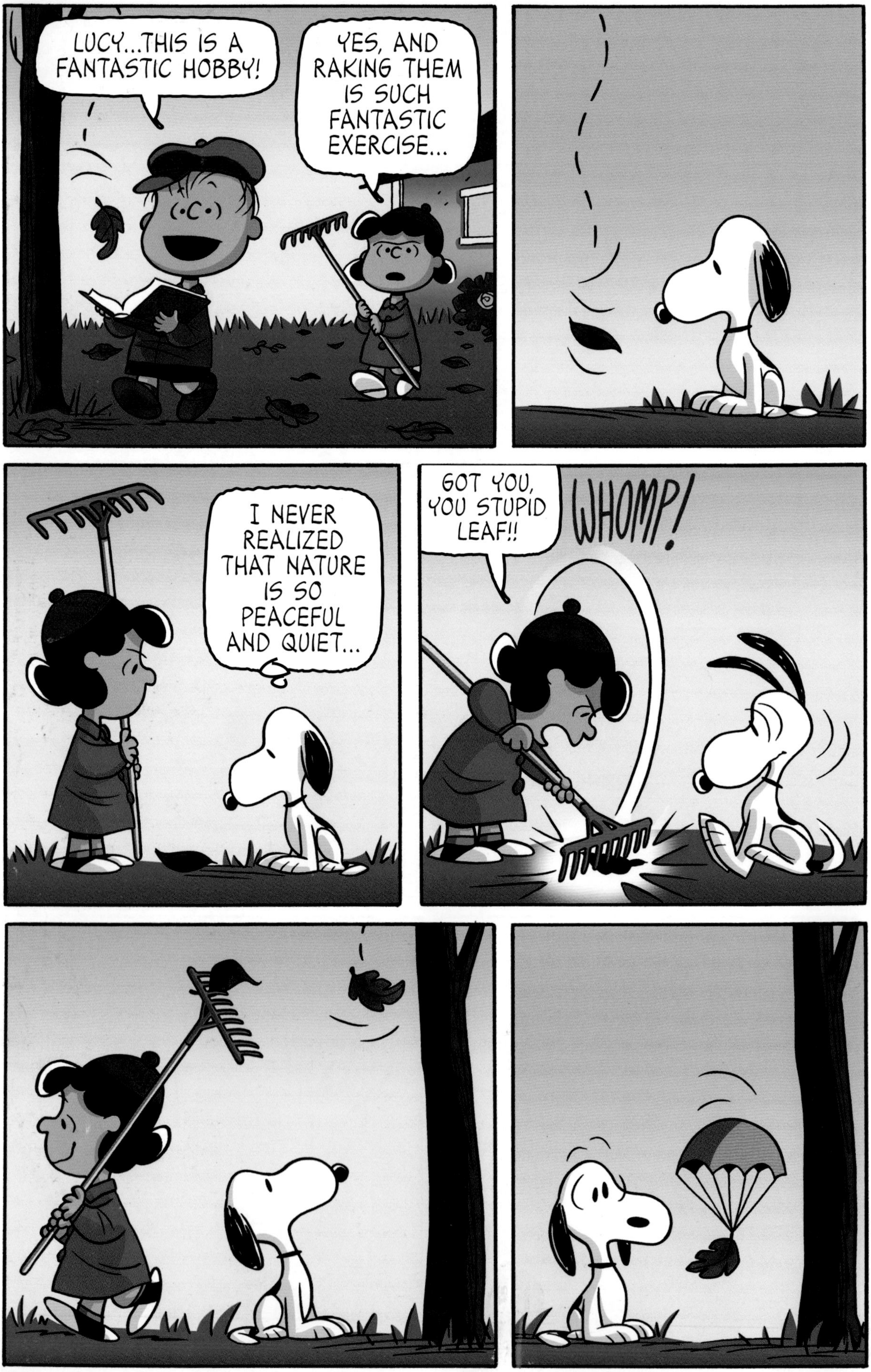
LUCY...THIS IS A FANTASTIC HOBBY!
YES, AND RAKING THEM IS SUCH FANTASTIC EXERCISE...
I NEVER REALIZED THAT NATURE IS SO PEACEFUL AND QUIET...
GOT YOU, YOU STUPID LEAF!!
WHOMP!

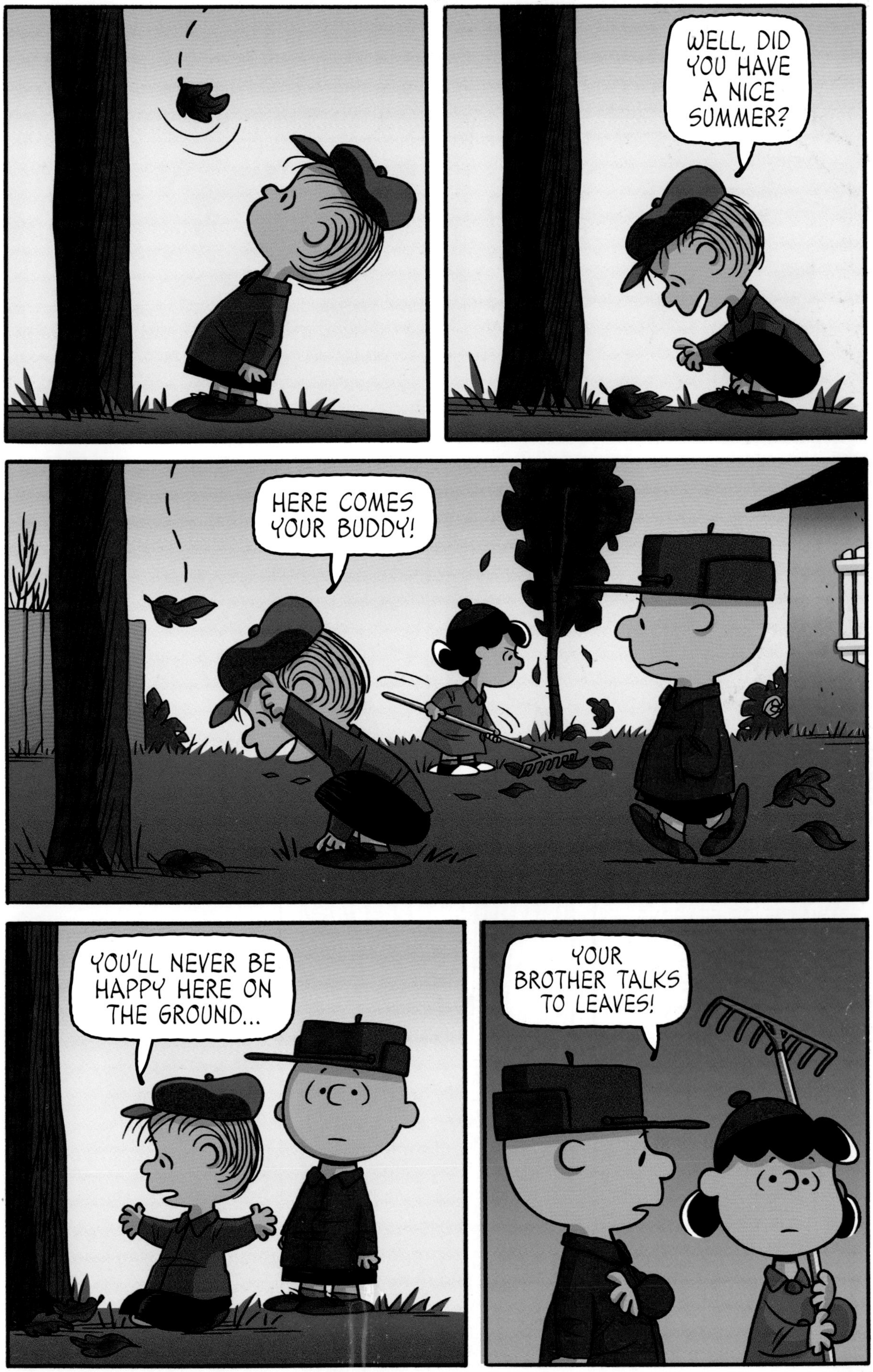
WELL, DID YOU HAVE A NICE SUMMER?
HERE COMES YOUR BUDDY!
YOU'LL NEVER BE HAPPY HERE ON THE GROUND...
YOUR BROTHER TALKS TO LEAVES!

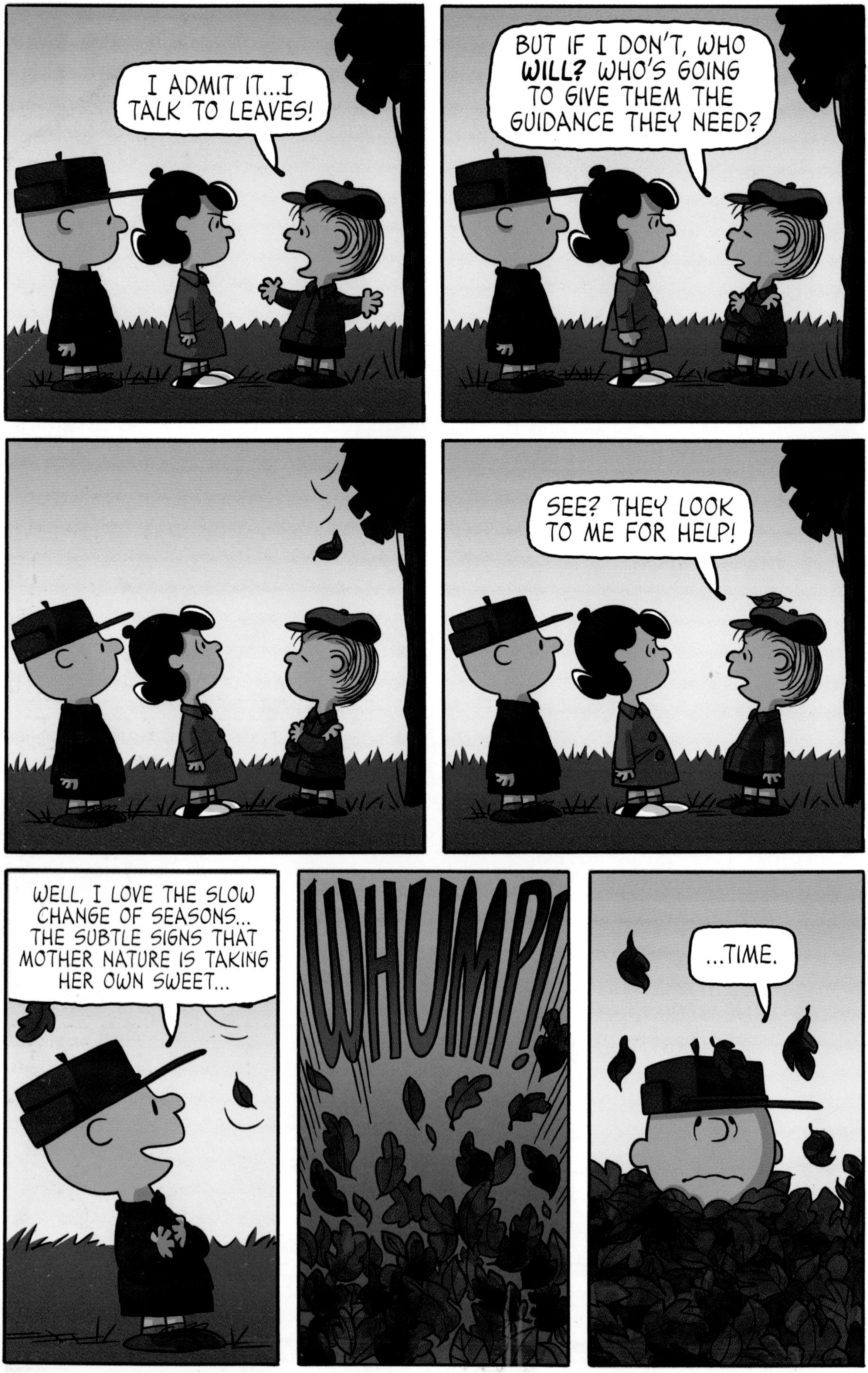
I ADMIT IT...I TALK TO LEAVES!
BUT IF I DON'T, WHO **WILL?** WHO'S GOING TO GIVE THEM THE GUIDANCE THEY NEED?
SEE? THEY LOOK TO ME FOR HELP!
WELL, I LOVE THE SLOW CHANGE OF SEASONS... THE SUBTLE SIGNS THAT MOTHER NATURE IS TAKING HER OWN SWEET...
WHUMP!
...TIME.

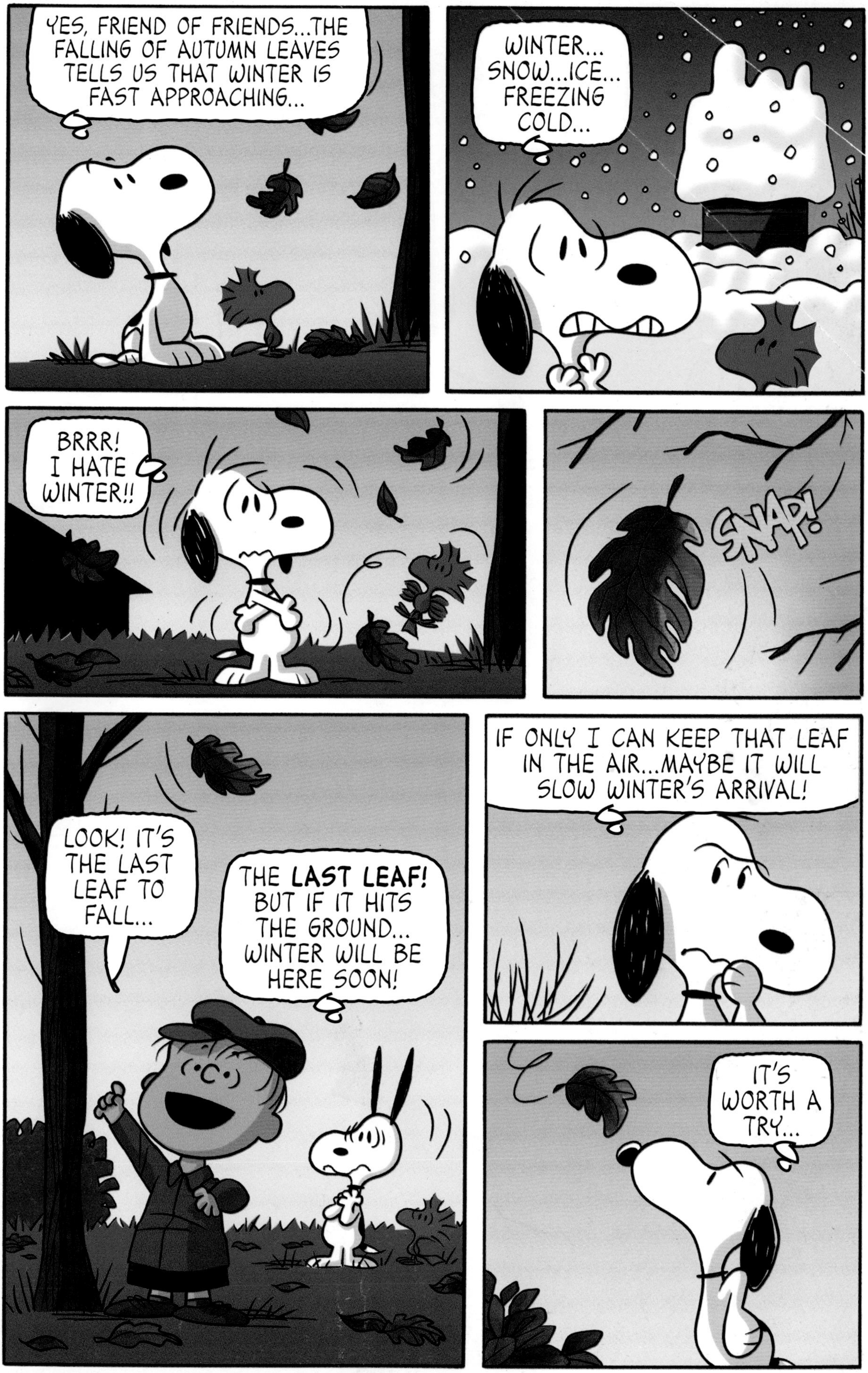
YES, FRIEND OF FRIENDS...THE FALLING OF AUTUMN LEAVES TELLS US THAT WINTER IS FAST APPROACHING...
WINTER... SNOW...ICE... FREEZING COLD...
BRRR! I HATE WINTER!!
SNAP!
LOOK! IT'S THE LAST LEAF TO FALL...
THE **LAST LEAF!** BUT IF IT HITS THE GROUND... WINTER WILL BE HERE SOON!
IF ONLY I CAN KEEP THAT LEAF IN THE AIR...MAYBE IT WILL SLOW WINTER'S ARRIVAL!
IT'S WORTH A TRY...

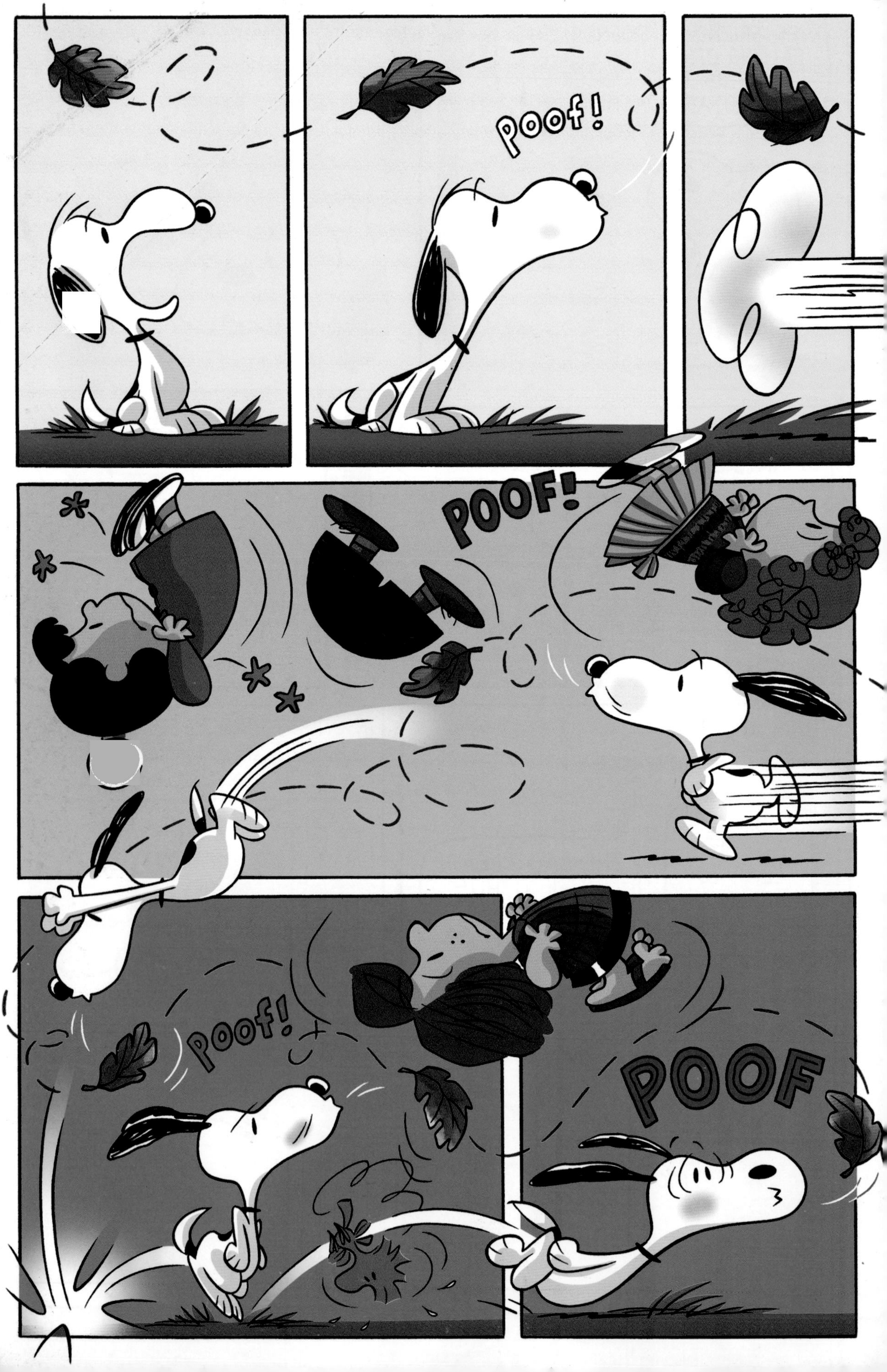
poof!
POOF!
poof!
POOF

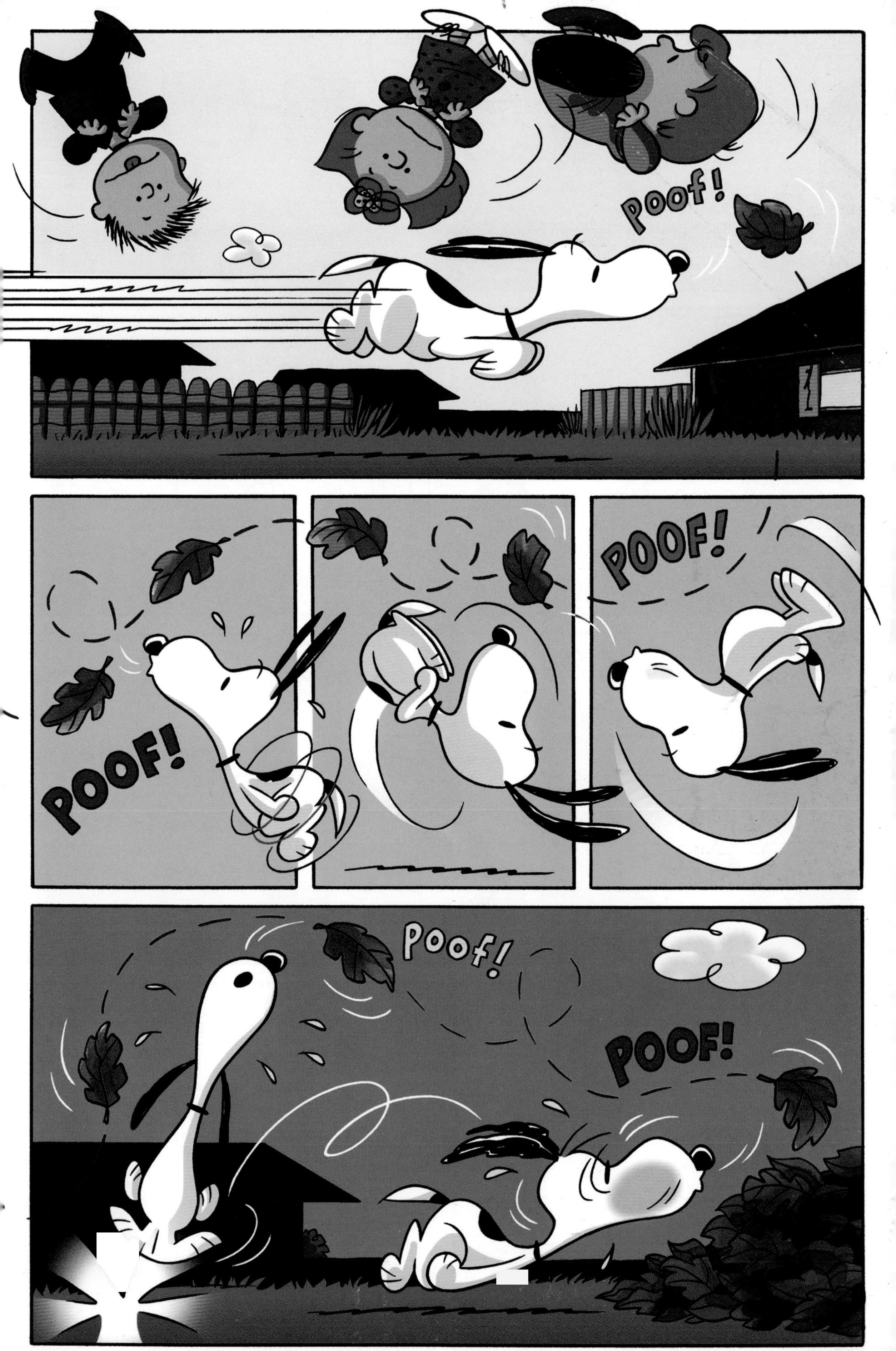
Poof!
POOF!
POOF!
Poof!
POOF!

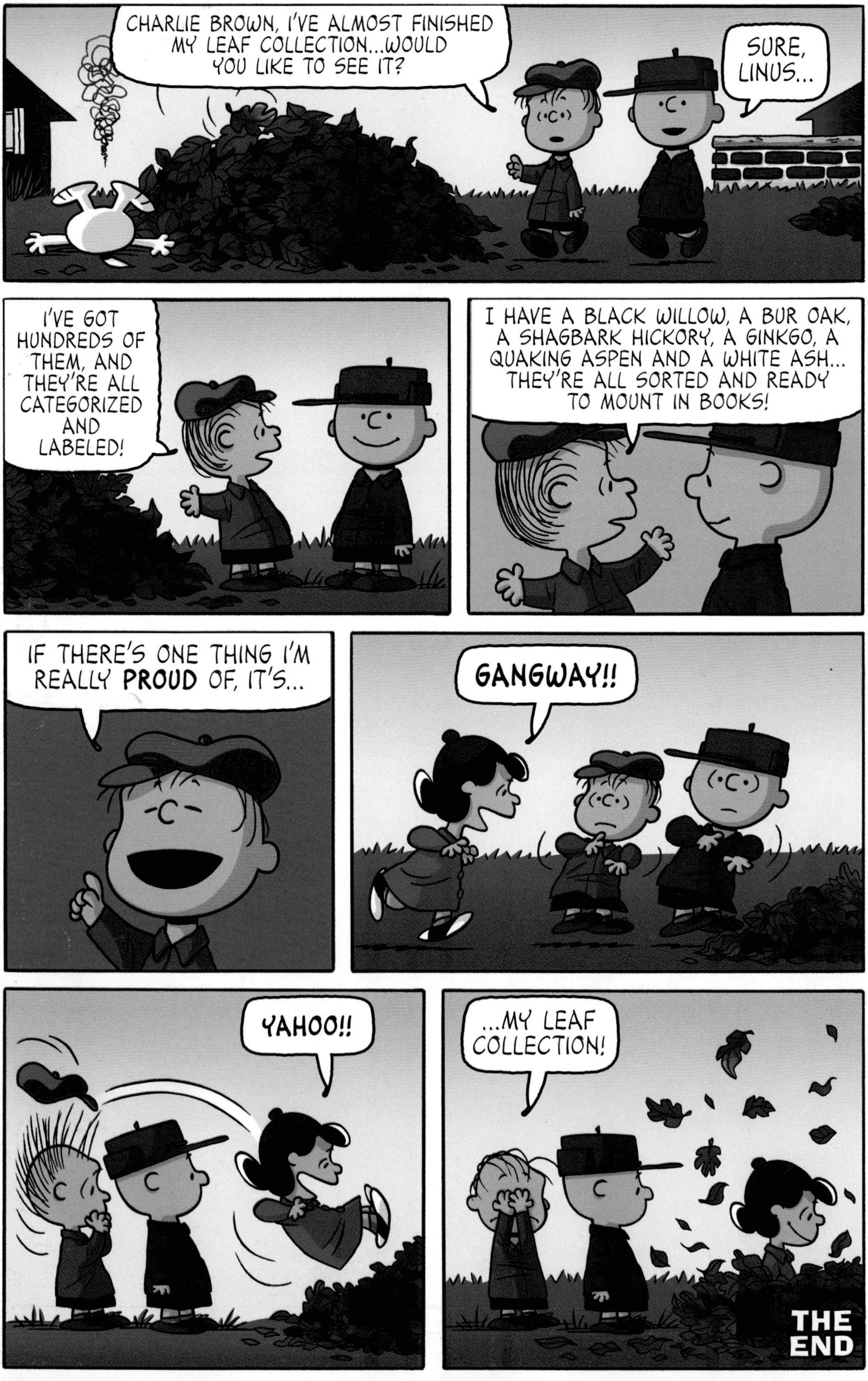
CHARLIE BROWN, I'VE ALMOST FINISHED MY LEAF COLLECTION...WOULD YOU LIKE TO SEE IT?
SURE, LINUS...
I'VE GOT HUNDREDS OF THEM, AND THEY'RE ALL CATEGORIZED AND LABELED!
I HAVE A BLACK WILLOW, A BUR OAK, A SHAGBARK HICKORY, A GINKGO, A QUAKING ASPEN AND A WHITE ASH... THEY'RE ALL SORTED AND READY TO MOUNT IN BOOKS!
IF THERE'S ONE THING I'M REALLY PROUD OF, IT'S...
GANGWAY!!
YAHOO!!
...MY LEAF COLLECTION!
THE END

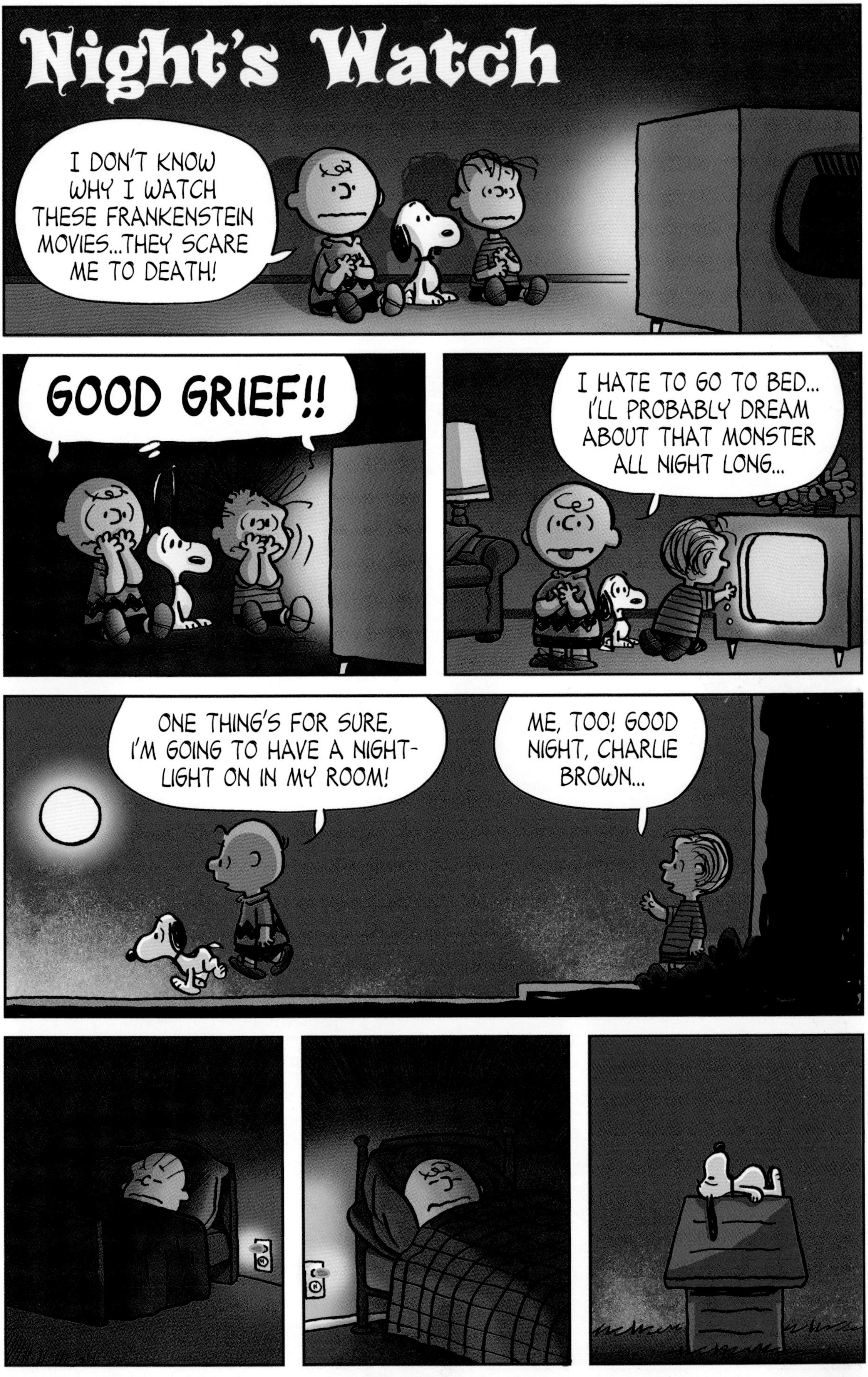
Night's Watch
I DON'T KNOW WHY I WATCH THESE FRANKENSTEIN MOVIES...THEY SCARE ME TO DEATH!
GOOD GRIEF!!
I HATE TO GO TO BED... I'LL PROBABLY DREAM ABOUT THAT MONSTER ALL NIGHT LONG...
ONE THING'S FOR SURE, I'M GOING TO HAVE A NIGHT-LIGHT ON IN MY ROOM!
ME, TOO! GOOD NIGHT, CHARLIE BROWN...

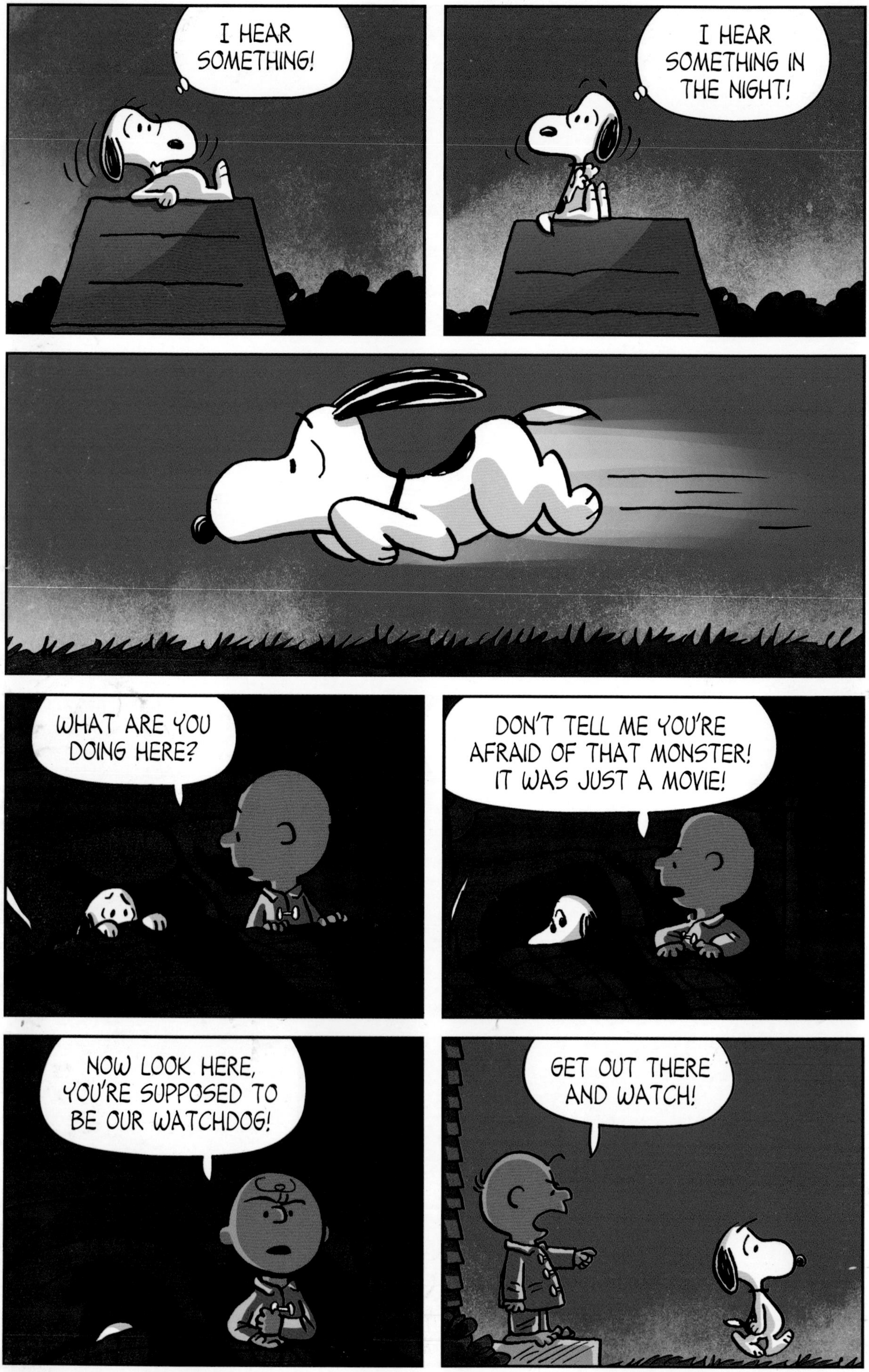
I HEAR SOMETHING!
I HEAR SOMETHING IN THE NIGHT!
WHAT ARE YOU DOING HERE?
DON'T TELL ME YOU'RE AFRAID OF THAT MONSTER! IT WAS JUST A MOVIE!
NOW LOOK HERE, YOU'RE SUPPOSED TO BE OUR WATCHDOG!
GET OUT THERE AND WATCH!

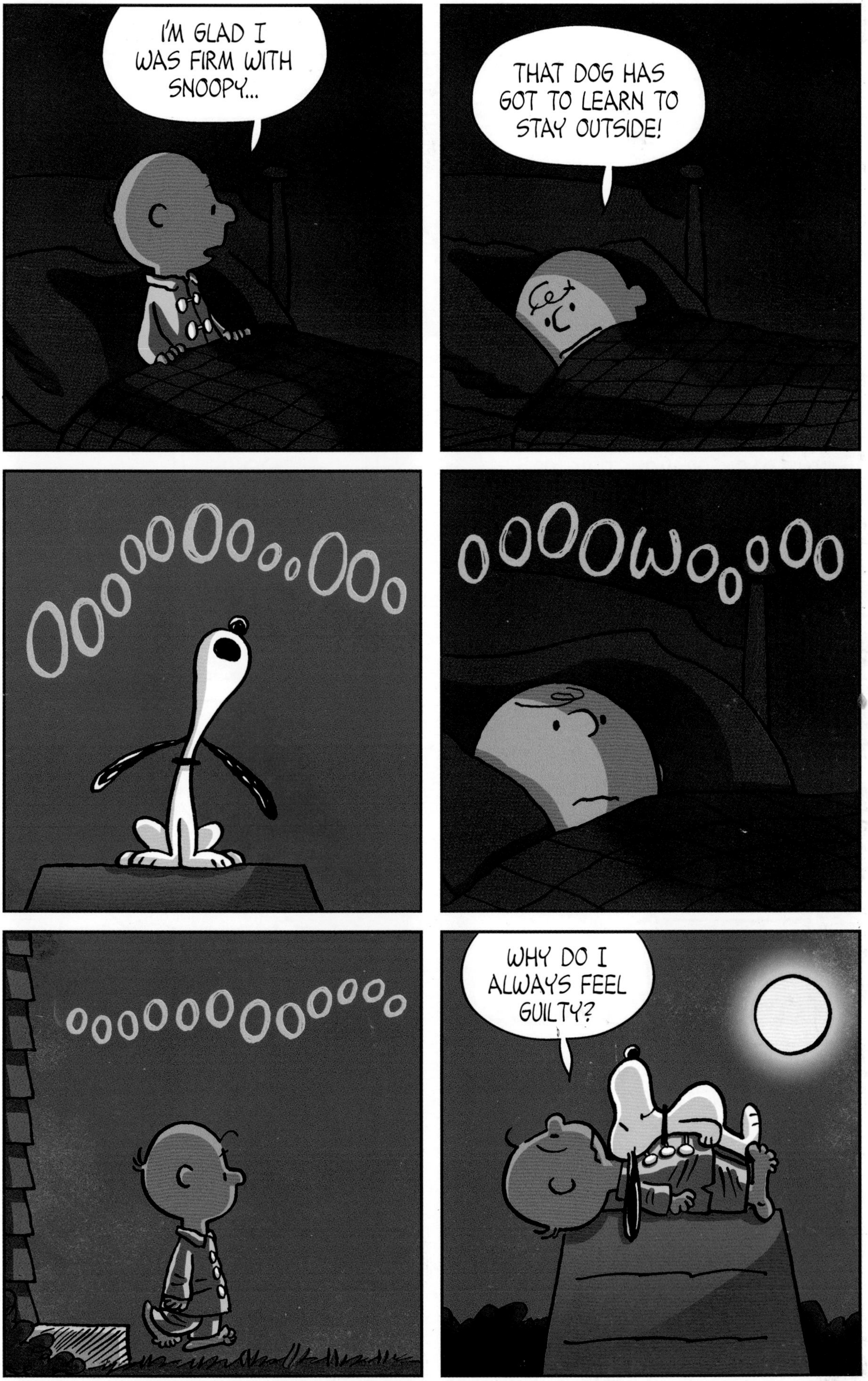
I'M GLAD I WAS FIRM WITH SNOOPY...
THAT DOG HAS GOT TO LEARN TO STAY OUTSIDE!
OOOOOOOOoOOOO
OOOOWOoOOO
OOOOOOOOOOOOO
WHY DO I ALWAYS FEEL GUILTY?

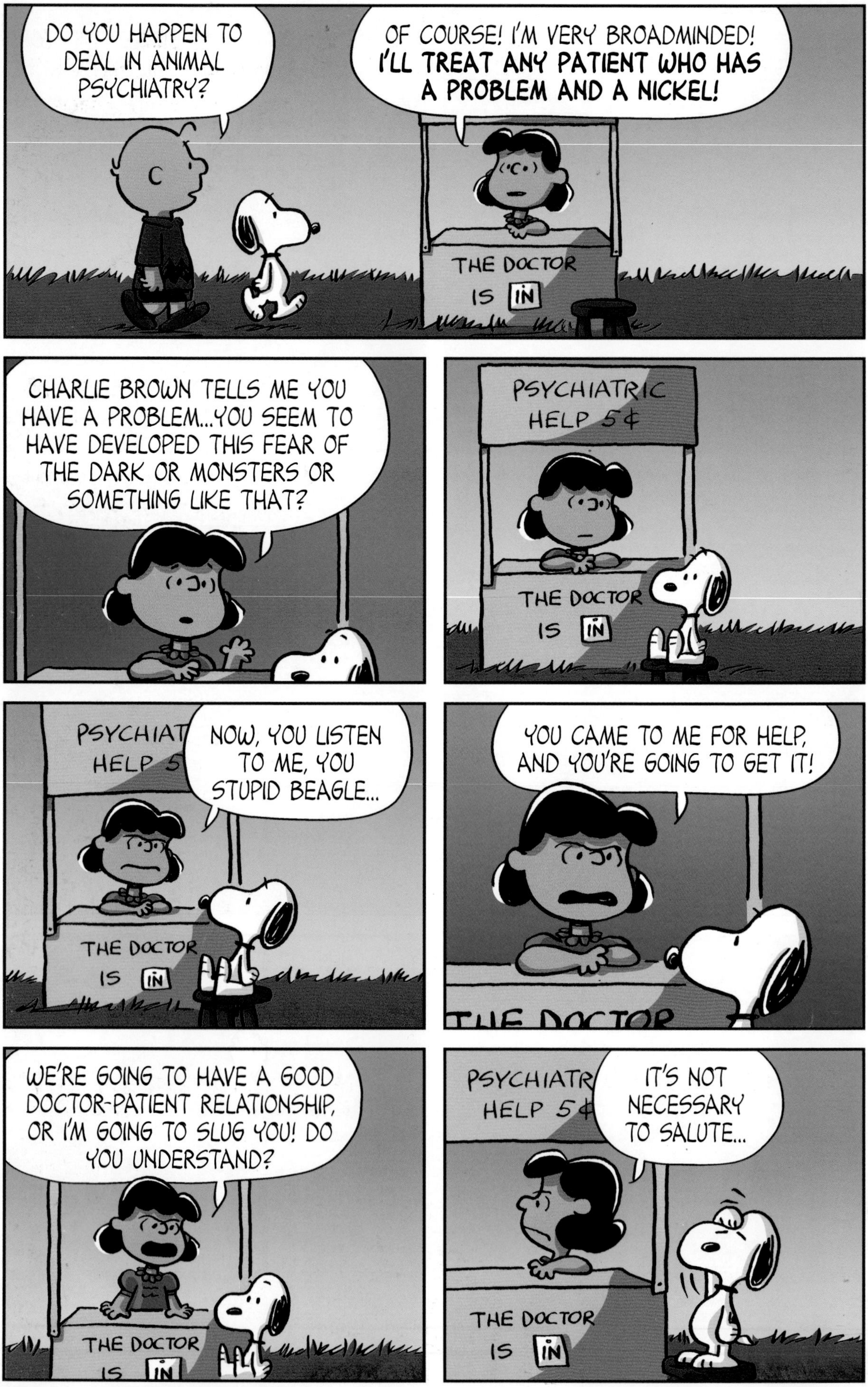
DO YOU HAPPEN TO DEAL IN ANIMAL PSYCHIATRY?
OF COURSE! I'M VERY BROADMINDED! **I'LL TREAT ANY PATIENT WHO HAS A PROBLEM AND A NICKEL!**
THE DOCTOR IS IN
CHARLIE BROWN TELLS ME YOU HAVE A PROBLEM...YOU SEEM TO HAVE DEVELOPED THIS FEAR OF THE DARK OR MONSTERS OR SOMETHING LIKE THAT?
PSYCHIATRIC HELP 5¢
THE DOCTOR IS IN
NOW, YOU LISTEN TO ME, YOU STUPID BEAGLE...
THE DOCTOR IS IN
YOU CAME TO ME FOR HELP, AND YOU'RE GOING TO GET IT!
WE'RE GOING TO HAVE A GOOD DOCTOR-PATIENT RELATIONSHIP, OR I'M GOING TO SLUG YOU! DO YOU UNDERSTAND?
THE DOCTOR IS IN
IT'S NOT NECESSARY TO SALUTE...
PSYCHIATR HELP 5¢
THE DOCTOR IS IN

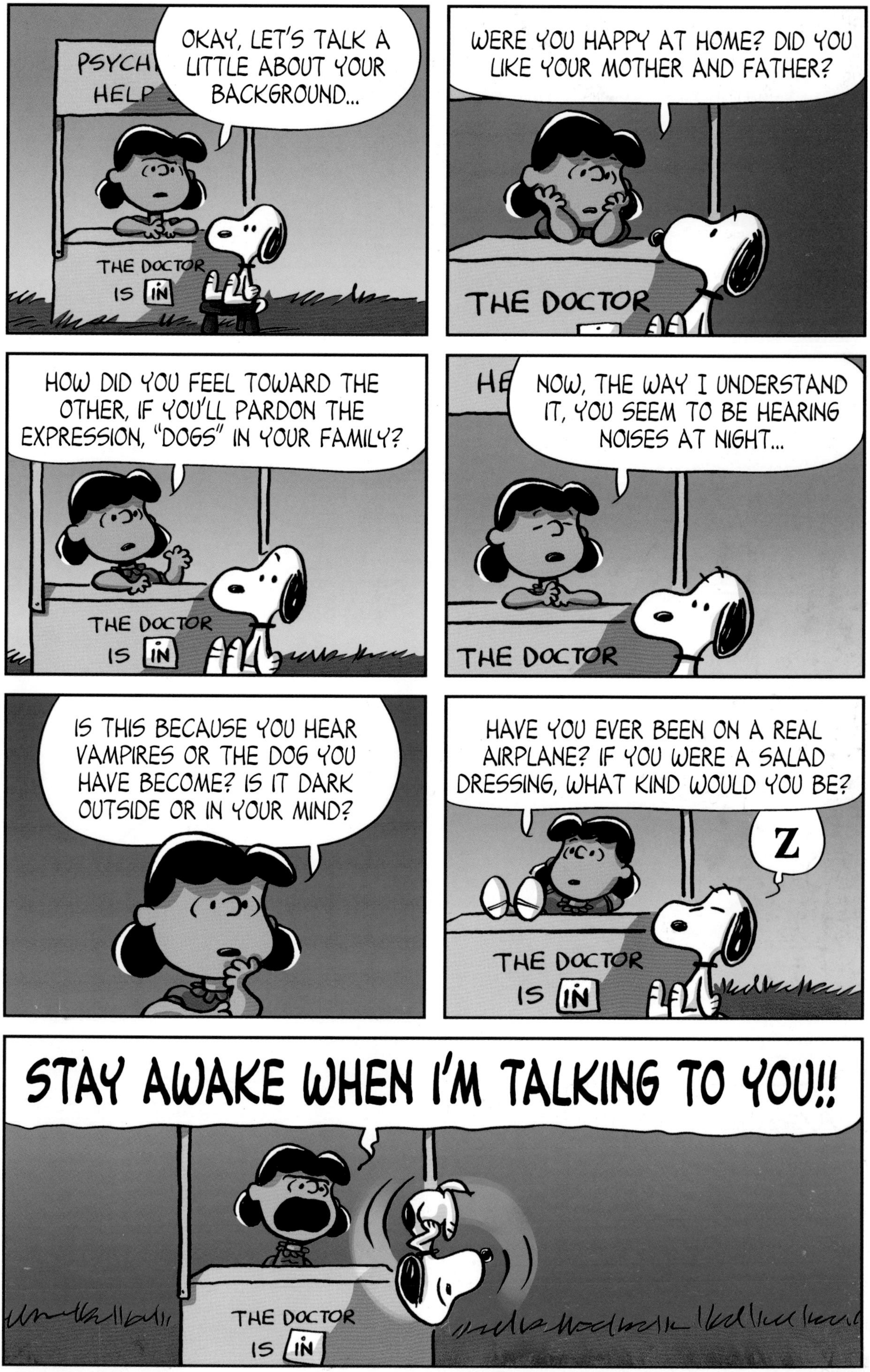
PSYCH
HELP
OKAY, LET'S TALK A LITTLE ABOUT YOUR BACKGROUND...
THE DOCTOR IS IN
WERE YOU HAPPY AT HOME? DID YOU LIKE YOUR MOTHER AND FATHER?
THE DOCTOR
HOW DID YOU FEEL TOWARD THE OTHER, IF YOU'LL PARDON THE EXPRESSION, "DOGS" IN YOUR FAMILY?
THE DOCTOR IS IN
NOW, THE WAY I UNDERSTAND IT, YOU SEEM TO BE HEARING NOISES AT NIGHT...
THE DOCTOR
IS THIS BECAUSE YOU HEAR VAMPIRES OR THE DOG YOU HAVE BECOME? IS IT DARK OUTSIDE OR IN YOUR MIND?
HAVE YOU EVER BEEN ON A REAL AIRPLANE? IF YOU WERE A SALAD DRESSING, WHAT KIND WOULD YOU BE?
Z
THE DOCTOR IS IN
STAY AWAKE WHEN I'M TALKING TO YOU!!
THE DOCTOR IS IN

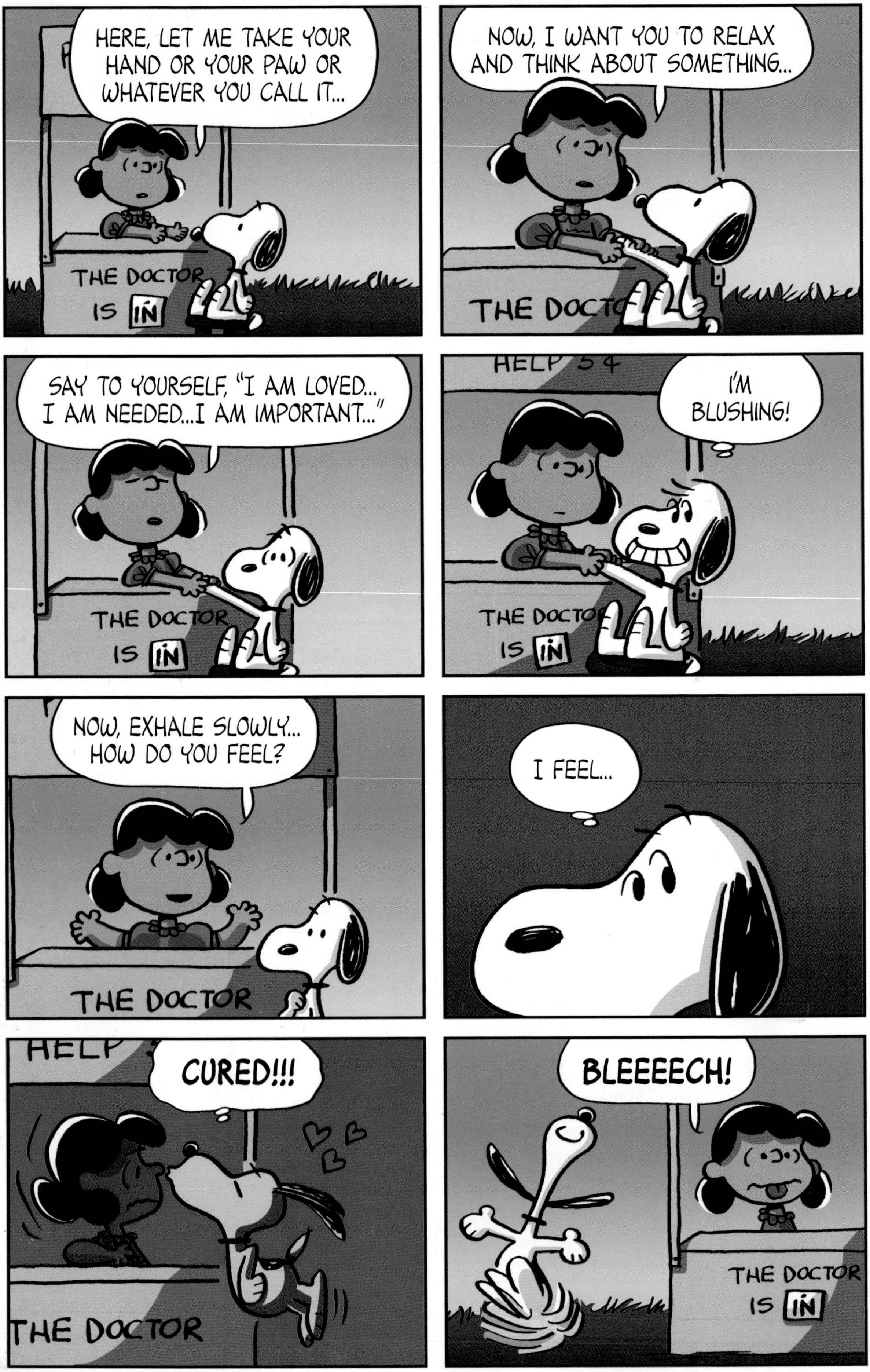
HERE, LET ME TAKE YOUR HAND OR YOUR PAW OR WHATEVER YOU CALL IT...
THE DOCTOR IS IN
NOW, I WANT YOU TO RELAX AND THINK ABOUT SOMETHING...
THE DOCTOR
SAY TO YOURSELF, "I AM LOVED... I AM NEEDED...I AM IMPORTANT..."
THE DOCTOR IS IN
HELP 5¢
I'M BLUSHING!
THE DOCTOR IS IN
NOW, EXHALE SLOWLY... HOW DO YOU FEEL?
THE DOCTOR
I FEEL...
HELP
CURED!!!
THE DOCTOR
BLEEEECH!
THE DOCTOR IS IN

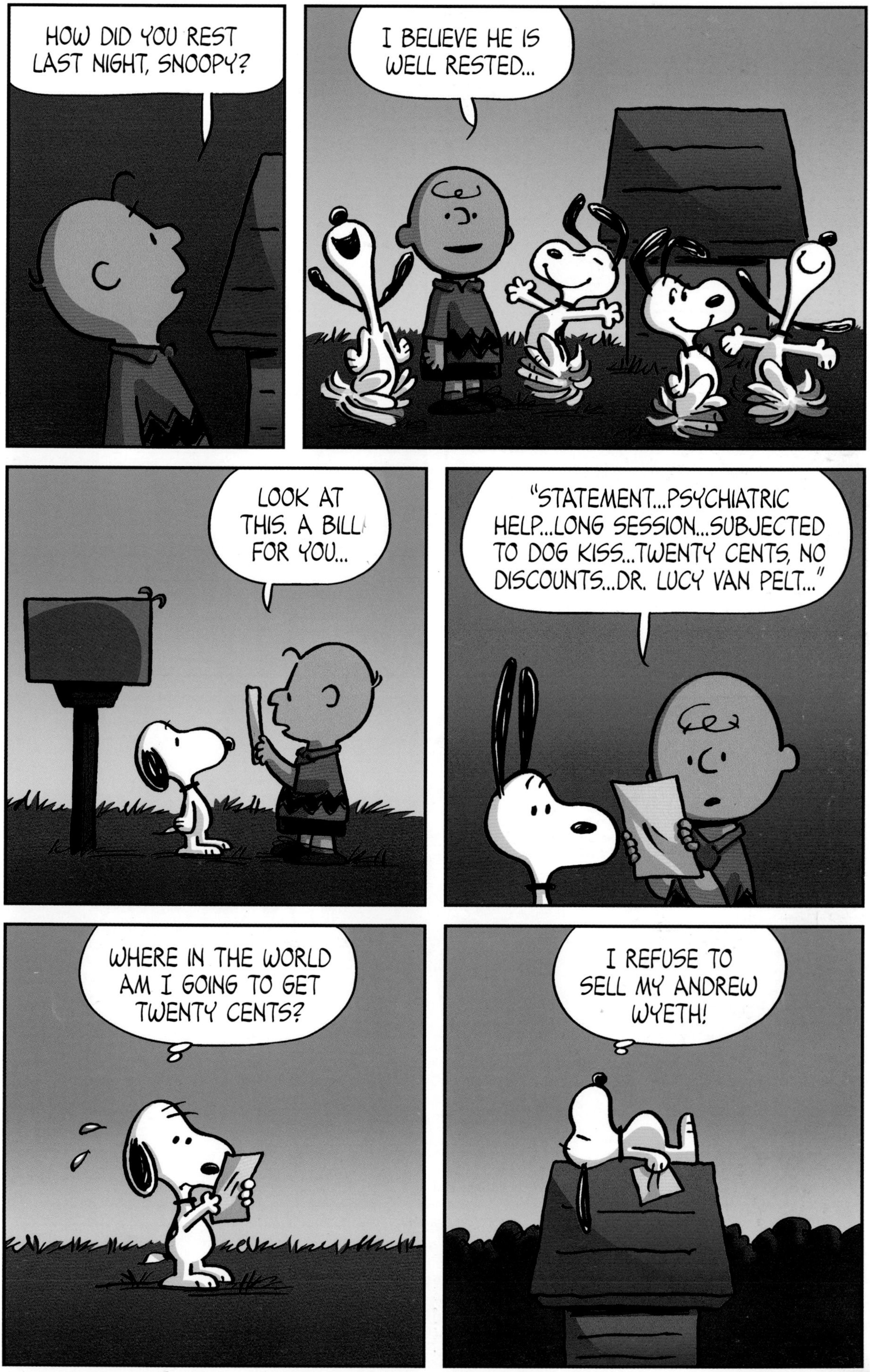
HOW DID YOU REST LAST NIGHT, SNOOPY?
I BELIEVE HE IS WELL RESTED...
LOOK AT THIS. A BILL FOR YOU...
"STATEMENT...PSYCHIATRIC HELP...LONG SESSION...SUBJECTED TO DOG KISS...TWENTY CENTS, NO DISCOUNTS...DR. LUCY VAN PELT..."
WHERE IN THE WORLD AM I GOING TO GET TWENTY CENTS?
I REFUSE TO SELL MY ANDREW WYETH!

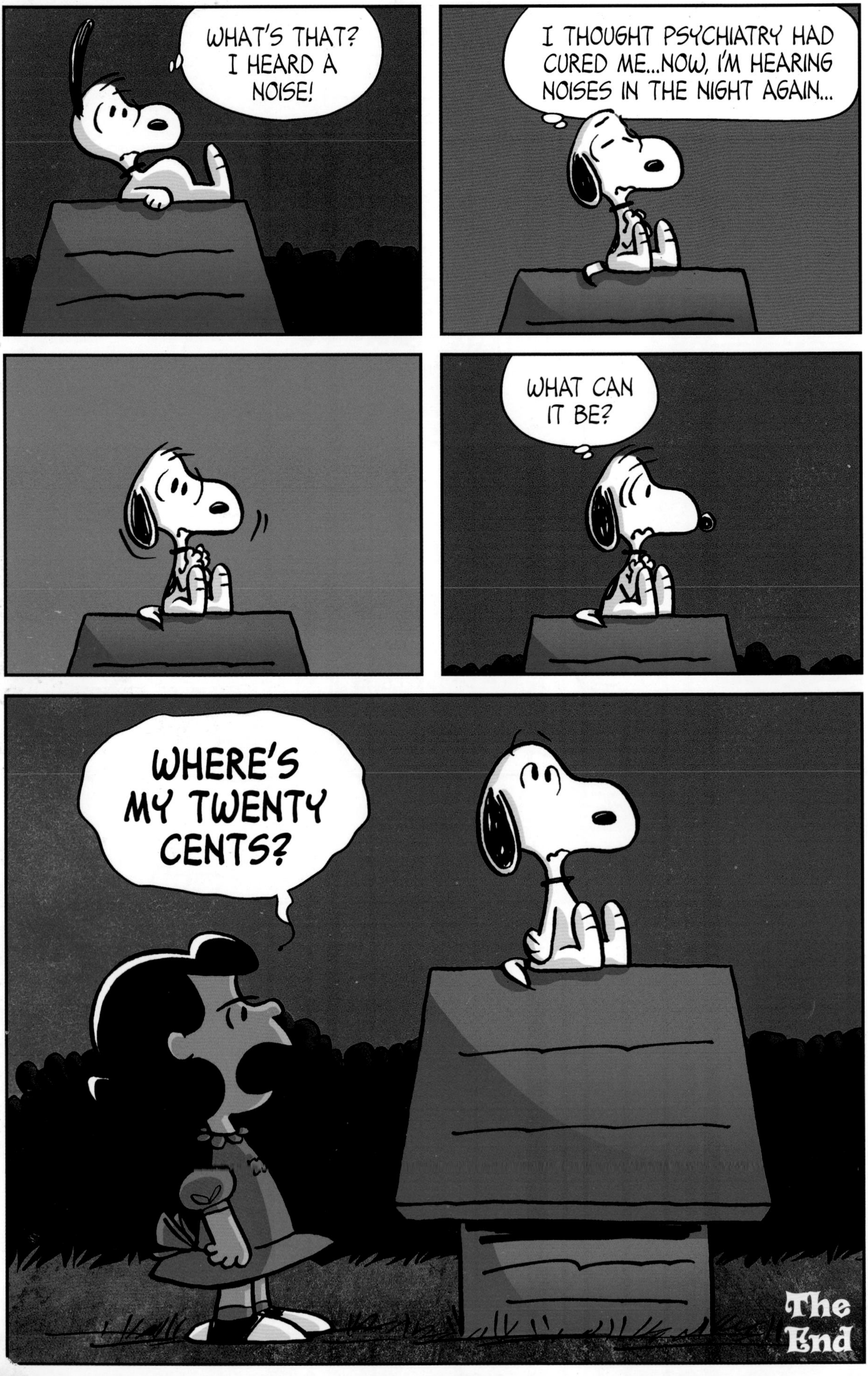
WHAT'S THAT? I HEARD A NOISE!
I THOUGHT PSYCHIATRY HAD CURED ME...NOW, I'M HEARING NOISES IN THE NIGHT AGAIN...
WHAT CAN IT BE?
WHERE'S MY TWENTY CENTS?
The End

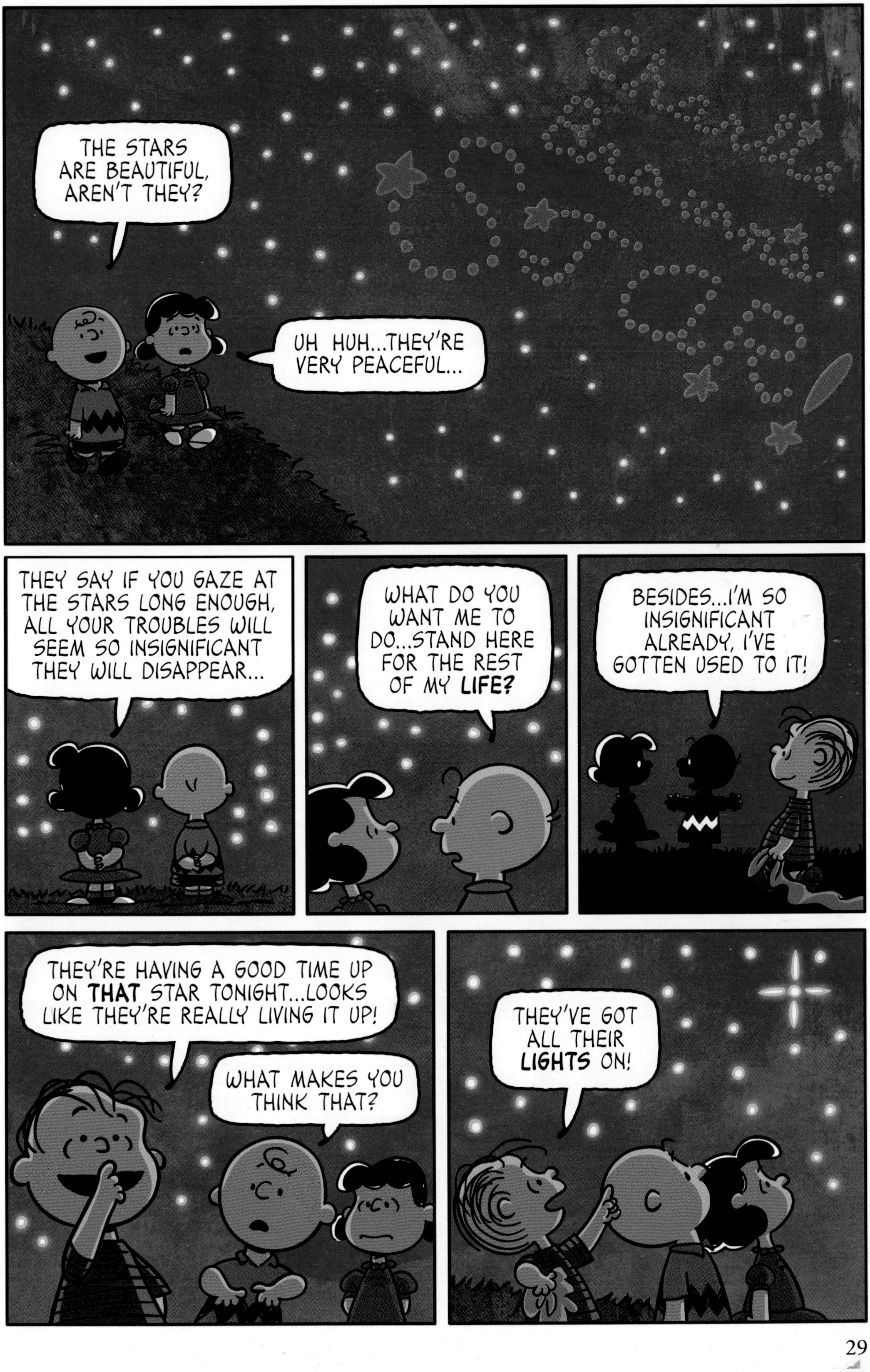
THE STARS ARE BEAUTIFUL, AREN'T THEY?
UH HUH...THEY'RE VERY PEACEFUL...
THEY SAY IF YOU GAZE AT THE STARS LONG ENOUGH, ALL YOUR TROUBLES WILL SEEM SO INSIGNIFICANT THEY WILL DISAPPEAR...
WHAT DO YOU WANT ME TO DO...STAND HERE FOR THE REST OF MY **LIFE?**
BESIDES...I'M SO INSIGNIFICANT ALREADY, I'VE GOTTEN USED TO IT!
THEY'RE HAVING A GOOD TIME UP ON **THAT** STAR TONIGHT...LOOKS LIKE THEY'RE REALLY LIVING IT UP!
WHAT MAKES YOU THINK THAT?
THEY'VE GOT ALL THEIR **LIGHTS** ON!

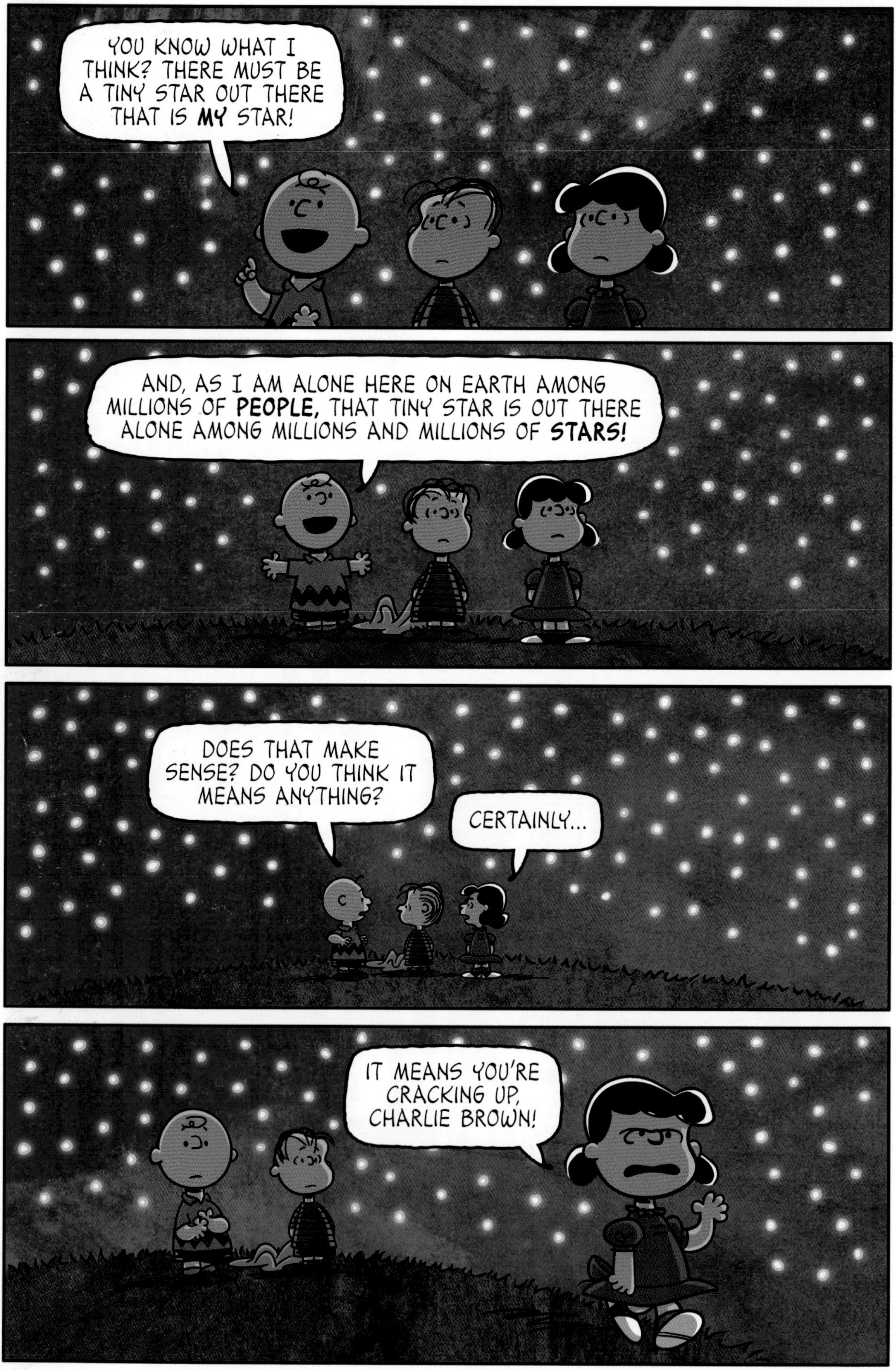
YOU KNOW WHAT I THINK? THERE MUST BE A TINY STAR OUT THERE THAT IS **MY** STAR!
AND, AS I AM ALONE HERE ON EARTH AMONG MILLIONS OF **PEOPLE,** THAT TINY STAR IS OUT THERE ALONE AMONG MILLIONS AND MILLIONS OF **STARS!**
DOES THAT MAKE SENSE? DO YOU THINK IT MEANS ANYTHING?
CERTAINLY...
IT MEANS YOU'RE CRACKING UP, CHARLIE BROWN!

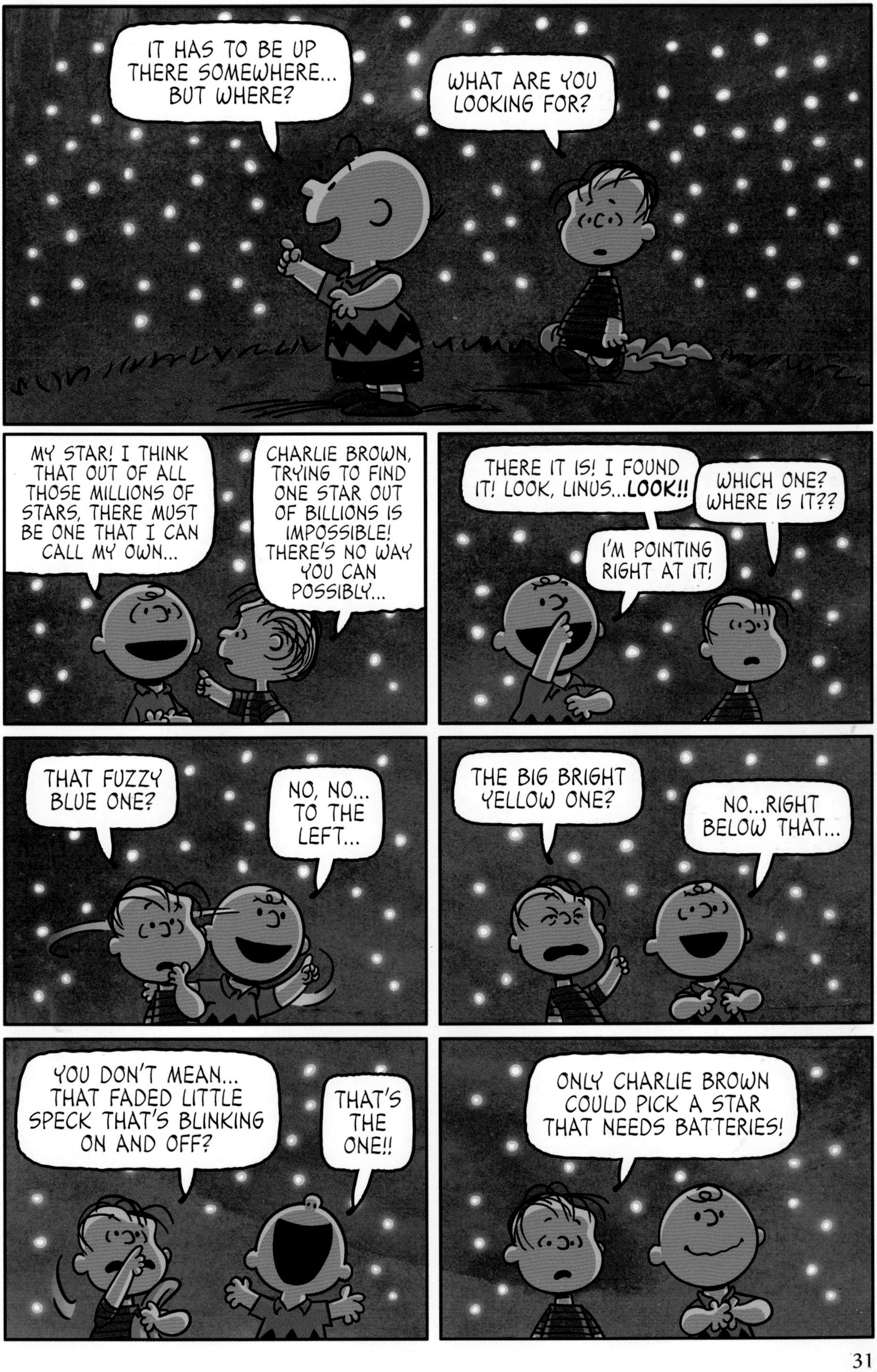

IT HAS TO BE UP THERE SOMEWHERE... BUT WHERE?
WHAT ARE YOU LOOKING FOR?
MY STAR! I THINK THAT OUT OF ALL THOSE MILLIONS OF STARS, THERE MUST BE ONE THAT I CAN CALL MY OWN...
CHARLIE BROWN, TRYING TO FIND ONE STAR OUT OF BILLIONS IS IMPOSSIBLE! THERE'S NO WAY YOU CAN POSSIBLY...
THERE IT IS! I FOUND IT! LOOK, LINUS...**LOOK!!**
WHICH ONE? WHERE IS IT??
I'M POINTING RIGHT AT IT!
THAT FUZZY BLUE ONE?
NO, NO... TO THE LEFT...
THE BIG BRIGHT YELLOW ONE?
NO...RIGHT BELOW THAT...
YOU DON'T MEAN... THAT FADED LITTLE SPECK THAT'S BLINKING ON AND OFF?
THAT'S THE ONE!!
ONLY CHARLIE BROWN COULD PICK A STAR THAT NEEDS BATTERIES!

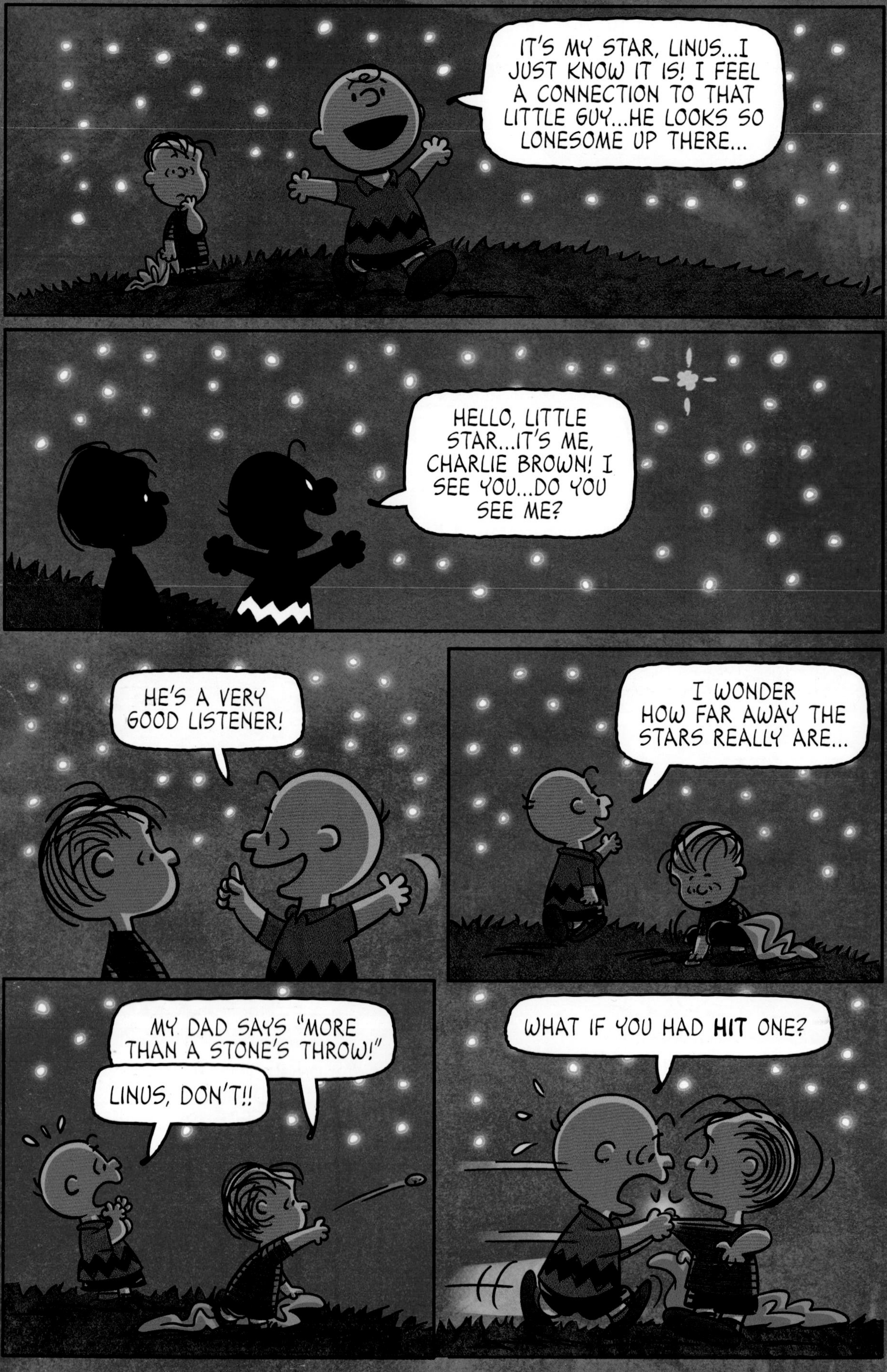
IT'S MY STAR, LINUS...I JUST KNOW IT IS! I FEEL A CONNECTION TO THAT LITTLE GUY...HE LOOKS SO LONESOME UP THERE...
HELLO, LITTLE STAR...IT'S ME, CHARLIE BROWN! I SEE YOU...DO YOU SEE ME?
HE'S A VERY GOOD LISTENER!
I WONDER HOW FAR AWAY THE STARS REALLY ARE...
MY DAD SAYS "MORE THAN A STONE'S THROW!"
LINUS, DON'T!!
WHAT IF YOU HAD **HIT** ONE?

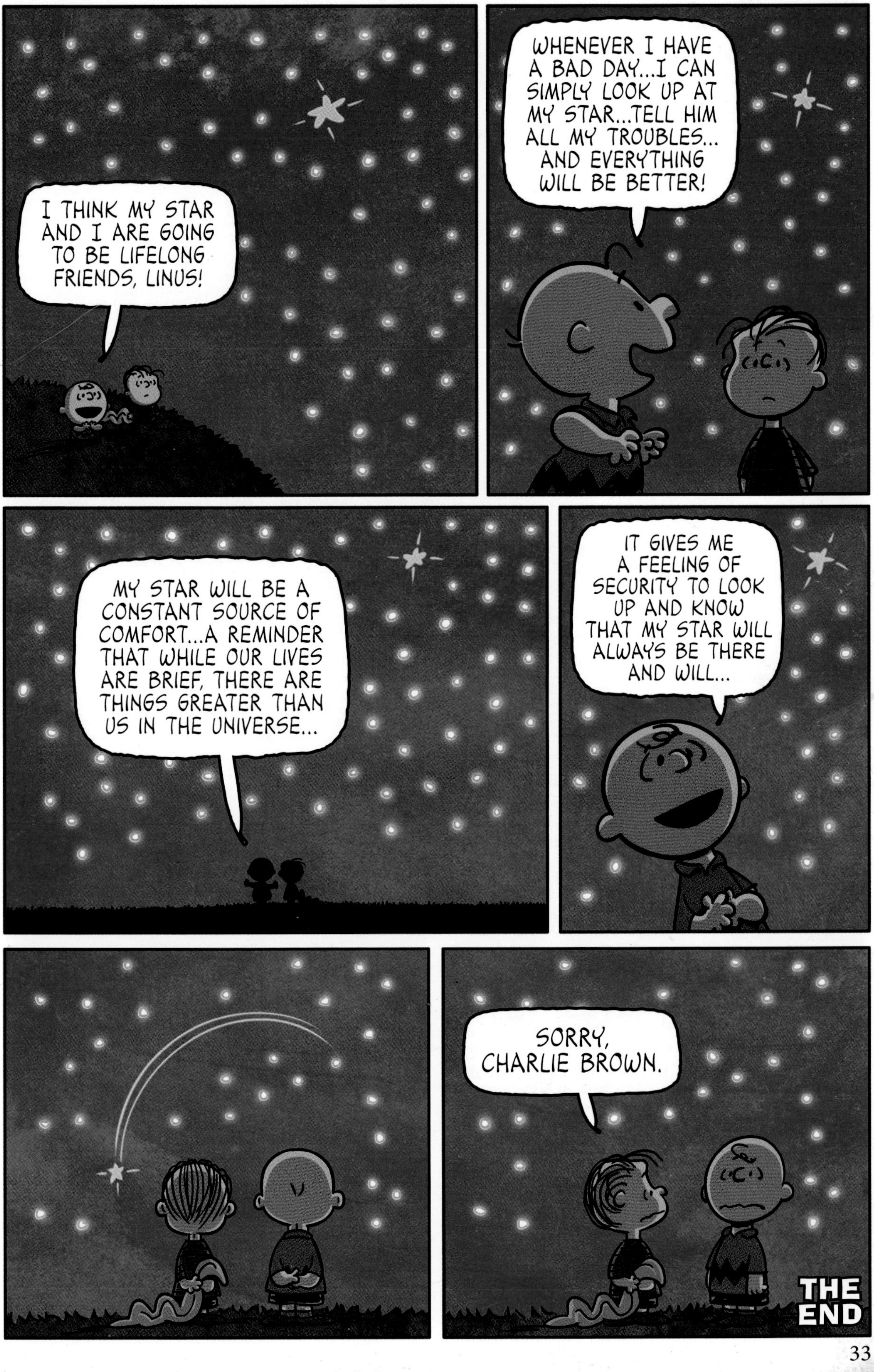
I THINK MY STAR AND I ARE GOING TO BE LIFELONG FRIENDS, LINUS!
WHENEVER I HAVE A BAD DAY...I CAN SIMPLY LOOK UP AT MY STAR...TELL HIM ALL MY TROUBLES... AND EVERYTHING WILL BE BETTER!
MY STAR WILL BE A CONSTANT SOURCE OF COMFORT...A REMINDER THAT WHILE OUR LIVES ARE BRIEF, THERE ARE THINGS GREATER THAN US IN THE UNIVERSE...
IT GIVES ME A FEELING OF SECURITY TO LOOK UP AND KNOW THAT MY STAR WILL ALWAYS BE THERE AND WILL...
SORRY, CHARLIE BROWN.
THE END

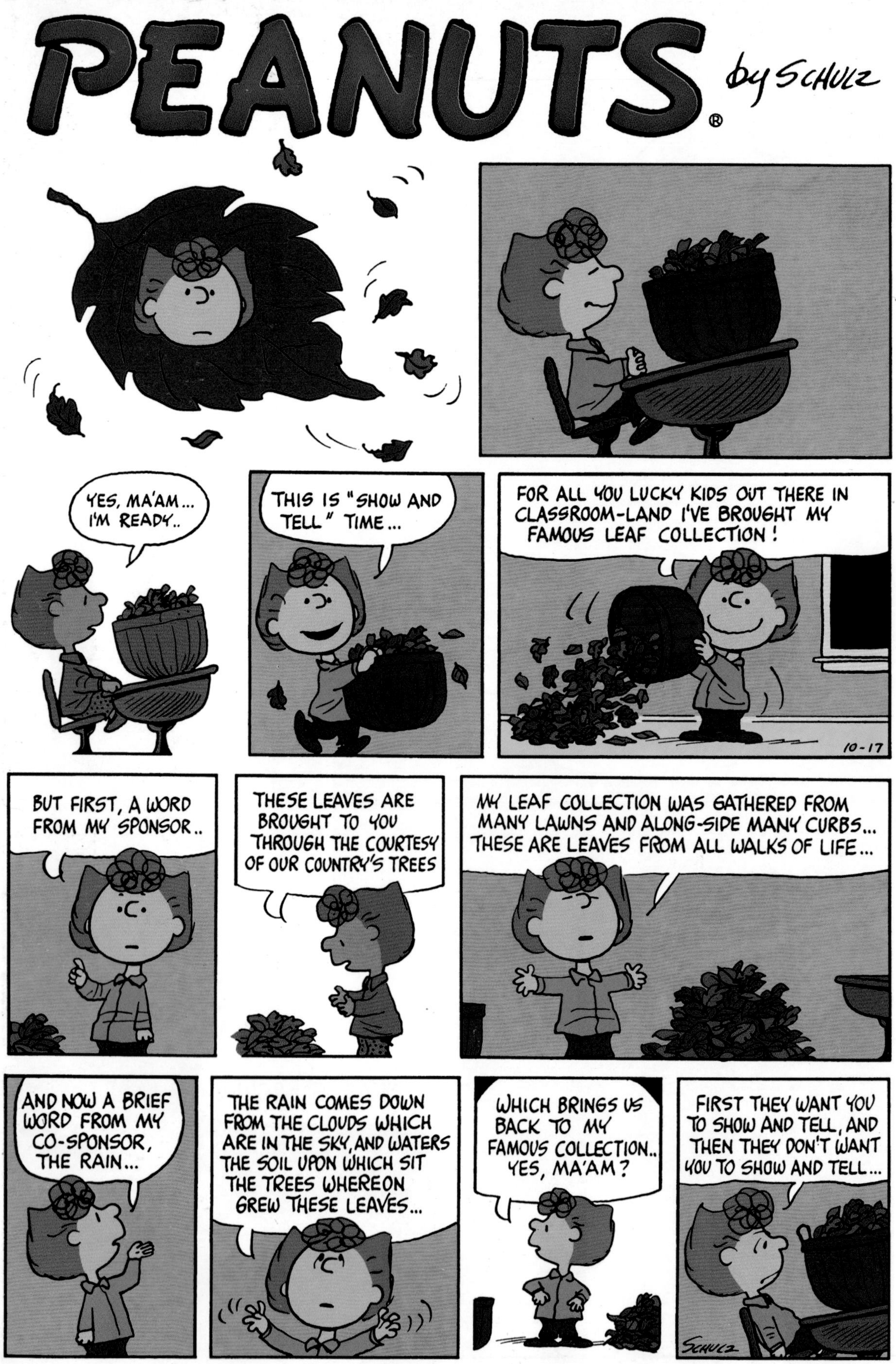
PEANUTS
by SCHULZ
YES, MA'AM... I'M READY..
THIS IS "SHOW AND TELL" TIME...
FOR ALL YOU LUCKY KIDS OUT THERE IN CLASSROOM-LAND I'VE BROUGHT MY FAMOUS LEAF COLLECTION!
10-17
BUT FIRST, A WORD FROM MY SPONSOR..
THESE LEAVES ARE BROUGHT TO YOU THROUGH THE COURTESY OF OUR COUNTRY'S TREES
MY LEAF COLLECTION WAS GATHERED FROM MANY LAWNS AND ALONG-SIDE MANY CURBS... THESE ARE LEAVES FROM ALL WALKS OF LIFE...
AND NOW A BRIEF WORD FROM MY CO-SPONSOR, THE RAIN...
THE RAIN COMES DOWN FROM THE CLOUDS WHICH ARE IN THE SKY, AND WATERS THE SOIL UPON WHICH SIT THE TREES WHEREON GREW THESE LEAVES...
WHICH BRINGS US BACK TO MY FAMOUS COLLECTION.. YES, MA'AM?
FIRST THEY WANT YOU TO SHOW AND TELL, AND THEN THEY DON'T WANT YOU TO SHOW AND TELL...
SCHULZ

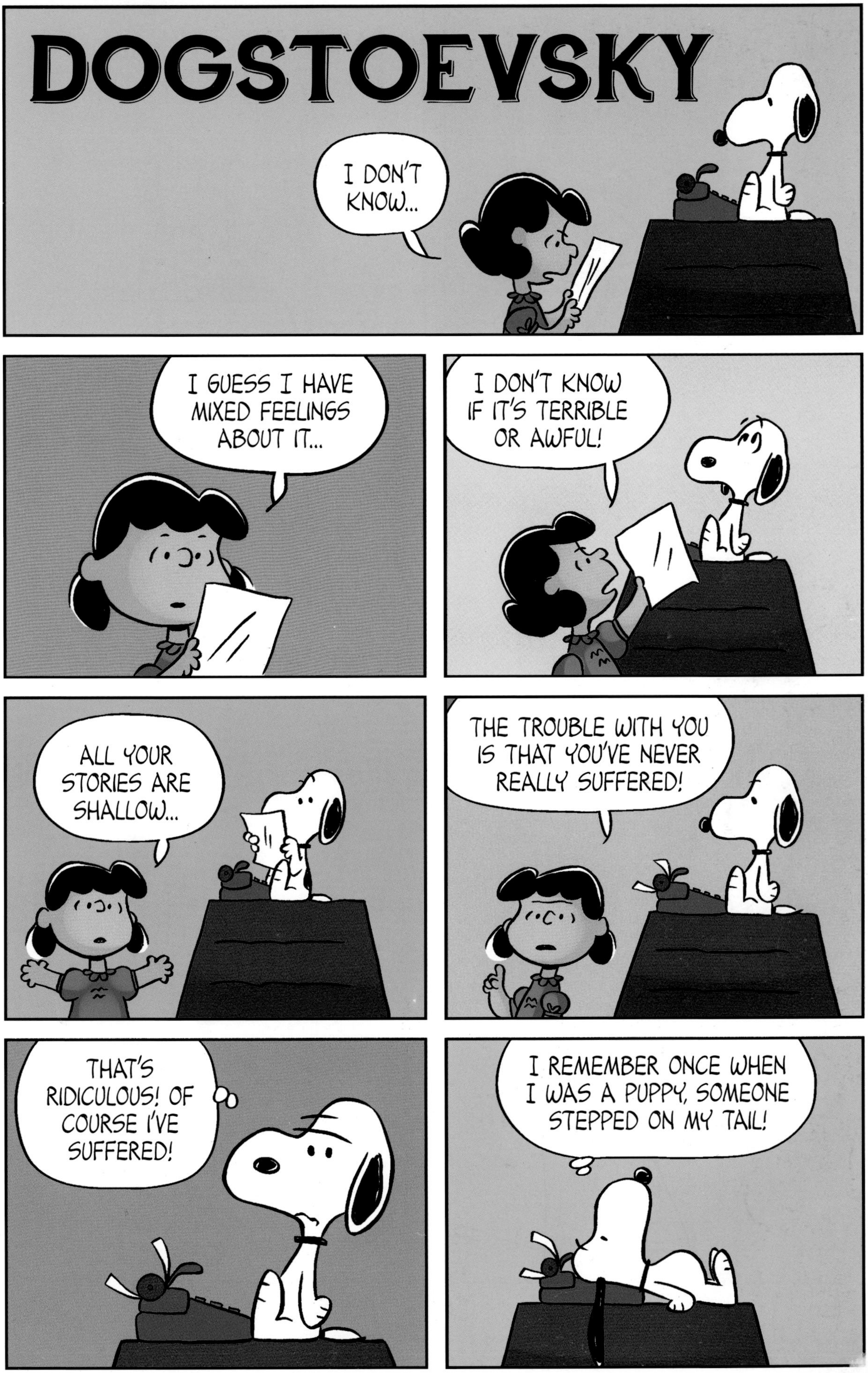
DOGSTOEVSKY
I DON'T KNOW...
I GUESS I HAVE MIXED FEELINGS ABOUT IT...
I DON'T KNOW IF IT'S TERRIBLE OR AWFUL!
ALL YOUR STORIES ARE SHALLOW...
THE TROUBLE WITH YOU IS THAT YOU'VE NEVER REALLY SUFFERED!
THAT'S RIDICULOUS! OF COURSE I'VE SUFFERED!
I REMEMBER ONCE WHEN I WAS A PUPPY, SOMEONE STEPPED ON MY TAIL!

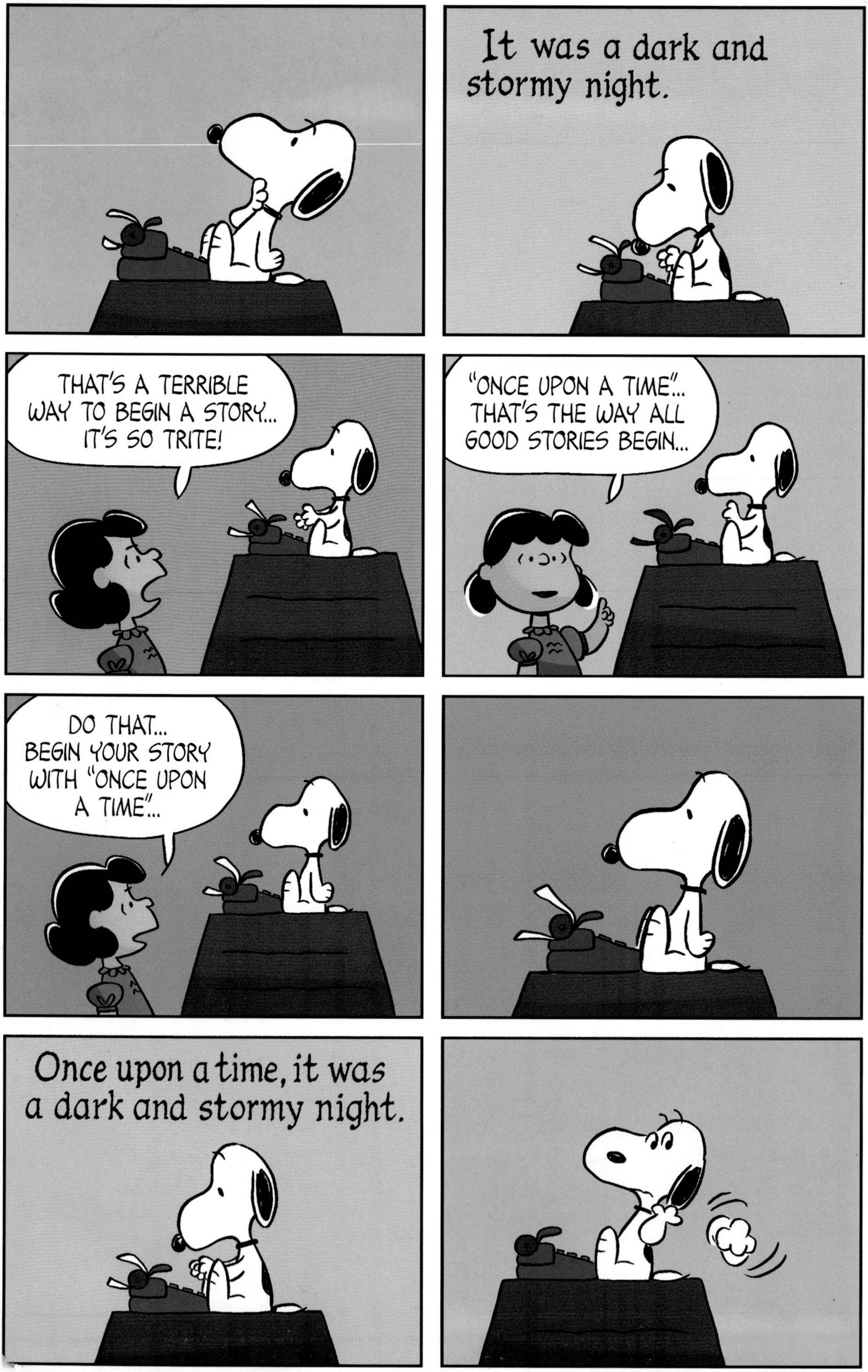

It was a dark and stormy night.
THAT'S A TERRIBLE WAY TO BEGIN A STORY... IT'S SO TRITE!
"ONCE UPON A TIME"... THAT'S THE WAY ALL GOOD STORIES BEGIN...
DO THAT... BEGIN YOUR STORY WITH "ONCE UPON A TIME"...
Once upon a time, it was a dark and stormy night.

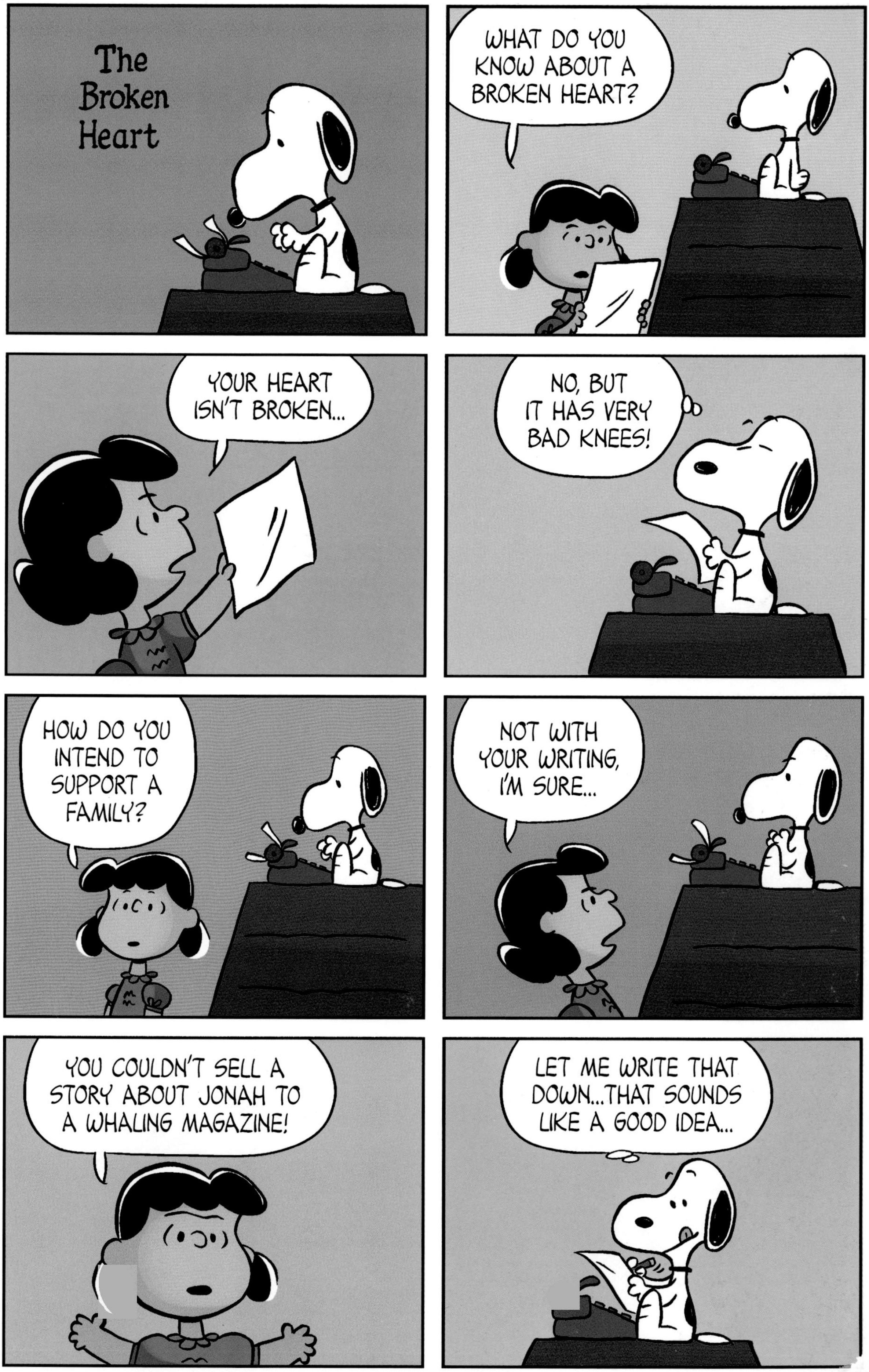
The Broken Heart
WHAT DO YOU KNOW ABOUT A BROKEN HEART?
YOUR HEART ISN'T BROKEN...
NO, BUT IT HAS VERY BAD KNEES!
HOW DO YOU INTEND TO SUPPORT A FAMILY?
NOT WITH YOUR WRITING, I'M SURE...
YOU COULDN'T SELL A STORY ABOUT JONAH TO A WHALING MAGAZINE!
LET ME WRITE THAT DOWN...THAT SOUNDS LIKE A GOOD IDEA...

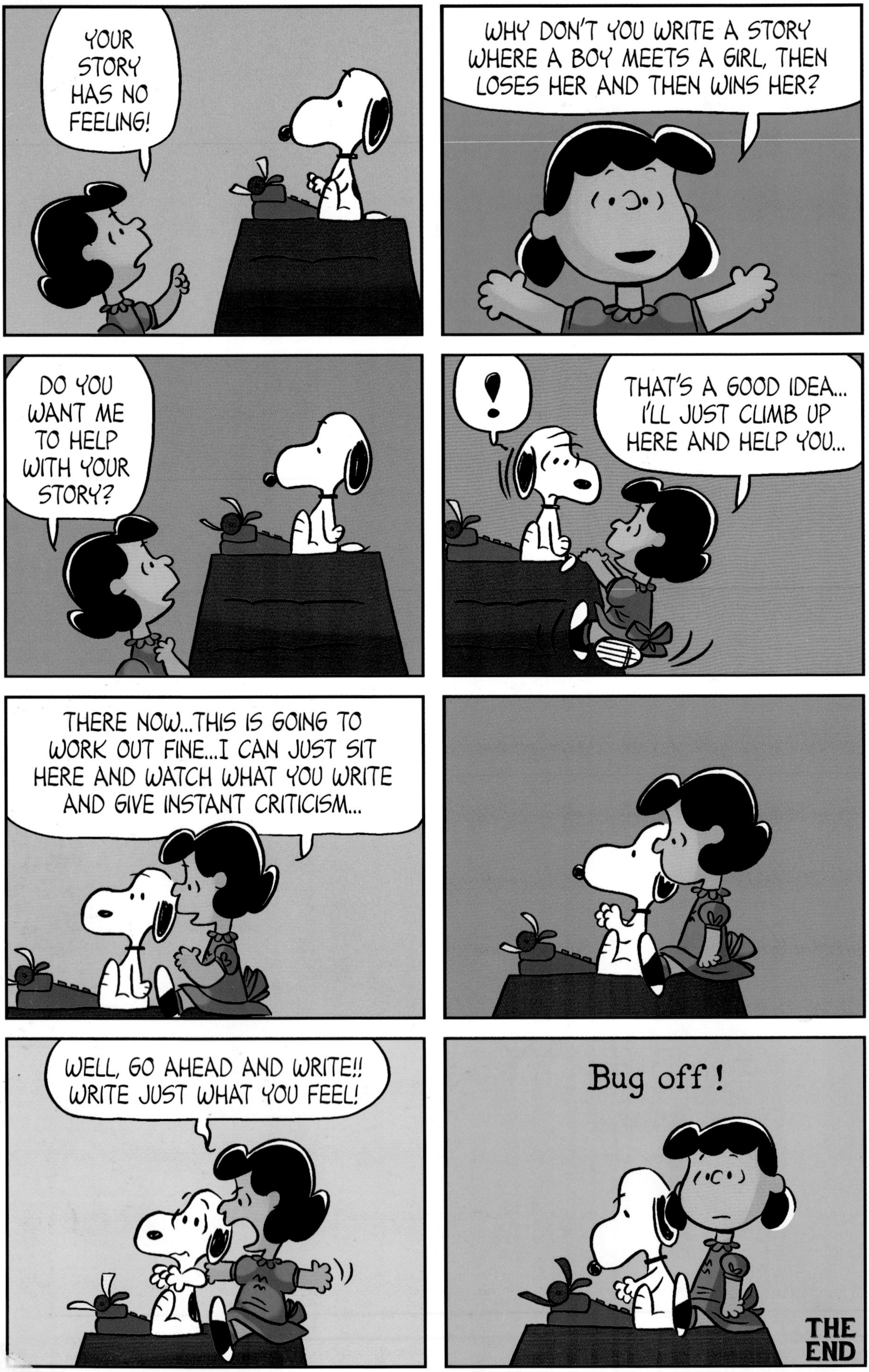
YOUR STORY HAS NO FEELING!
WHY DON'T YOU WRITE A STORY WHERE A BOY MEETS A GIRL, THEN LOSES HER AND THEN WINS HER?
DO YOU WANT ME TO HELP WITH YOUR STORY?
!
THAT'S A GOOD IDEA... I'LL JUST CLIMB UP HERE AND HELP YOU...
THERE NOW...THIS IS GOING TO WORK OUT FINE...I CAN JUST SIT HERE AND WATCH WHAT YOU WRITE AND GIVE INSTANT CRITICISM...
WELL, GO AHEAD AND WRITE!! WRITE JUST WHAT YOU FEEL!
Bug off !
THE END

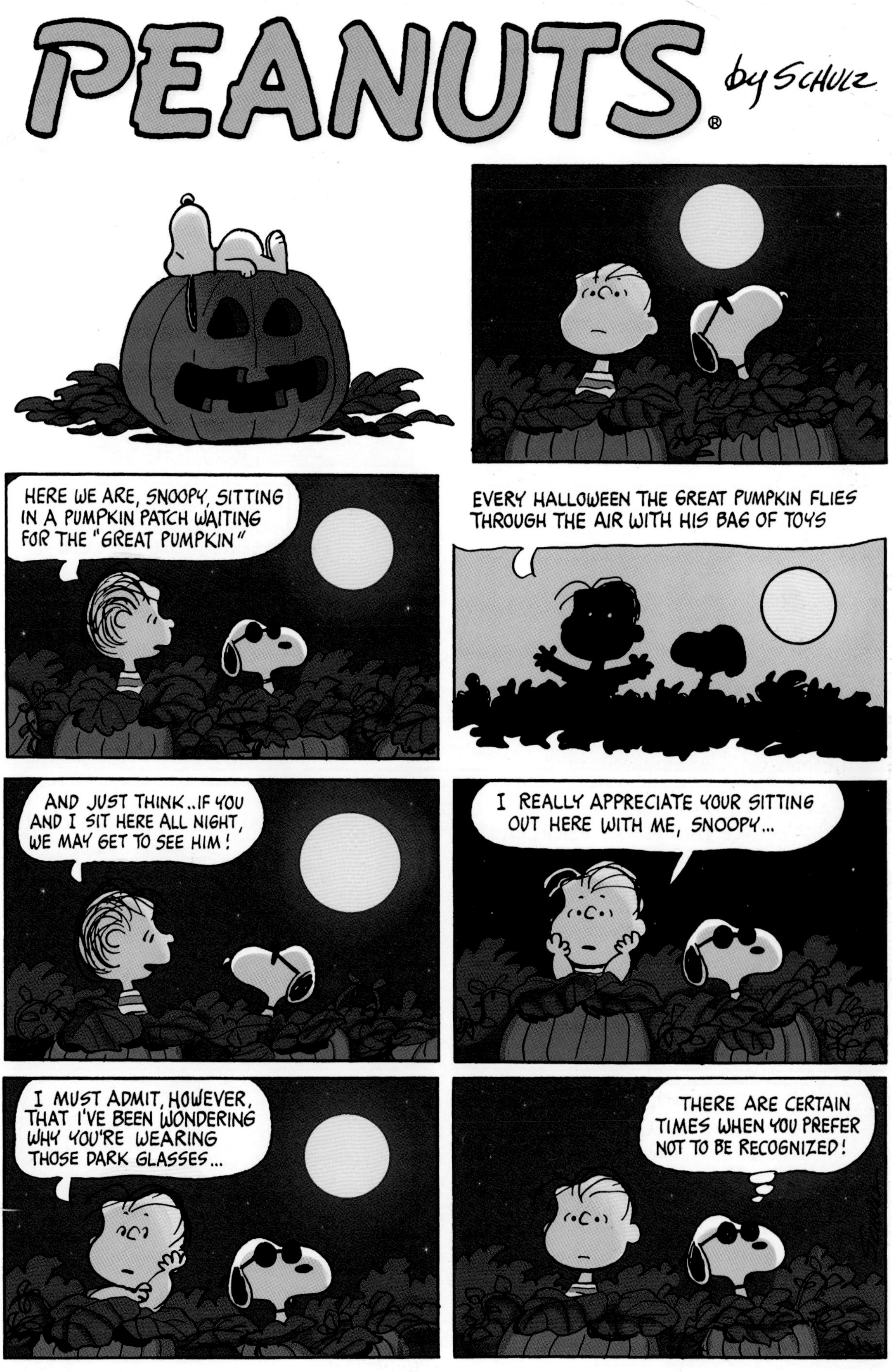
PEANUTS
by SCHULZ
HERE WE ARE, SNOOPY, SITTING IN A PUMPKIN PATCH WAITING FOR THE "GREAT PUMPKIN"
EVERY HALLOWEEN THE GREAT PUMPKIN FLIES THROUGH THE AIR WITH HIS BAG OF TOYS
AND JUST THINK..IF YOU AND I SIT HERE ALL NIGHT, WE MAY GET TO SEE HIM!
I REALLY APPRECIATE YOUR SITTING OUT HERE WITH ME, SNOOPY...
I MUST ADMIT, HOWEVER, THAT I'VE BEEN WONDERING WHY YOU'RE WEARING THOSE DARK GLASSES...
THERE ARE CERTAIN TIMES WHEN YOU PREFER NOT TO BE RECOGNIZED!

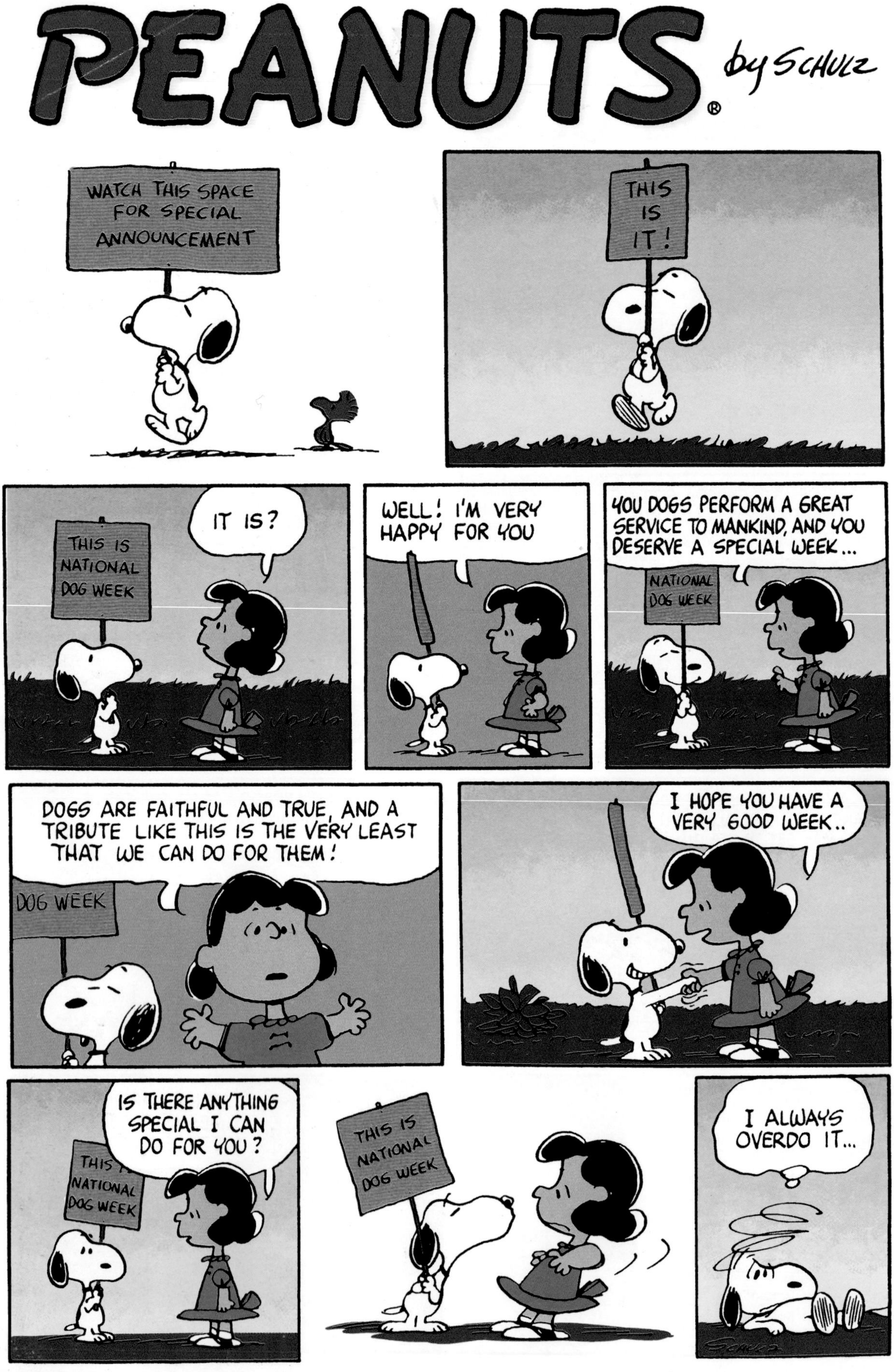
PEANUTS
by SCHULZ
WATCH THIS SPACE FOR SPECIAL ANNOUNCEMENT
THIS IS IT!
THIS IS NATIONAL DOG WEEK
IT IS?
WELL! I'M VERY HAPPY FOR YOU
YOU DOGS PERFORM A GREAT SERVICE TO MANKIND, AND YOU DESERVE A SPECIAL WEEK...
NATIONAL DOG WEEK
DOGS ARE FAITHFUL AND TRUE, AND A TRIBUTE LIKE THIS IS THE VERY LEAST THAT WE CAN DO FOR THEM!
DOG WEEK
I HOPE YOU HAVE A VERY GOOD WEEK..
IS THERE ANYTHING SPECIAL I CAN DO FOR YOU?
NATIONAL DOG WEEK
THIS IS NATIONAL DOG WEEK
I ALWAYS OVERDO IT...
SCHULZ

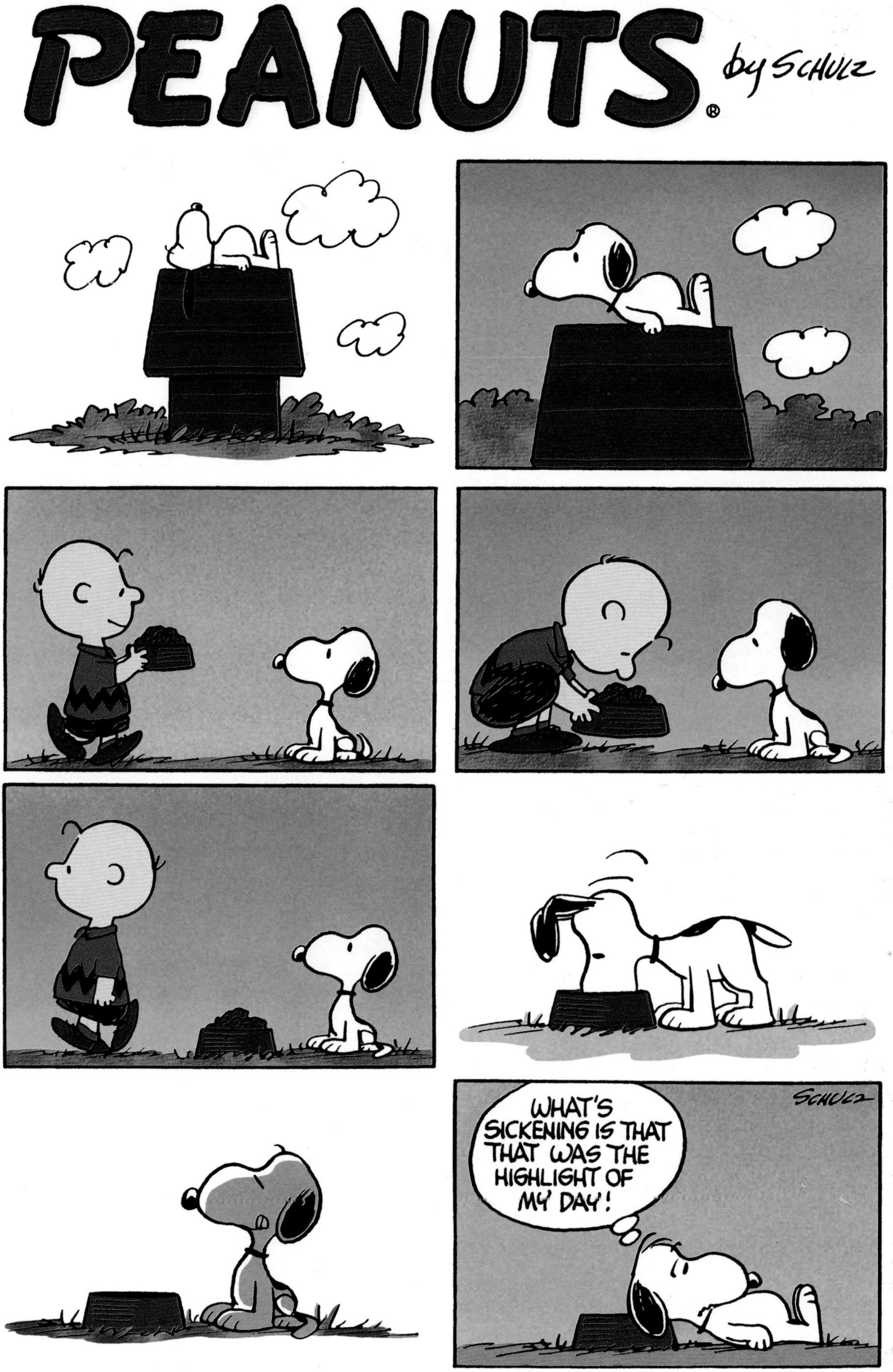
PEANUTS
by SCHULZ
SCHULZ
WHAT'S SICKENING IS THAT THAT WAS THE HIGHLIGHT OF MY DAY!

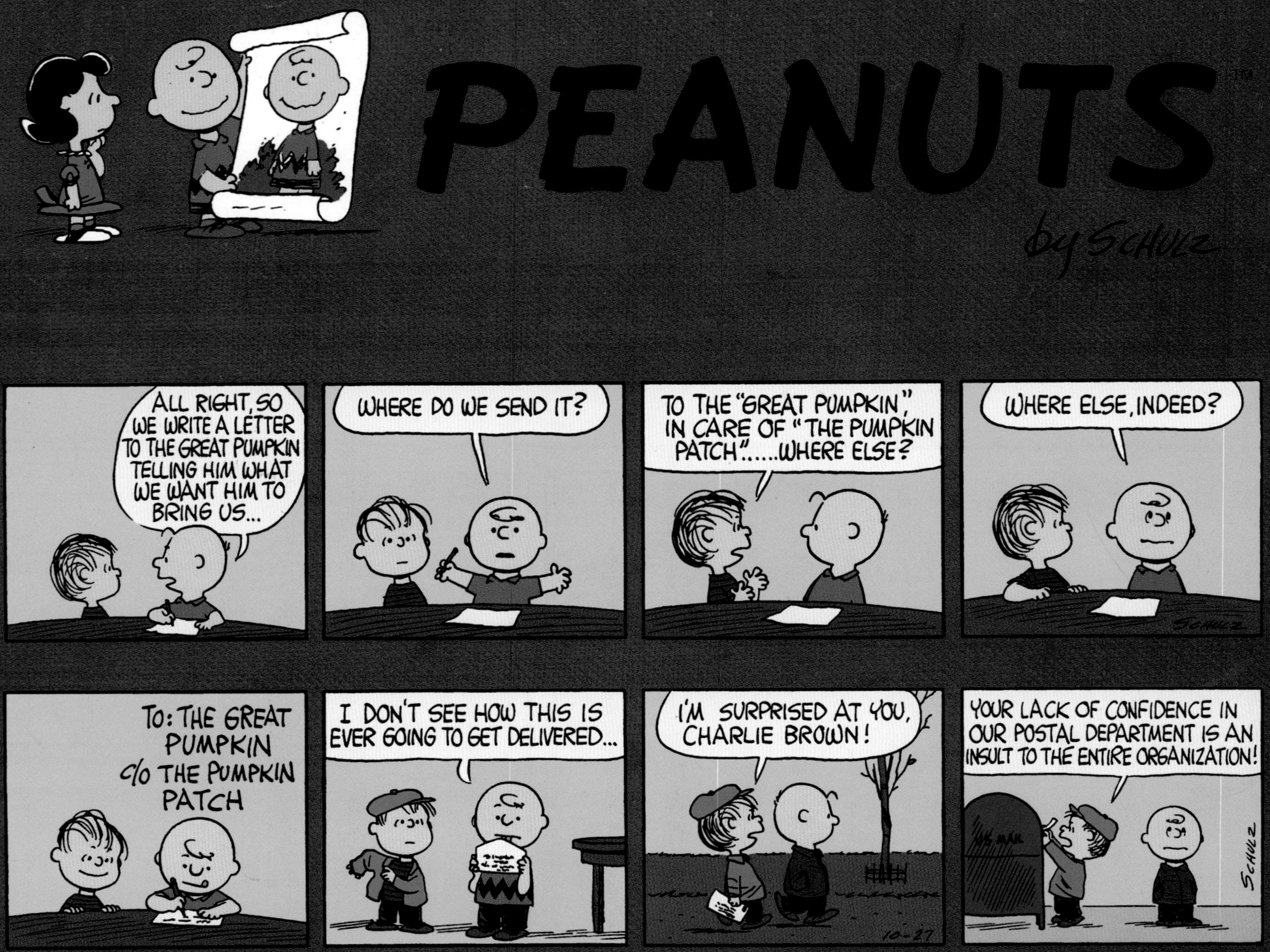
PEANUTS™
by SCHULZ
ALL RIGHT, SO WE WRITE A LETTER TO THE GREAT PUMPKIN TELLING HIM WHAT WE WANT HIM TO BRING US...
WHERE DO WE SEND IT?
TO THE "GREAT PUMPKIN," IN CARE OF "THE PUMPKIN PATCH"......WHERE ELSE?
WHERE ELSE, INDEED?
SCHULZ
TO: THE GREAT PUMPKIN c/o THE PUMPKIN PATCH
I DON'T SEE HOW THIS IS EVER GOING TO GET DELIVERED...
I'M SURPRISED AT YOU, CHARLIE BROWN!
10-27
YOUR LACK OF CONFIDENCE IN OUR POSTAL DEPARTMENT IS AN INSULT TO THE ENTIRE ORGANIZATION!
US MAIL
SCHULZ

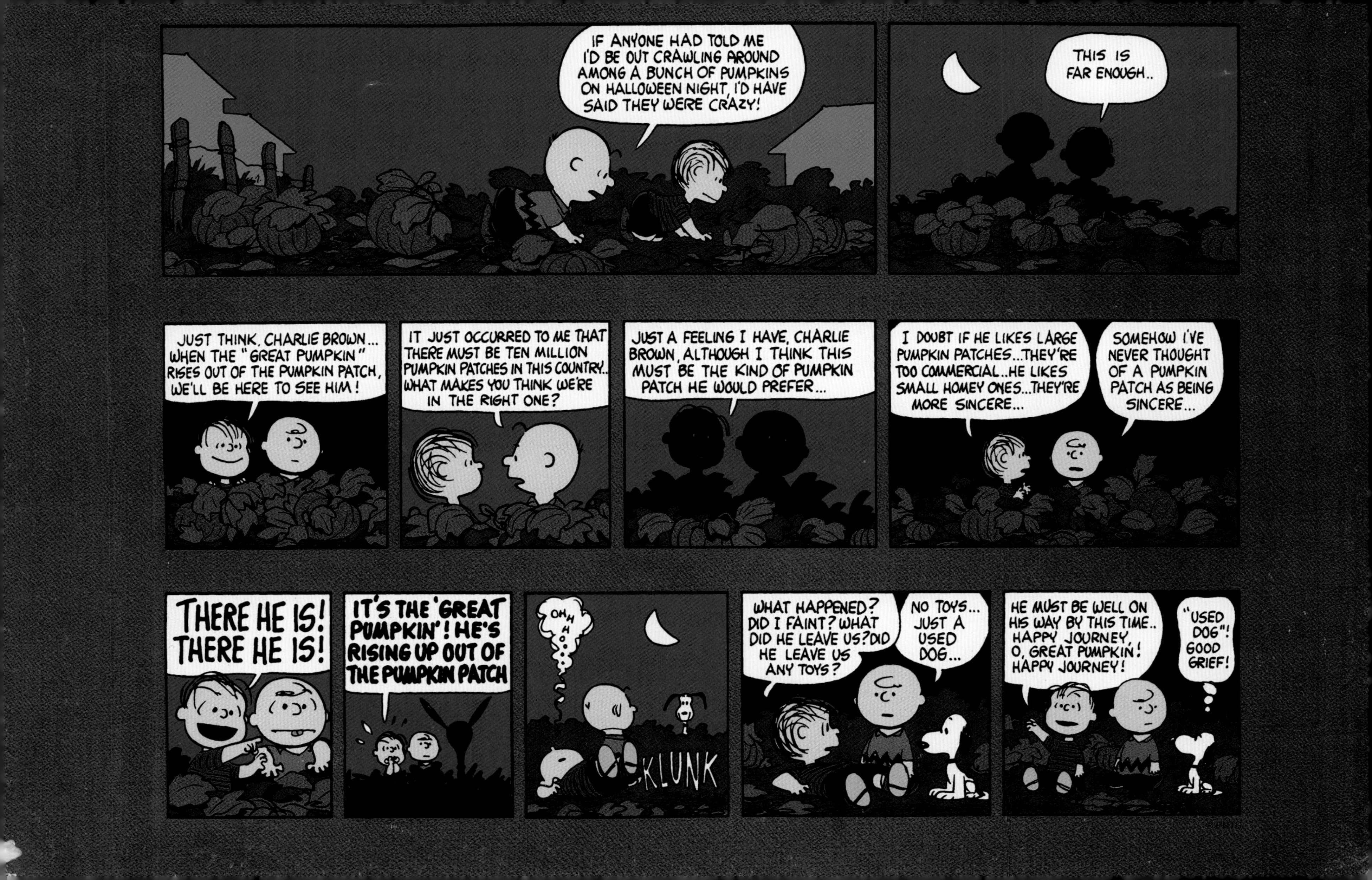

IF ANYONE HAD TOLD ME I'D BE OUT CRAWLING AROUND AMONG A BUNCH OF PUMPKINS ON HALLOWEEN NIGHT, I'D HAVE SAID THEY WERE CRAZY!
THIS IS FAR ENOUGH..
JUST THINK, CHARLIE BROWN... WHEN THE "GREAT PUMPKIN" RISES OUT OF THE PUMPKIN PATCH, WE'LL BE HERE TO SEE HIM!
IT JUST OCCURRED TO ME THAT THERE MUST BE TEN MILLION PUMPKIN PATCHES IN THIS COUNTRY.. WHAT MAKES YOU THINK WE'RE IN THE RIGHT ONE?
JUST A FEELING I HAVE, CHARLIE BROWN, ALTHOUGH I THINK THIS MUST BE THE KIND OF PUMPKIN PATCH HE WOULD PREFER...
I DOUBT IF HE LIKES LARGE PUMPKIN PATCHES...THEY'RE TOO COMMERCIAL..HE LIKES SMALL HOMEY ONES...THEY'RE MORE SINCERE...
SOMEHOW I'VE NEVER THOUGHT OF A PUMPKIN PATCH AS BEING SINCERE...
THERE HE IS! THERE HE IS!
IT'S THE 'GREAT PUMPKIN'! HE'S RISING UP OUT OF THE PUMPKIN PATCH
OHHH
KLUNK
WHAT HAPPENED? DID I FAINT? WHAT DID HE LEAVE US? DID HE LEAVE US ANY TOYS?
NO TOYS... JUST A USED DOG...
HE MUST BE WELL ON HIS WAY BY THIS TIME.. HAPPY JOURNEY, O, GREAT PUMPKIN! HAPPY JOURNEY!
"USED DOG"! GOOD GRIEF!

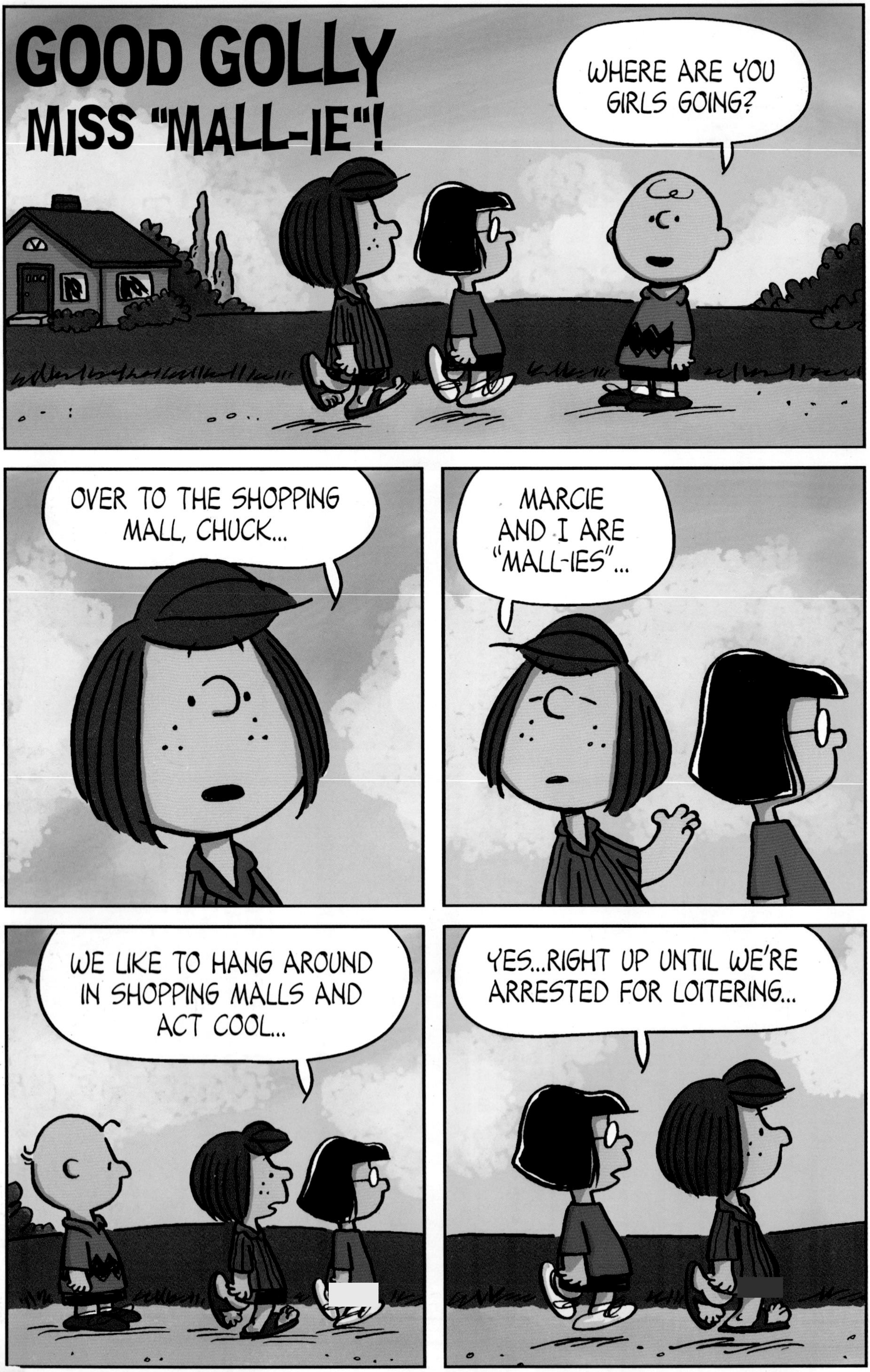
GOOD GOLLY MISS "MALL-IE"!
WHERE ARE YOU GIRLS GOING?
OVER TO THE SHOPPING MALL, CHUCK...
MARCIE AND I ARE "MALL-IES"...
WE LIKE TO HANG AROUND IN SHOPPING MALLS AND ACT COOL...
YES...RIGHT UP UNTIL WE'RE ARRESTED FOR LOITERING...

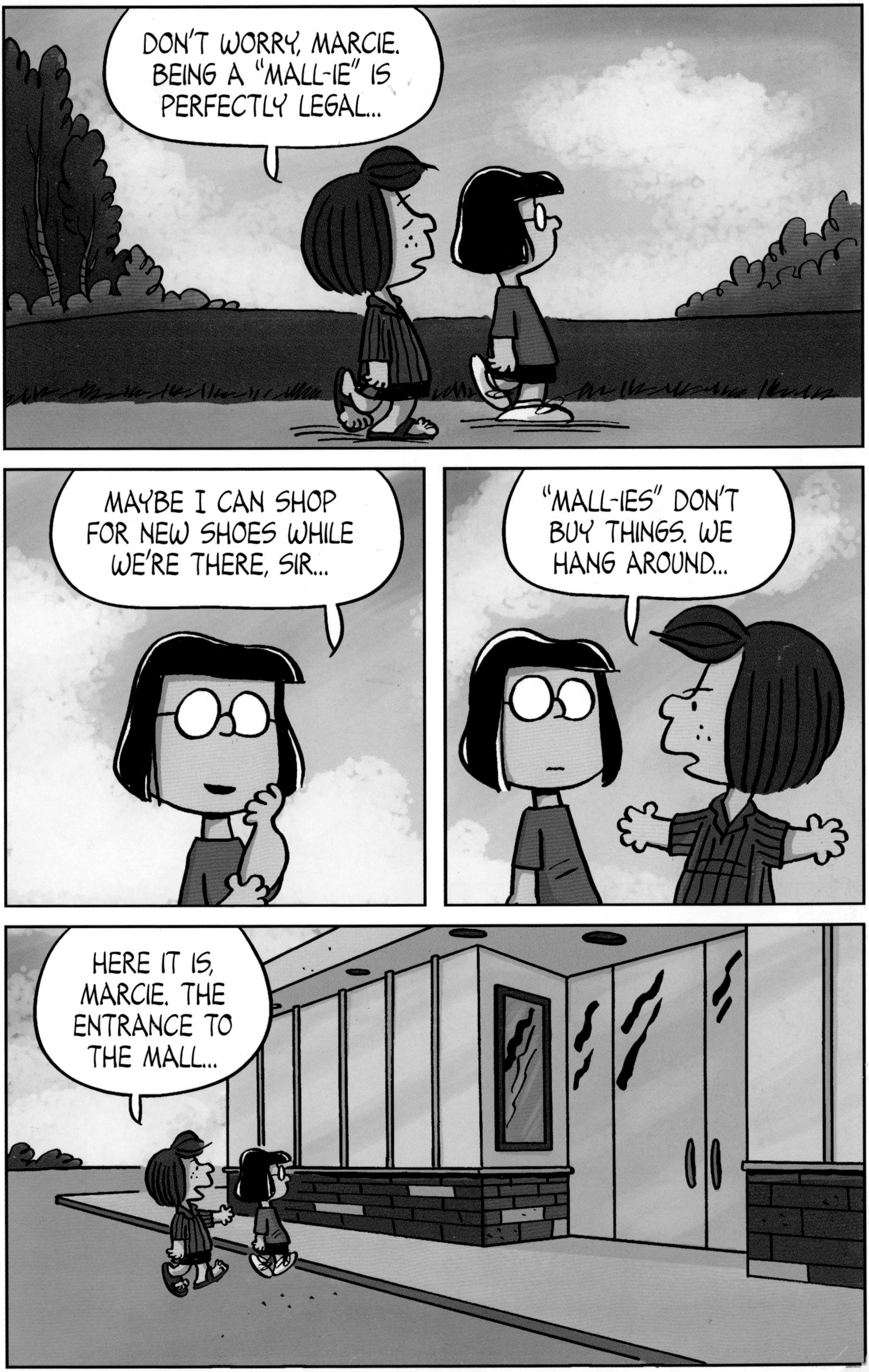
DON'T WORRY, MARCIE. BEING A "MALL-IE" IS PERFECTLY LEGAL...
MAYBE I CAN SHOP FOR NEW SHOES WHILE WE'RE THERE, SIR...
"MALL-IES" DON'T BUY THINGS. WE HANG AROUND...
HERE IT IS, MARCIE. THE ENTRANCE TO THE MALL...

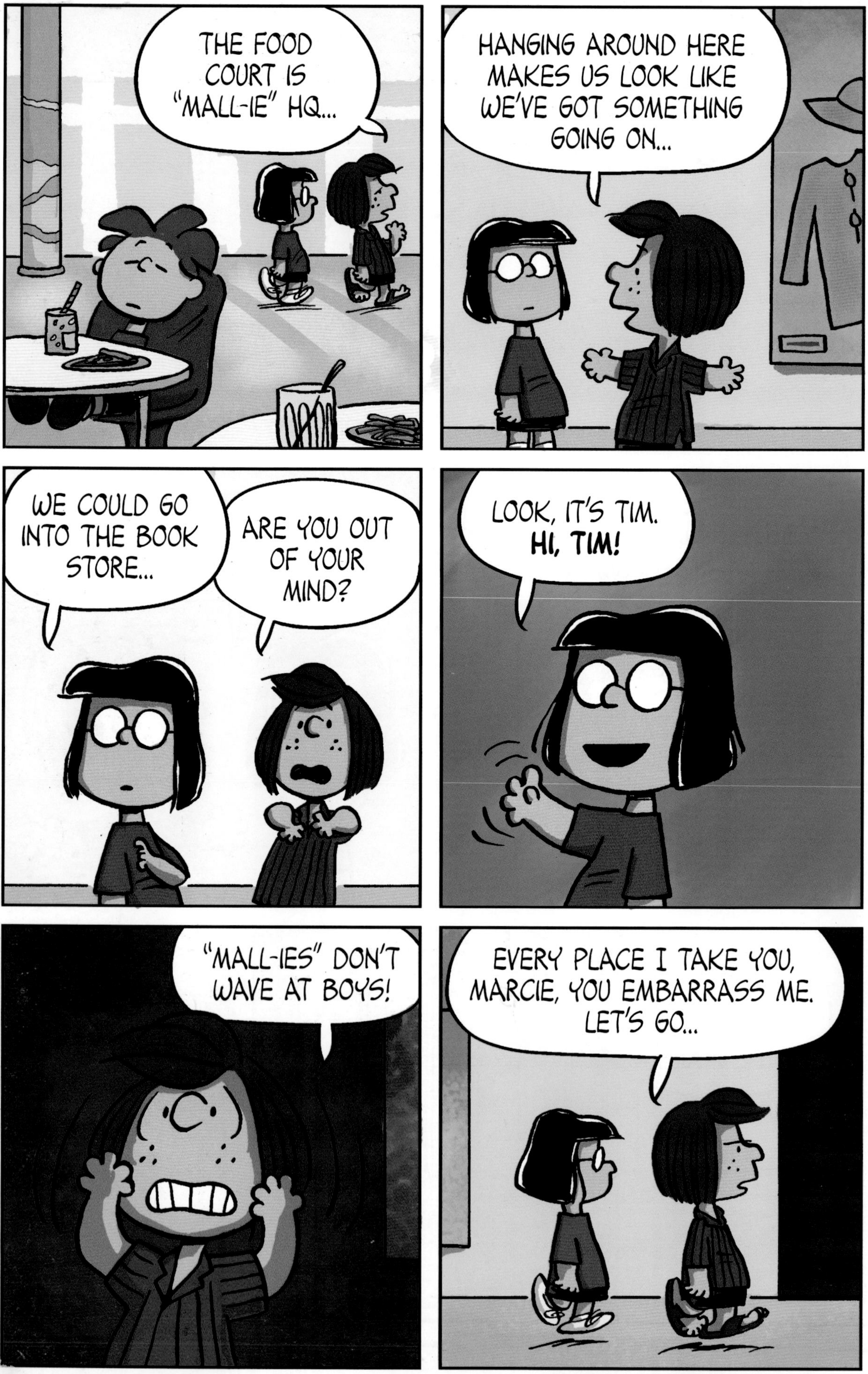
THE FOOD COURT IS "MALL-IE" HQ...
HANGING AROUND HERE MAKES US LOOK LIKE WE'VE GOT SOMETHING GOING ON...
WE COULD GO INTO THE BOOK STORE...
ARE YOU OUT OF YOUR MIND?
LOOK, IT'S TIM. **HI, TIM!**
"MALL-IES" DON'T WAVE AT BOYS!
EVERY PLACE I TAKE YOU, MARCIE, YOU EMBARRASS ME. LET'S GO...

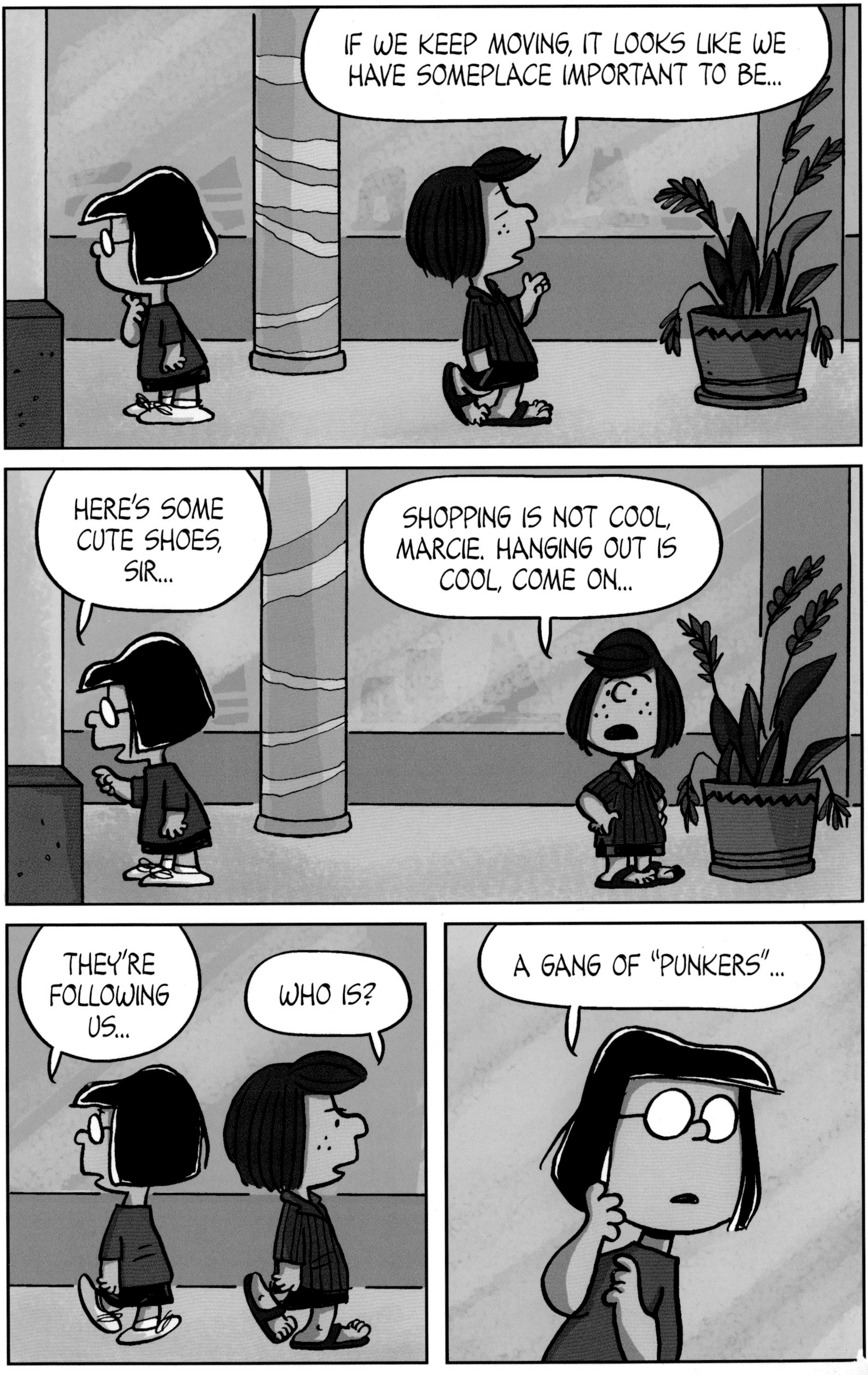
IF WE KEEP MOVING, IT LOOKS LIKE WE HAVE SOMEPLACE IMPORTANT TO BE...
HERE'S SOME CUTE SHOES, SIR...
SHOPPING IS NOT COOL, MARCIE. HANGING OUT IS COOL, COME ON...
THEY'RE FOLLOWING US...
WHO IS?
A GANG OF "PUNKERS"...

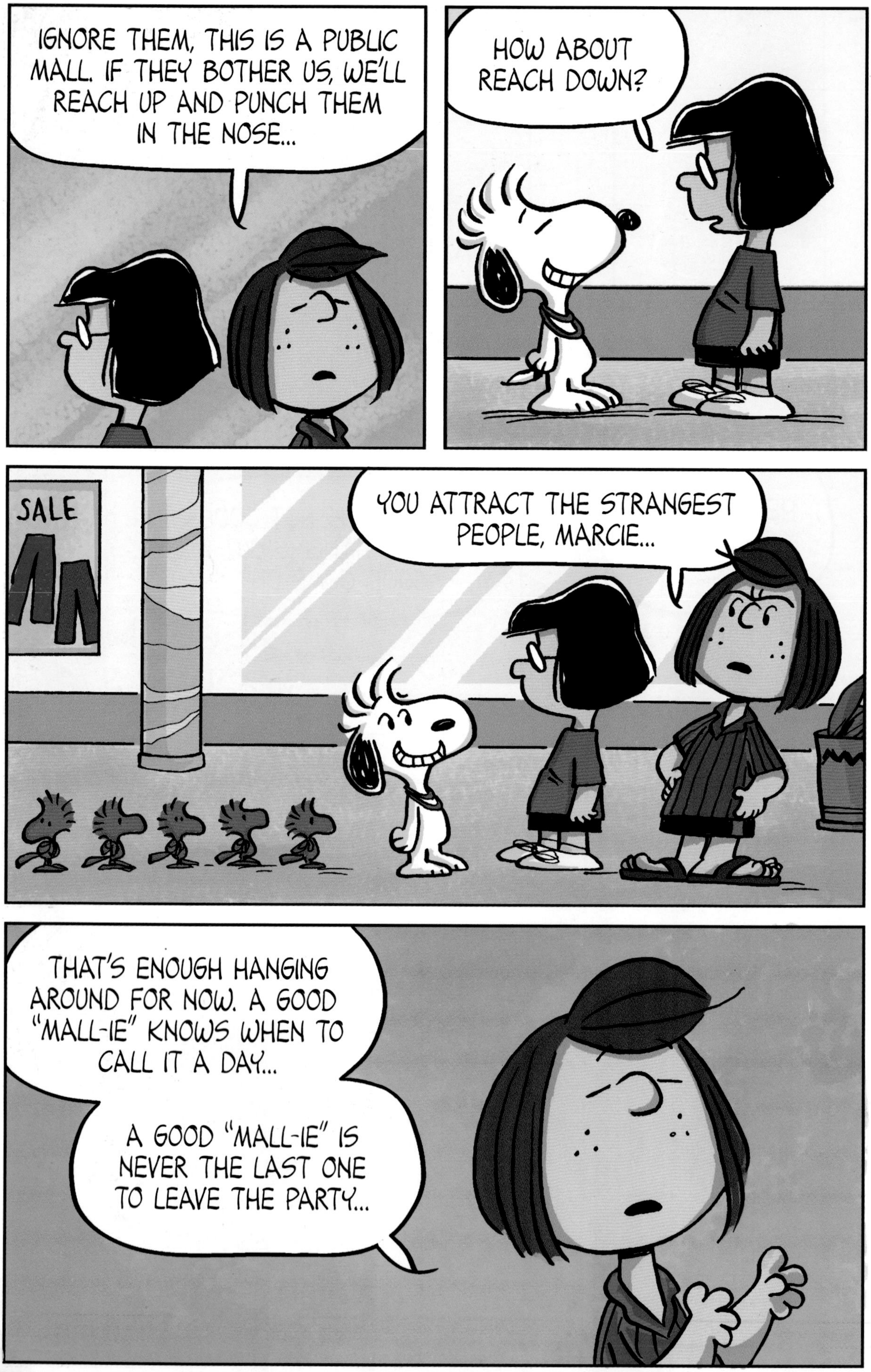
IGNORE THEM, THIS IS A PUBLIC MALL. IF THEY BOTHER US, WE'LL REACH UP AND PUNCH THEM IN THE NOSE...
HOW ABOUT REACH DOWN?
SALE
YOU ATTRACT THE STRANGEST PEOPLE, MARCIE...
THAT'S ENOUGH HANGING AROUND FOR NOW. A GOOD "MALL-IE" KNOWS WHEN TO CALL IT A DAY...
A GOOD "MALL-IE" IS NEVER THE LAST ONE TO LEAVE THE PARTY...

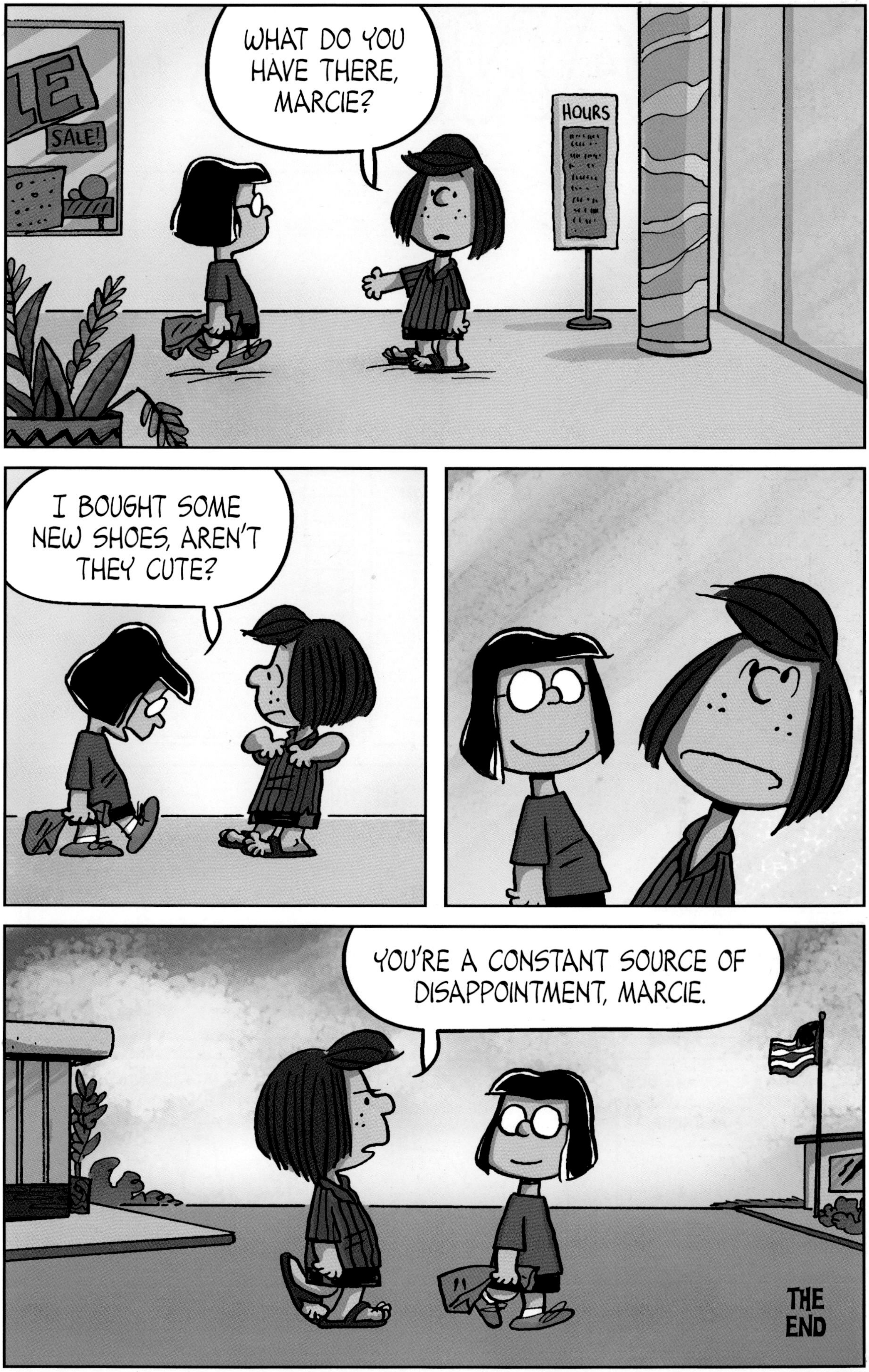
SALE!
HOURS
WHAT DO YOU HAVE THERE, MARCIE?
I BOUGHT SOME NEW SHOES, AREN'T THEY CUTE?
YOU'RE A CONSTANT SOURCE OF DISAPPOINTMENT, MARCIE.
THE END

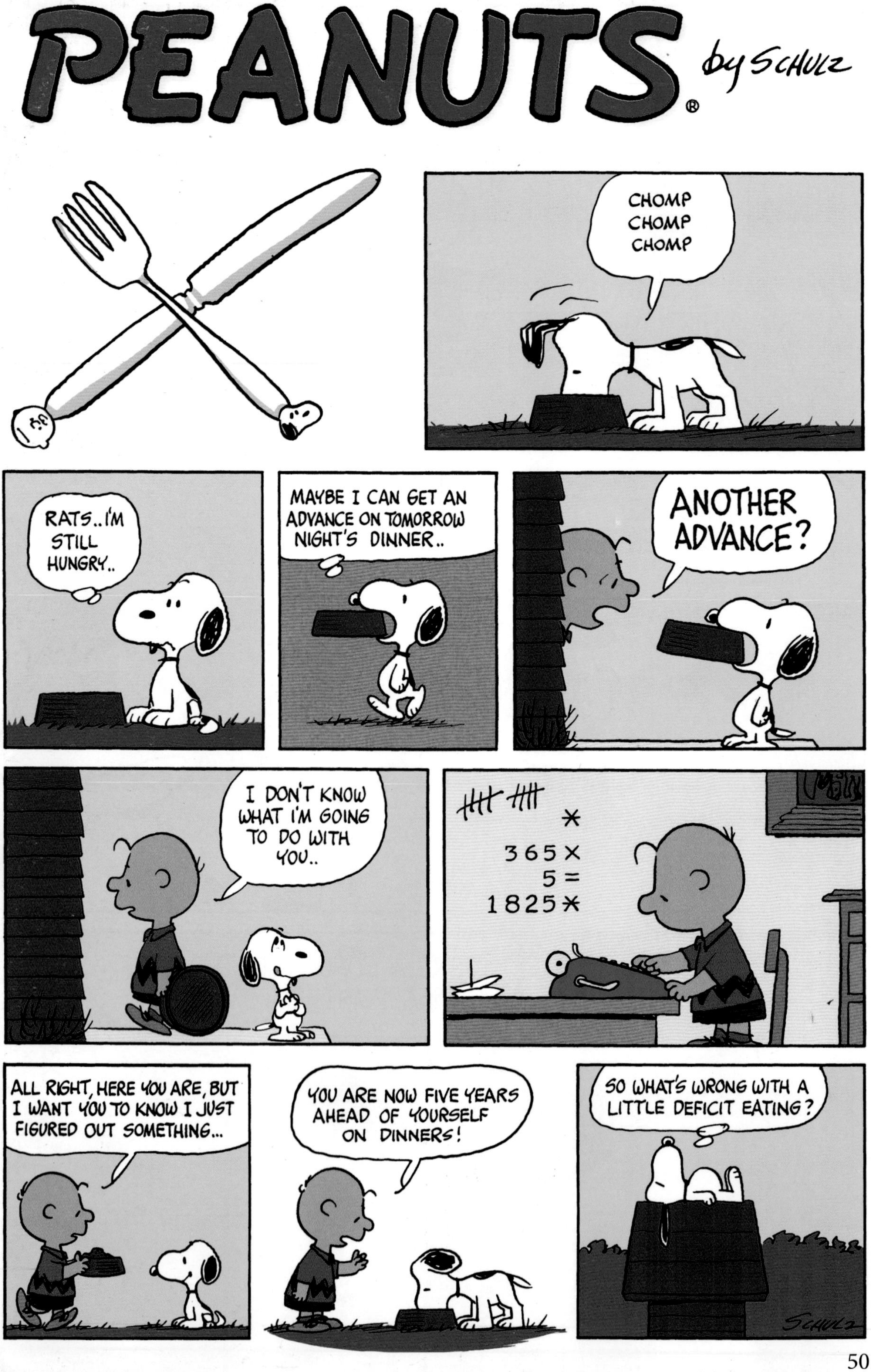
PEANUTS
by SCHULZ
CHOMP CHOMP CHOMP
RATS..I'M STILL HUNGRY..
MAYBE I CAN GET AN ADVANCE ON TOMORROW NIGHT'S DINNER..
ANOTHER ADVANCE?
I DON'T KNOW WHAT I'M GOING TO DO WITH YOU..
365 ×
5 =
1825
ALL RIGHT, HERE YOU ARE, BUT I WANT YOU TO KNOW I JUST FIGURED OUT SOMETHING...
YOU ARE NOW FIVE YEARS AHEAD OF YOURSELF ON DINNERS!
SO WHAT'S WRONG WITH A LITTLE DEFICIT EATING?
SCHULZ

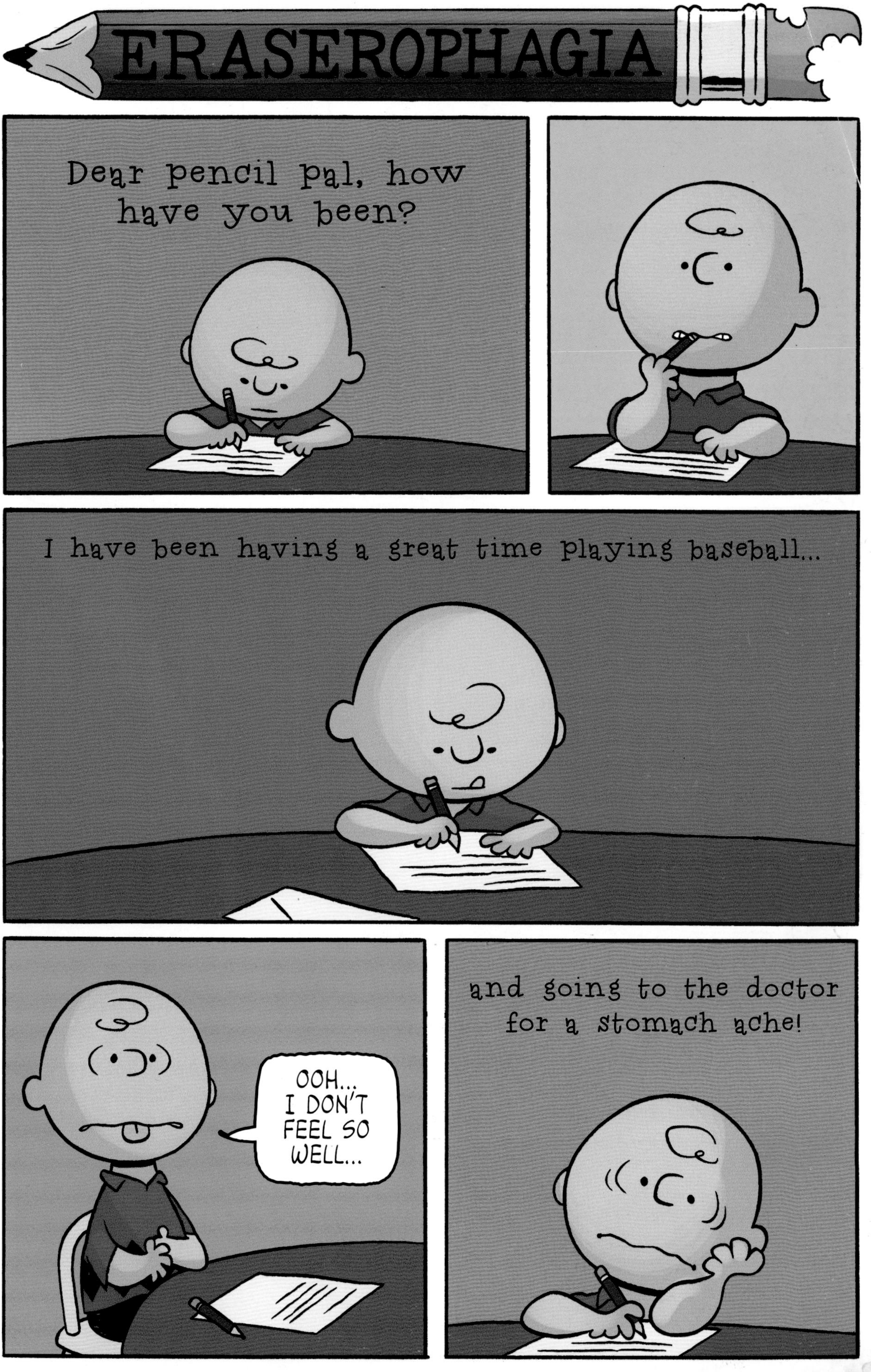
ERASEROPHAGIA
Dear pencil pal, how have you been?
I have been having a great time playing baseball...
OOH... I DON'T FEEL SO WELL...
and going to the doctor for a stomach ache!

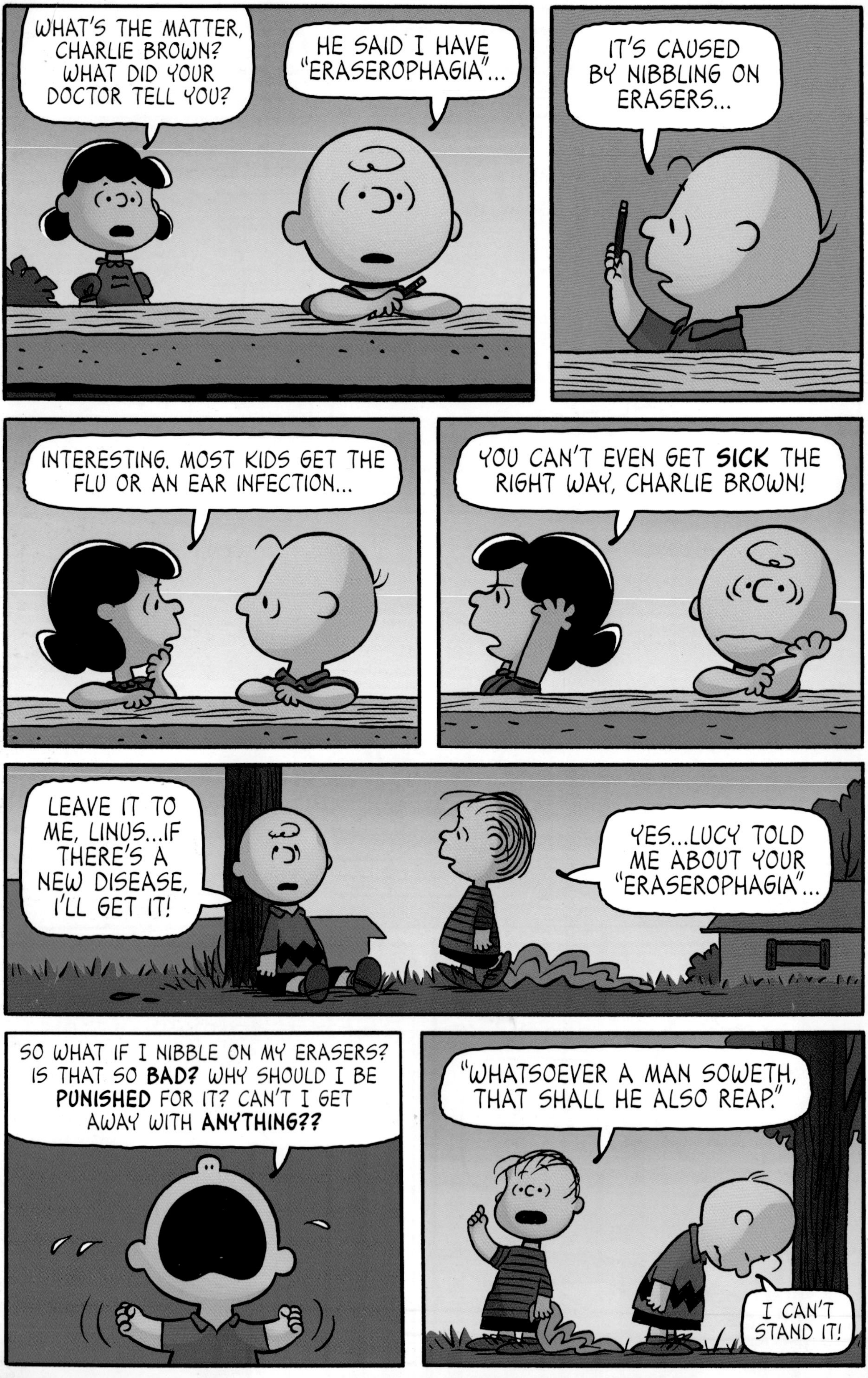

WHAT'S THE MATTER, CHARLIE BROWN? WHAT DID YOUR DOCTOR TELL YOU?
HE SAID I HAVE "ERASEROPHAGIA"...
IT'S CAUSED BY NIBBLING ON ERASERS...
INTERESTING. MOST KIDS GET THE FLU OR AN EAR INFECTION...
YOU CAN'T EVEN GET **SICK** THE RIGHT WAY, CHARLIE BROWN!
YES...LUCY TOLD ME ABOUT YOUR "ERASEROPHAGIA"...
LEAVE IT TO ME, LINUS...IF THERE'S A NEW DISEASE, I'LL GET IT!
SO WHAT IF I NIBBLE ON MY ERASERS? IS THAT SO **BAD?** WHY SHOULD I BE **PUNISHED** FOR IT? CAN'T I GET AWAY WITH **ANYTHING??**
"WHATSOEVER A MAN SOWETH, THAT SHALL HE ALSO REAP."
I CAN'T STAND IT!

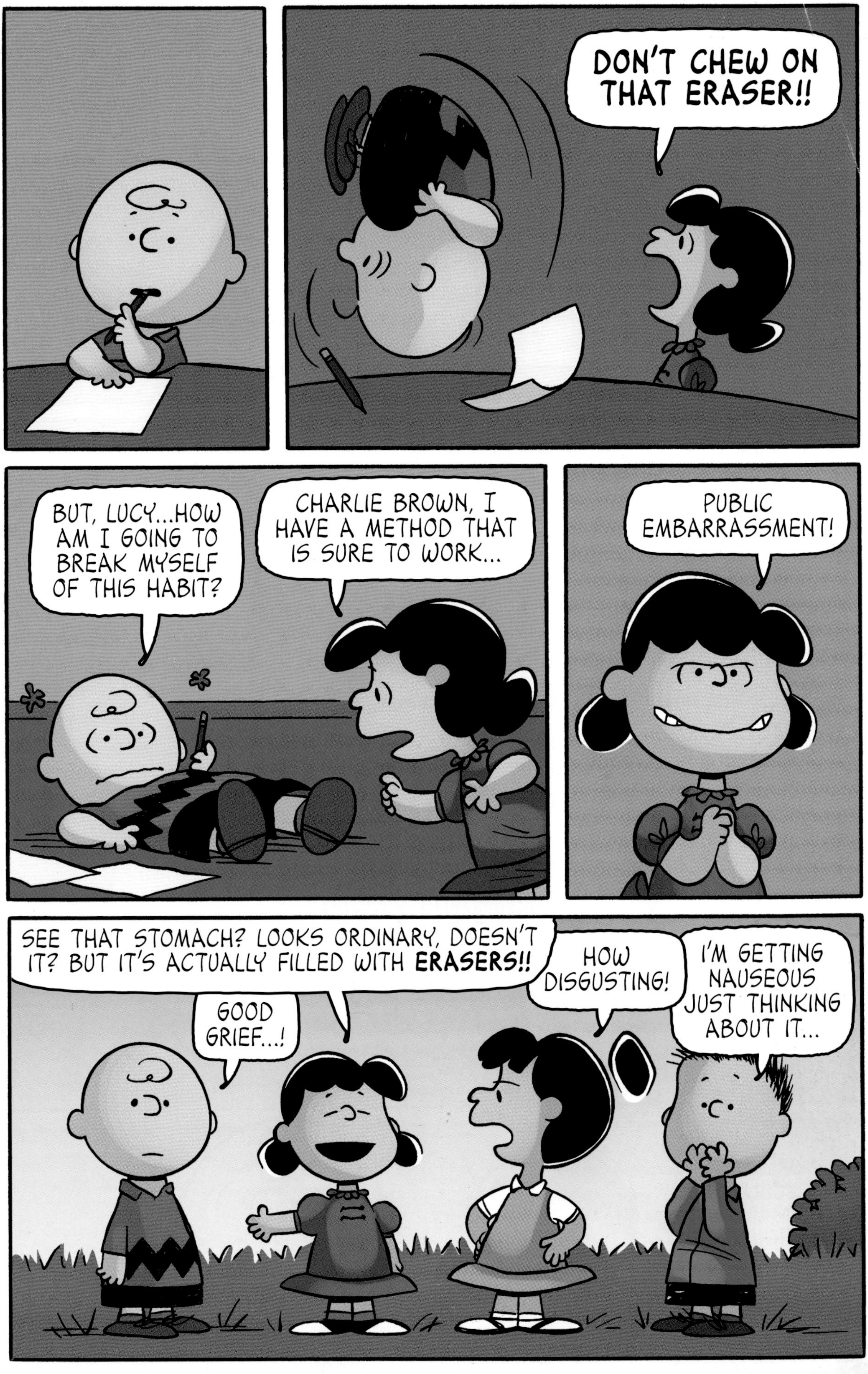
DON'T CHEW ON THAT ERASER!!
BUT, LUCY...HOW AM I GOING TO BREAK MYSELF OF THIS HABIT?
CHARLIE BROWN, I HAVE A METHOD THAT IS SURE TO WORK...
PUBLIC EMBARRASSMENT!
SEE THAT STOMACH? LOOKS ORDINARY, DOESN'T IT? BUT IT'S ACTUALLY FILLED WITH **ERASERS!!**
GOOD GRIEF...!
HOW DISGUSTING!
I'M GETTING NAUSEOUS JUST THINKING ABOUT IT...

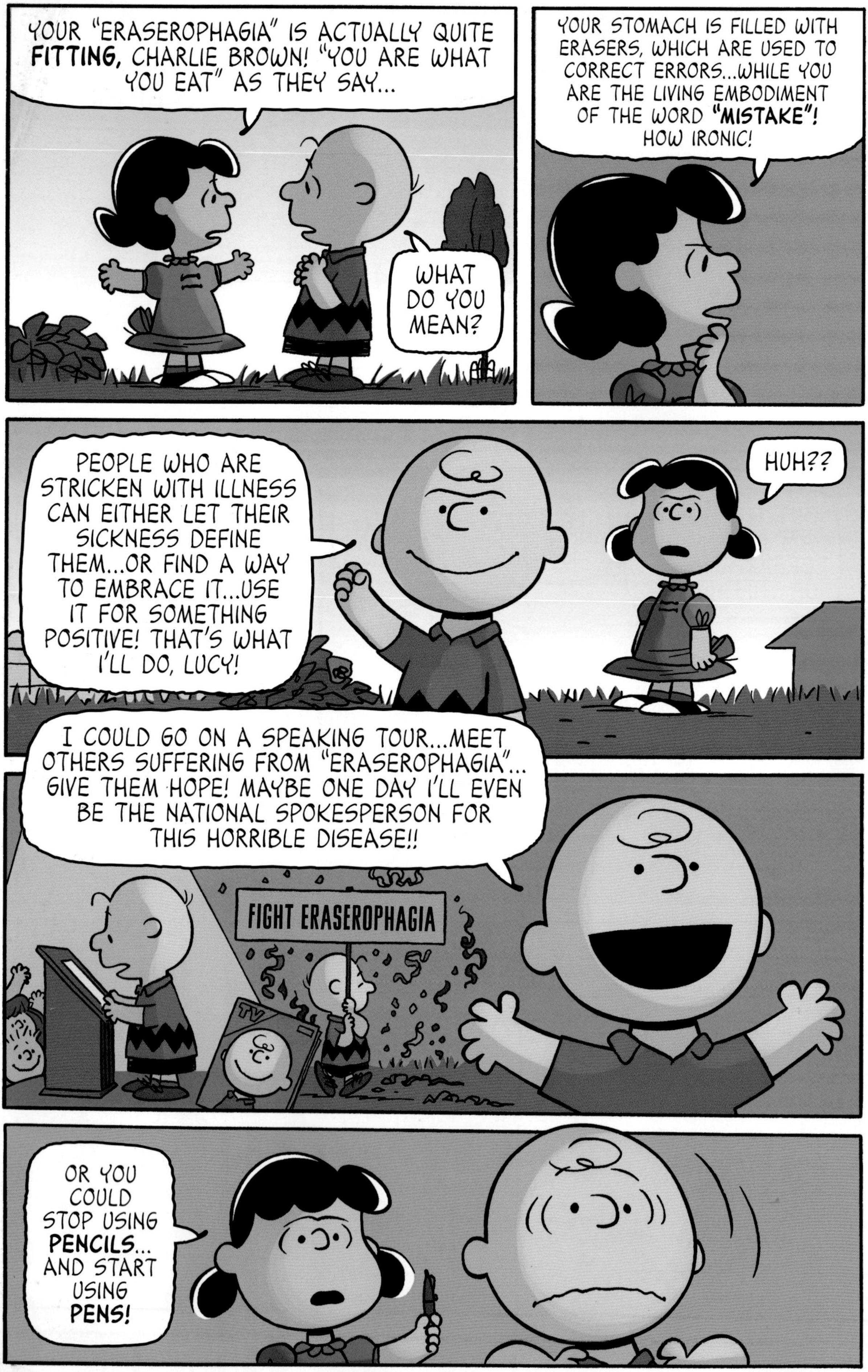
YOUR "ERASEROPHAGIA" IS ACTUALLY QUITE **FITTING,** CHARLIE BROWN! "YOU ARE WHAT YOU EAT" AS THEY SAY...
WHAT DO YOU MEAN?
YOUR STOMACH IS FILLED WITH ERASERS, WHICH ARE USED TO CORRECT ERRORS...WHILE YOU ARE THE LIVING EMBODIMENT OF THE WORD **"MISTAKE"!** HOW IRONIC!
PEOPLE WHO ARE STRICKEN WITH ILLNESS CAN EITHER LET THEIR SICKNESS DEFINE THEM...OR FIND A WAY TO EMBRACE IT...USE IT FOR SOMETHING POSITIVE! THAT'S WHAT I'LL DO, LUCY!
HUH??
I COULD GO ON A SPEAKING TOUR...MEET OTHERS SUFFERING FROM "ERASEROPHAGIA"... GIVE THEM HOPE! MAYBE ONE DAY I'LL EVEN BE THE NATIONAL SPOKESPERSON FOR THIS HORRIBLE DISEASE!!
FIGHT ERASEROPHAGIA
TV
OR YOU COULD STOP USING **PENCILS...** AND START USING **PENS!**

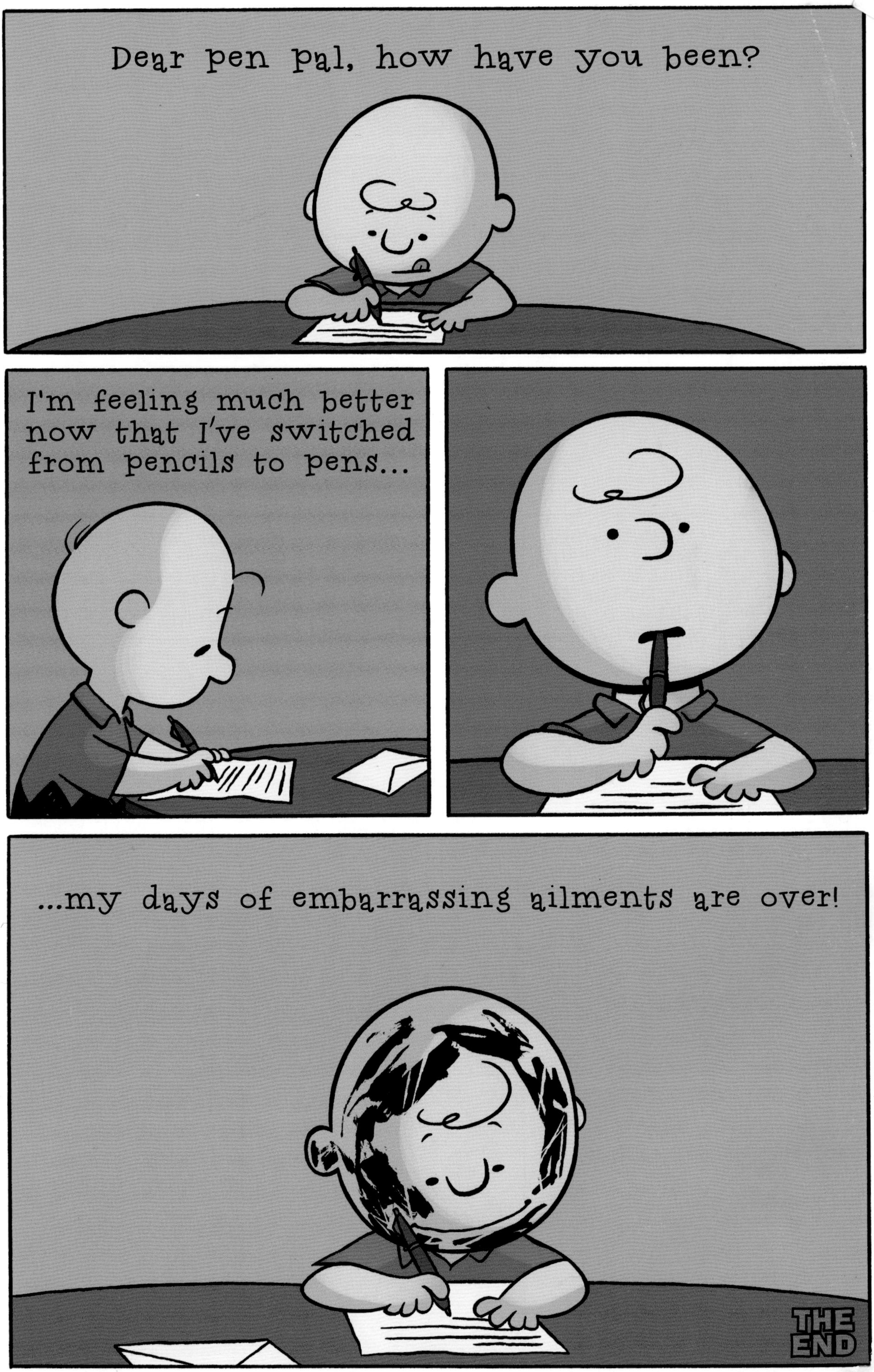
Dear pen pal, how have you been?
I'm feeling much better now that I've switched from pencils to pens...
...my days of embarrassing ailments are over!
THE END

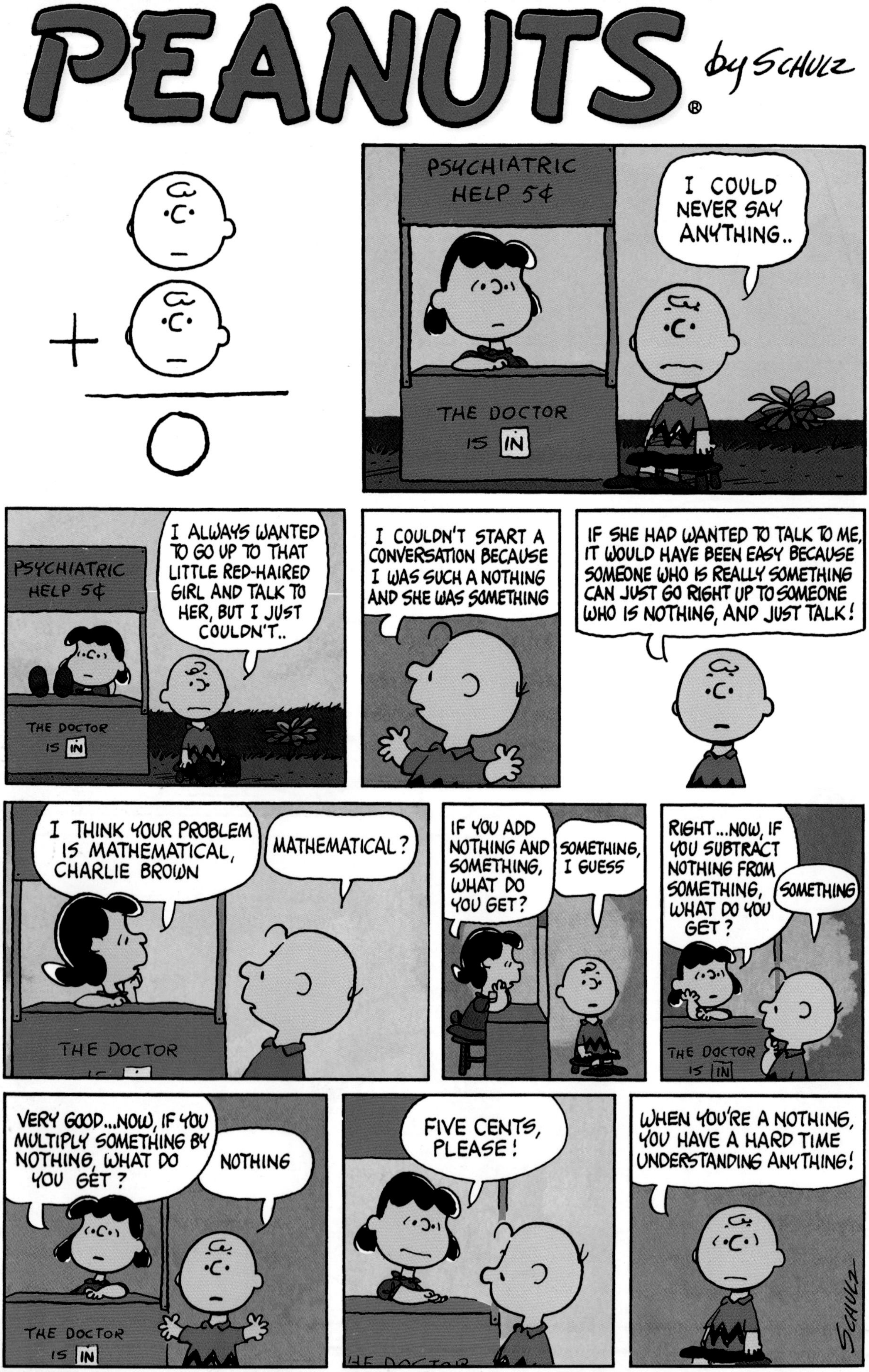
PEANUTS
by SCHULZ
PSYCHIATRIC HELP 5¢
I COULD NEVER SAY ANYTHING..
THE DOCTOR IS IN
I ALWAYS WANTED TO GO UP TO THAT LITTLE RED-HAIRED GIRL AND TALK TO HER, BUT I JUST COULDN'T..
I COULDN'T START A CONVERSATION BECAUSE I WAS SUCH A NOTHING AND SHE WAS SOMETHING
IF SHE HAD WANTED TO TALK TO ME, IT WOULD HAVE BEEN EASY BECAUSE SOMEONE WHO IS REALLY SOMETHING CAN JUST GO RIGHT UP TO SOMEONE WHO IS NOTHING, AND JUST TALK!
I THINK YOUR PROBLEM IS MATHEMATICAL, CHARLIE BROWN
MATHEMATICAL?
IF YOU ADD NOTHING AND SOMETHING, WHAT DO YOU GET?
SOMETHING, I GUESS
RIGHT...NOW, IF YOU SUBTRACT NOTHING FROM SOMETHING, WHAT DO YOU GET?
SOMETHING
VERY GOOD...NOW, IF YOU MULTIPLY SOMETHING BY NOTHING, WHAT DO YOU GET?
NOTHING
FIVE CENTS, PLEASE!
WHEN YOU'RE A NOTHING, YOU HAVE A HARD TIME UNDERSTANDING ANYTHING!
SCHULZ

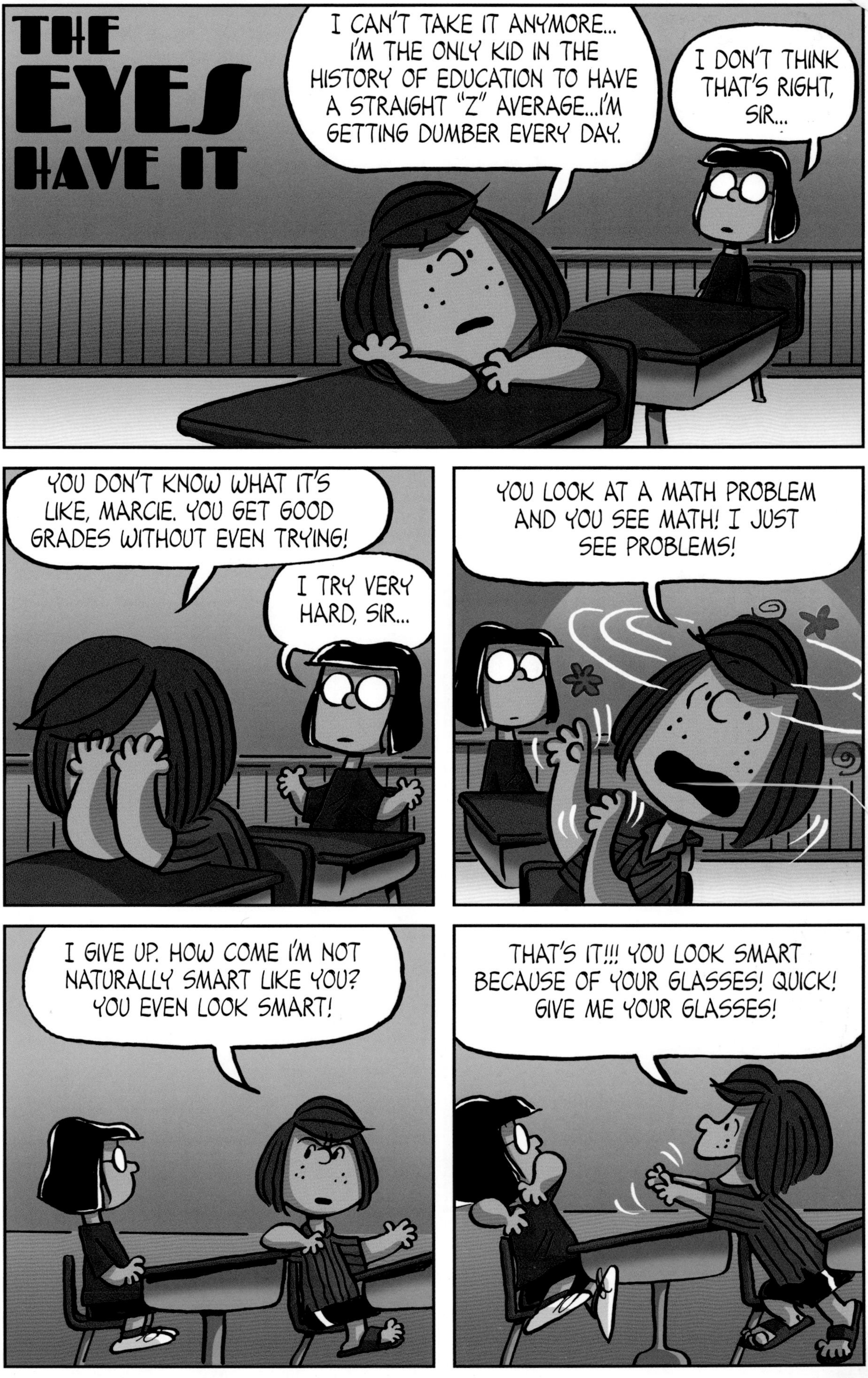
THE EYES HAVE IT
I CAN'T TAKE IT ANYMORE... I'M THE ONLY KID IN THE HISTORY OF EDUCATION TO HAVE A STRAIGHT "Z" AVERAGE...I'M GETTING DUMBER EVERY DAY.
I DON'T THINK THAT'S RIGHT, SIR...
YOU DON'T KNOW WHAT IT'S LIKE, MARCIE. YOU GET GOOD GRADES WITHOUT EVEN TRYING!
I TRY VERY HARD, SIR...
YOU LOOK AT A MATH PROBLEM AND YOU SEE MATH! I JUST SEE PROBLEMS!
I GIVE UP. HOW COME I'M NOT NATURALLY SMART LIKE YOU? YOU EVEN LOOK SMART!
THAT'S IT!!! YOU LOOK SMART BECAUSE OF YOUR GLASSES! QUICK! GIVE ME YOUR GLASSES!

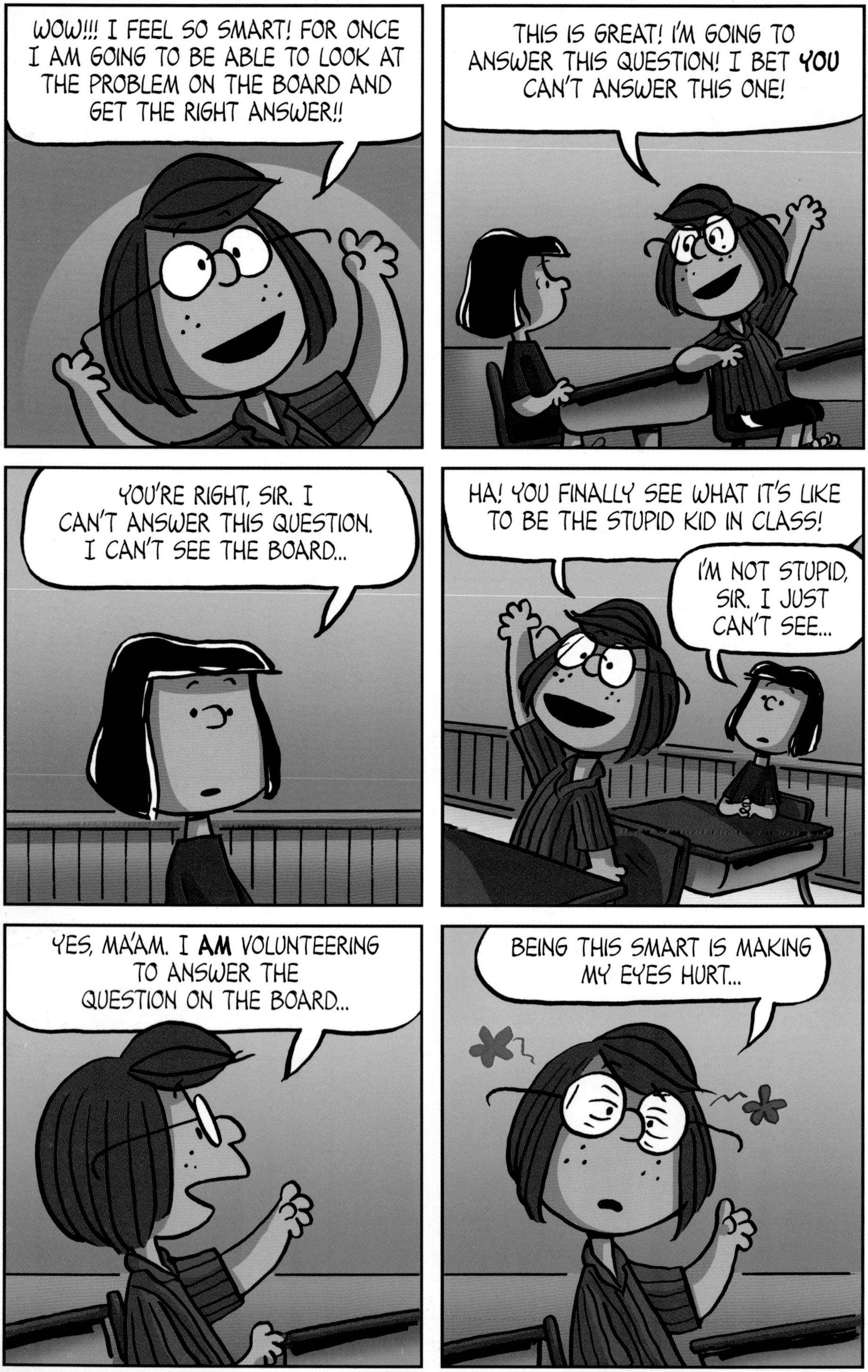
WOW!!! I FEEL SO SMART! FOR ONCE I AM GOING TO BE ABLE TO LOOK AT THE PROBLEM ON THE BOARD AND GET THE RIGHT ANSWER!!
THIS IS GREAT! I'M GOING TO ANSWER THIS QUESTION! I BET **YOU** CAN'T ANSWER THIS ONE!
YOU'RE RIGHT, SIR. I CAN'T ANSWER THIS QUESTION. I CAN'T SEE THE BOARD...
HA! YOU FINALLY SEE WHAT IT'S LIKE TO BE THE STUPID KID IN CLASS!
I'M NOT STUPID, SIR. I JUST CAN'T SEE...
YES, MA'AM. I **AM** VOLUNTEERING TO ANSWER THE QUESTION ON THE BOARD...
BEING THIS SMART IS MAKING MY EYES HURT...

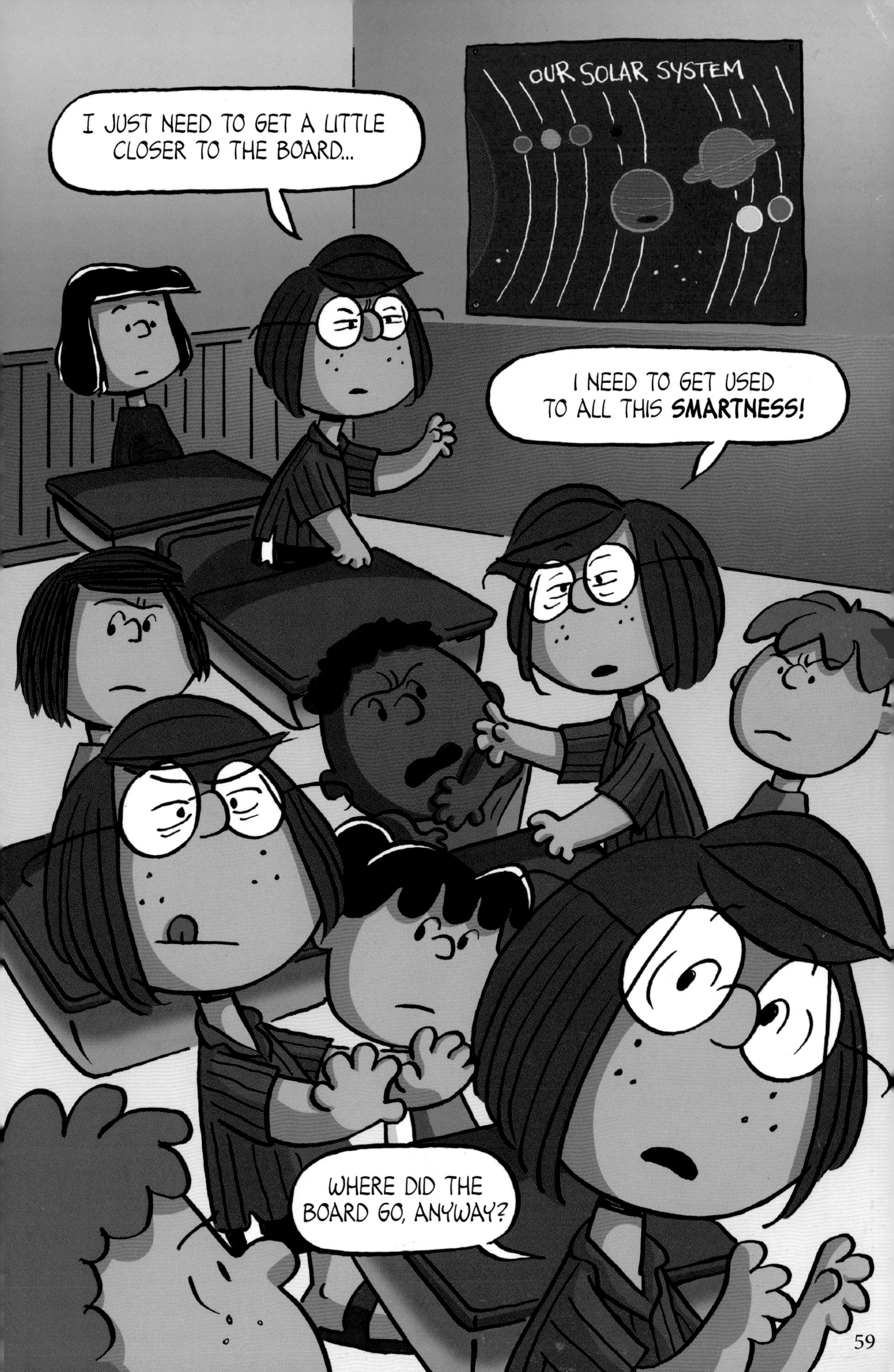
OUR SOLAR SYSTEM
I JUST NEED TO GET A LITTLE CLOSER TO THE BOARD...
I NEED TO GET USED TO ALL THIS **SMARTNESS!**
WHERE DID THE BOARD GO, ANYWAY?

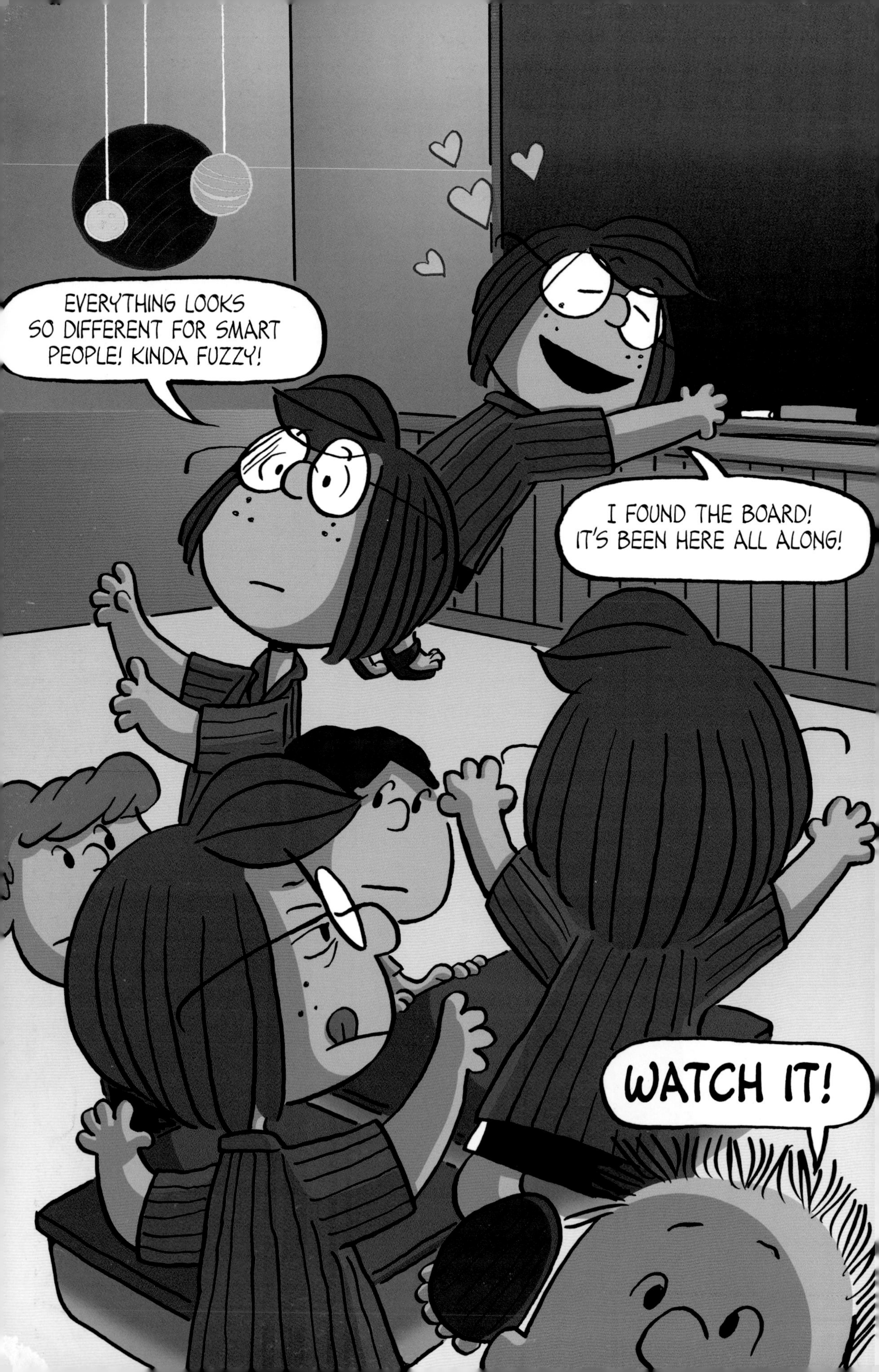
EVERYTHING LOOKS SO DIFFERENT FOR SMART PEOPLE! KINDA FUZZY!
I FOUND THE BOARD! IT'S BEEN HERE ALL ALONG!
WATCH IT!

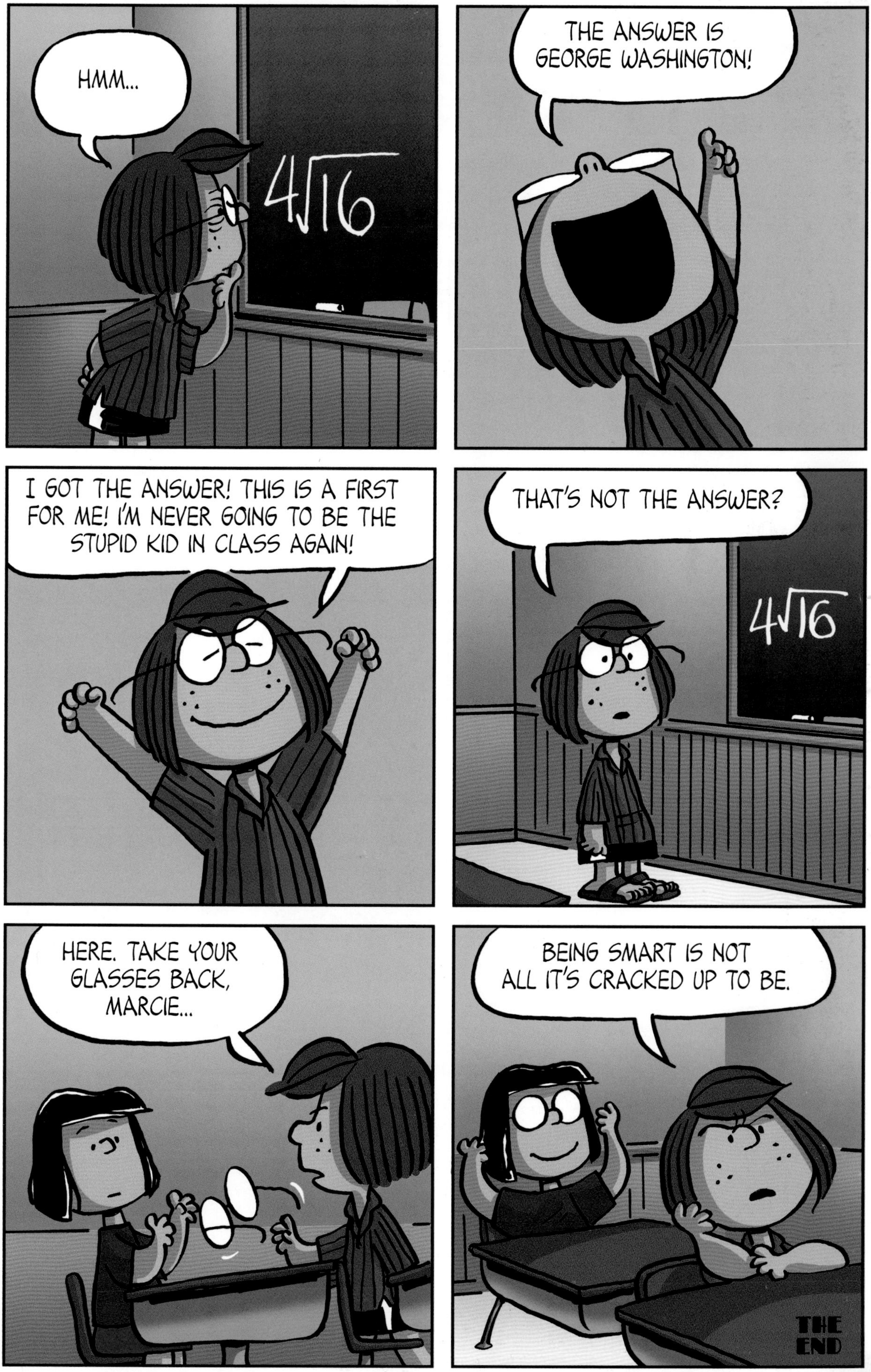
HMM...
4√16
THE ANSWER IS GEORGE WASHINGTON!
I GOT THE ANSWER! THIS IS A FIRST FOR ME! I'M NEVER GOING TO BE THE STUPID KID IN CLASS AGAIN!
THAT'S NOT THE ANSWER?
4√16
HERE. TAKE YOUR GLASSES BACK, MARCIE...
BEING SMART IS NOT ALL IT'S CRACKED UP TO BE.
THE END

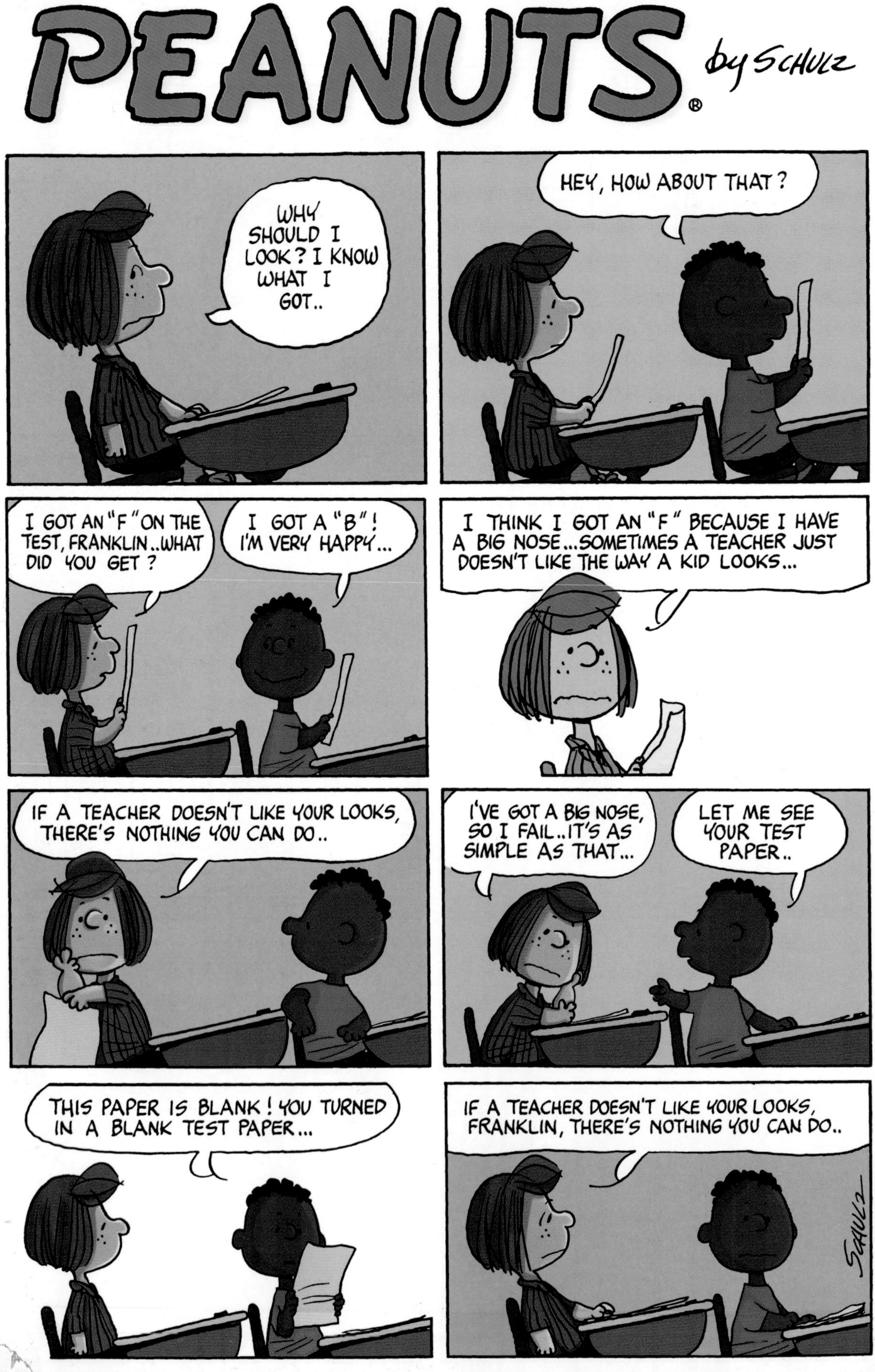
PEANUTS
by SCHULZ
WHY SHOULD I LOOK? I KNOW WHAT I GOT..
HEY, HOW ABOUT THAT?
I GOT AN "F" ON THE TEST, FRANKLIN..WHAT DID YOU GET?
I GOT A "B"! I'M VERY HAPPY...
I THINK I GOT AN "F" BECAUSE I HAVE A BIG NOSE...SOMETIMES A TEACHER JUST DOESN'T LIKE THE WAY A KID LOOKS...
IF A TEACHER DOESN'T LIKE YOUR LOOKS, THERE'S NOTHING YOU CAN DO..
I'VE GOT A BIG NOSE, SO I FAIL..IT'S AS SIMPLE AS THAT...
LET ME SEE YOUR TEST PAPER..
THIS PAPER IS BLANK! YOU TURNED IN A BLANK TEST PAPER...
IF A TEACHER DOESN'T LIKE YOUR LOOKS, FRANKLIN, THERE'S NOTHING YOU CAN DO..
SCHULZ

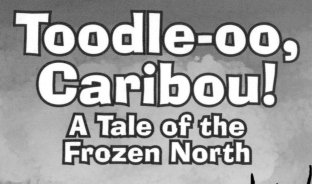

Toodle-oo, Caribou!
A Tale of the Frozen North

EXCITED FOR OUR ANNUAL WINTER HIKING TRIP, WOODSTOCK?

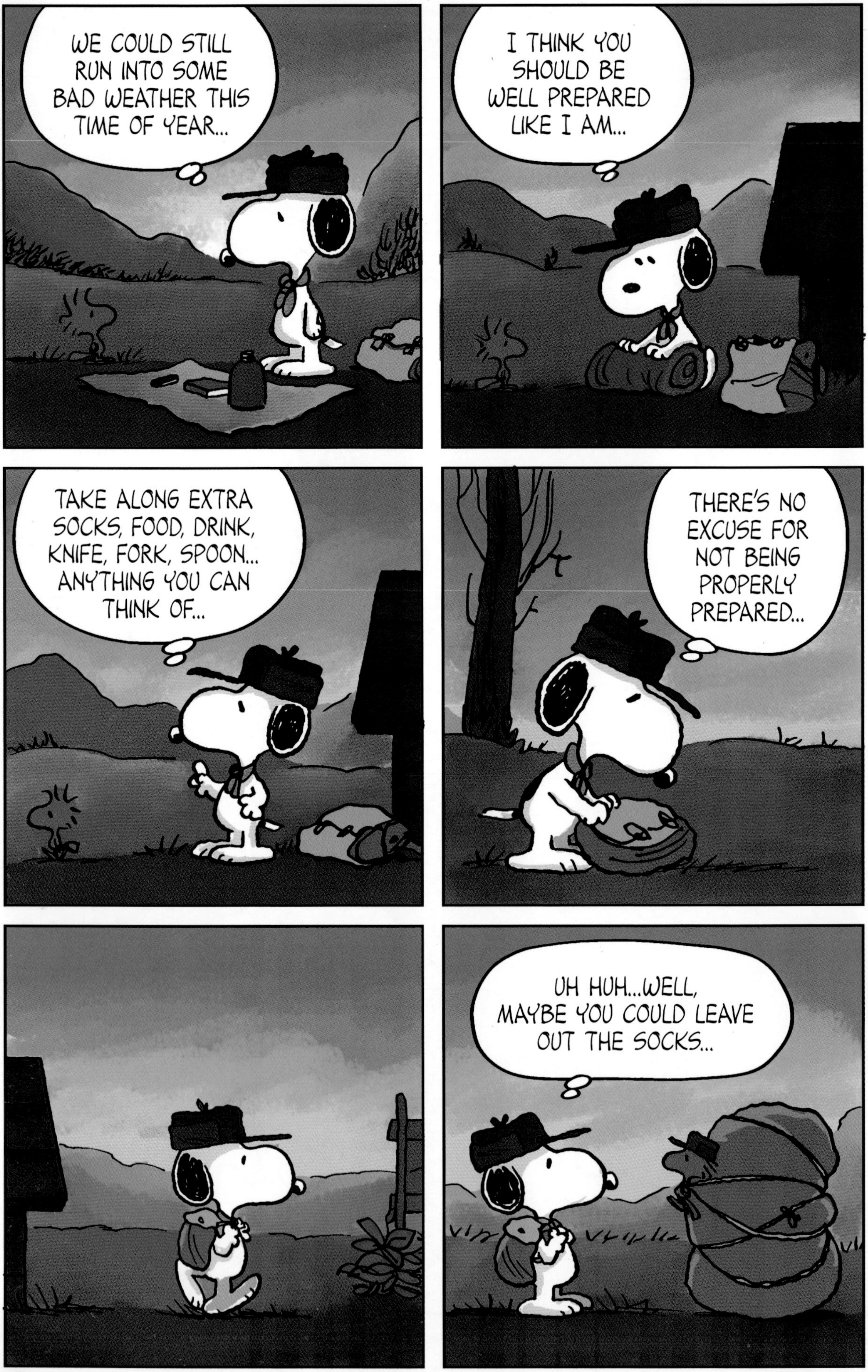
WE COULD STILL RUN INTO SOME BAD WEATHER THIS TIME OF YEAR...
I THINK YOU SHOULD BE WELL PREPARED LIKE I AM...
TAKE ALONG EXTRA SOCKS, FOOD, DRINK, KNIFE, FORK, SPOON... ANYTHING YOU CAN THINK OF...
THERE'S NO EXCUSE FOR NOT BEING PROPERLY PREPARED...
UH HUH...WELL, MAYBE YOU COULD LEAVE OUT THE SOCKS...

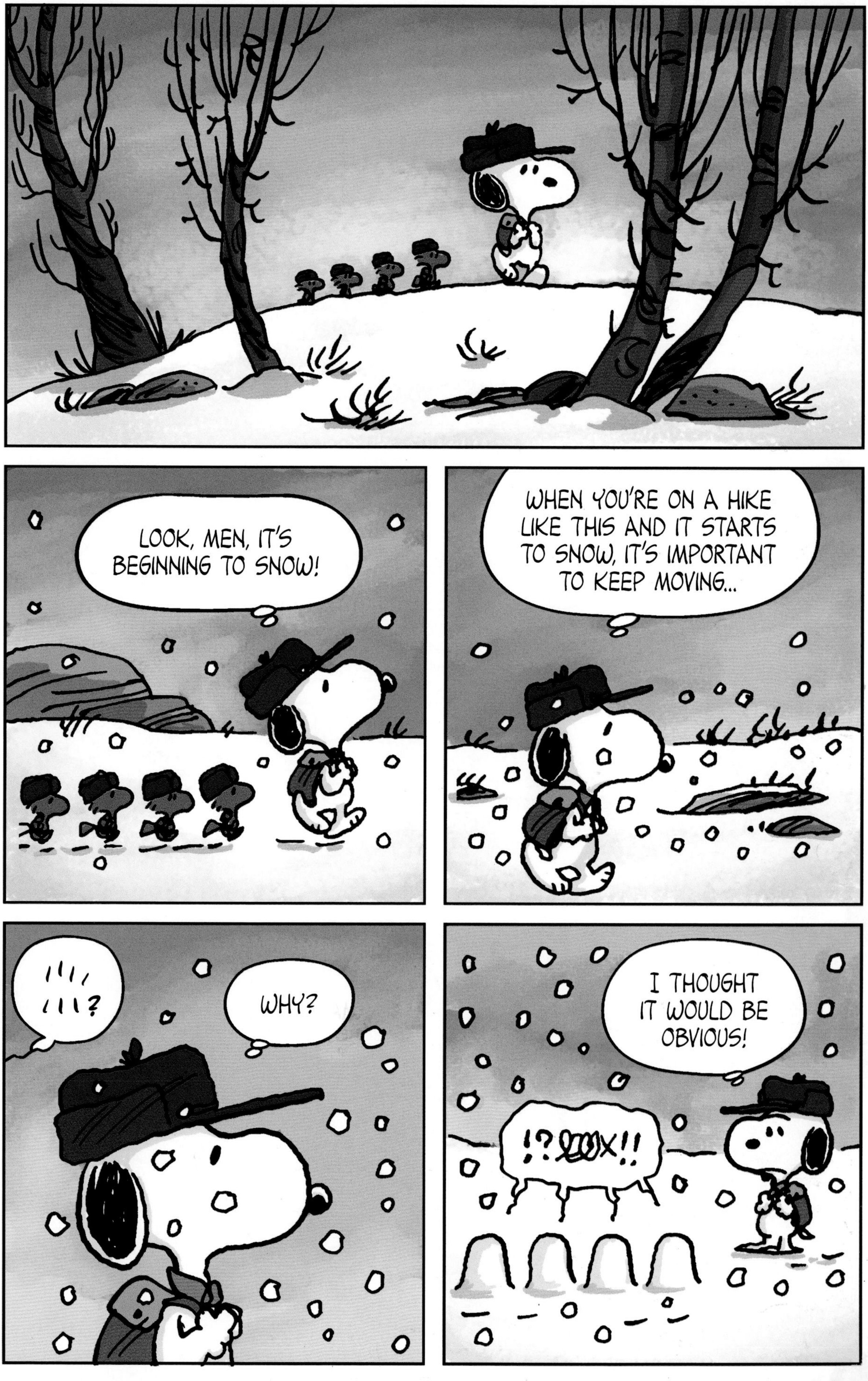
LOOK, MEN, IT'S BEGINNING TO SNOW!
WHEN YOU'RE ON A HIKE LIKE THIS AND IT STARTS TO SNOW, IT'S IMPORTANT TO KEEP MOVING...
WHY?
I THOUGHT IT WOULD BE OBVIOUS!

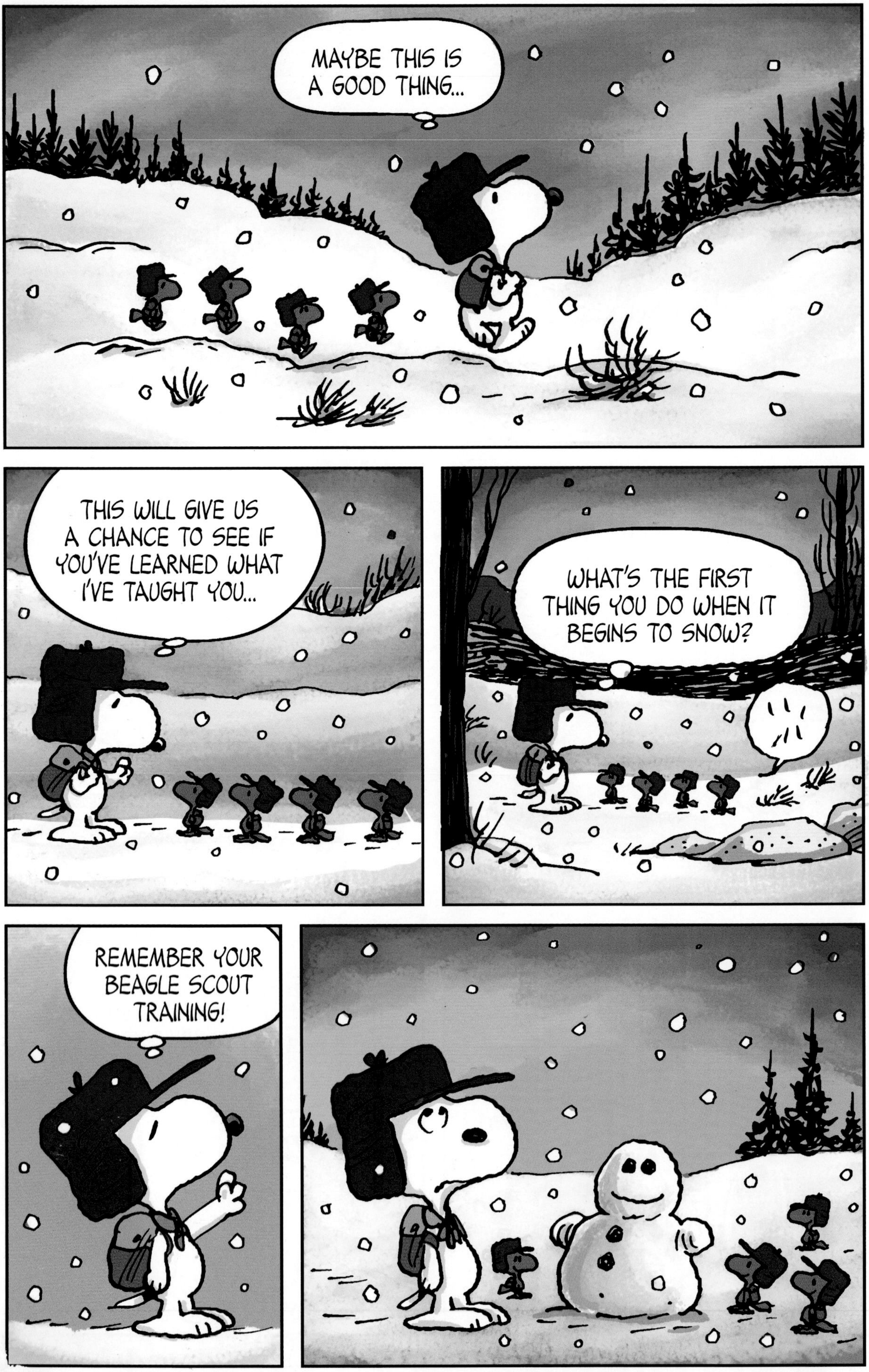
MAYBE THIS IS A GOOD THING...
THIS WILL GIVE US A CHANCE TO SEE IF YOU'VE LEARNED WHAT I'VE TAUGHT YOU...
WHAT'S THE FIRST THING YOU DO WHEN IT BEGINS TO SNOW?
REMEMBER YOUR BEAGLE SCOUT TRAINING!

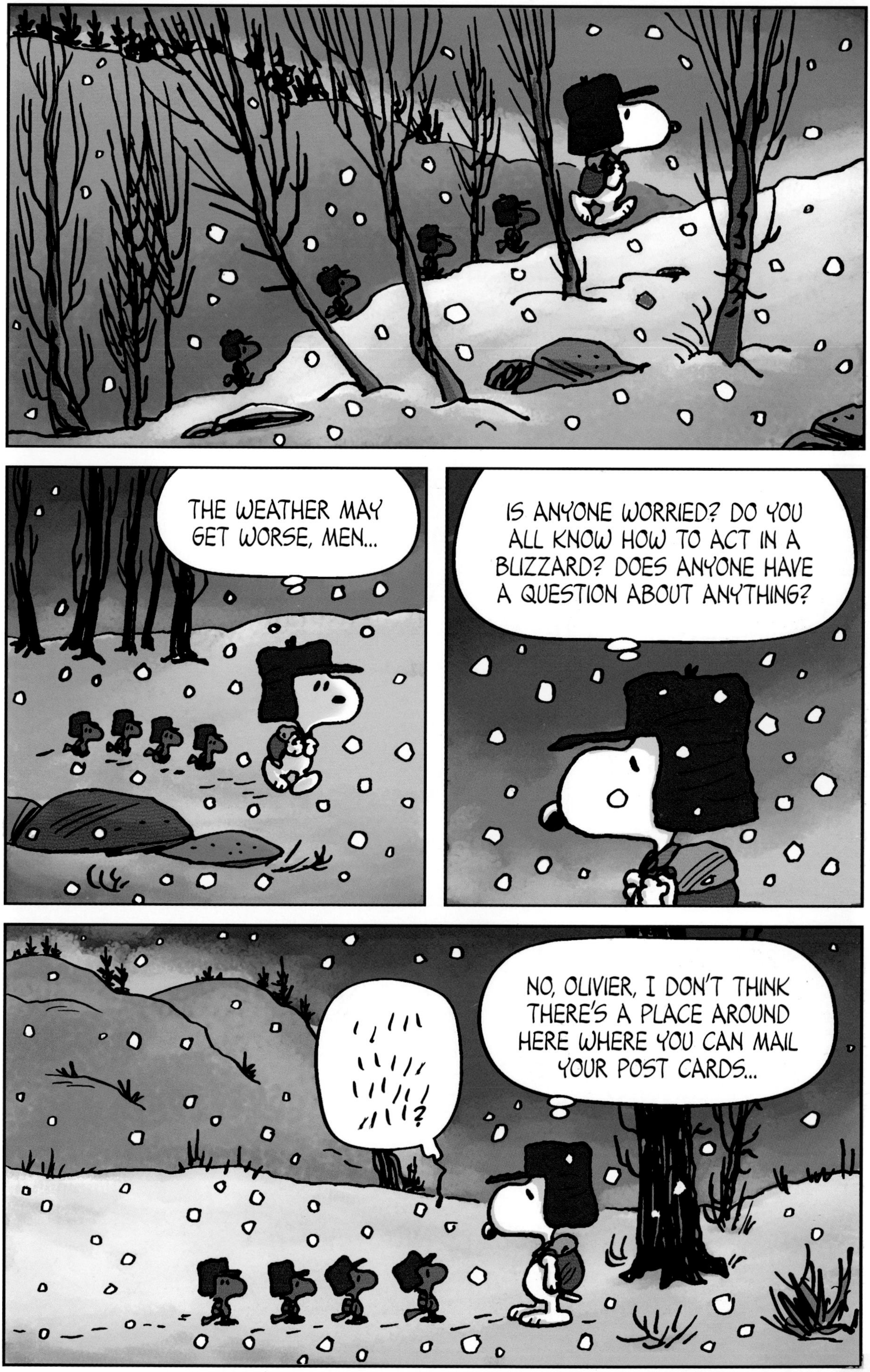
THE WEATHER MAY GET WORSE, MEN...
IS ANYONE WORRIED? DO YOU ALL KNOW HOW TO ACT IN A BLIZZARD? DOES ANYONE HAVE A QUESTION ABOUT ANYTHING?
NO, OLIVIER, I DON'T THINK THERE'S A PLACE AROUND HERE WHERE YOU CAN MAIL YOUR POST CARDS...

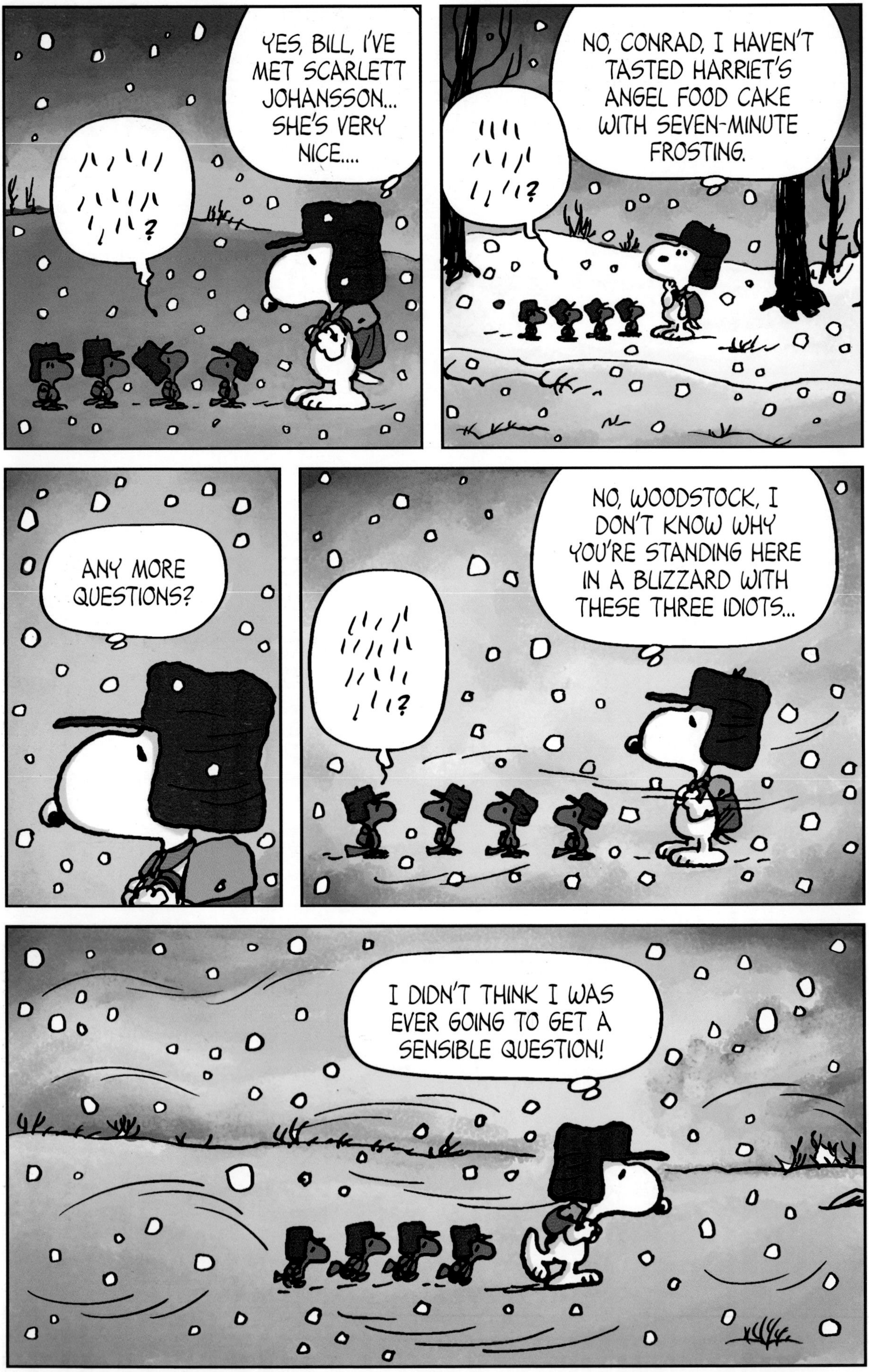
YES, BILL, I'VE MET SCARLETT JOHANSSON... SHE'S VERY NICE....
NO, CONRAD, I HAVEN'T TASTED HARRIET'S ANGEL FOOD CAKE WITH SEVEN-MINUTE FROSTING.
ANY MORE QUESTIONS?
NO, WOODSTOCK, I DON'T KNOW WHY YOU'RE STANDING HERE IN A BLIZZARD WITH THESE THREE IDIOTS...
I DIDN'T THINK I WAS EVER GOING TO GET A SENSIBLE QUESTION!

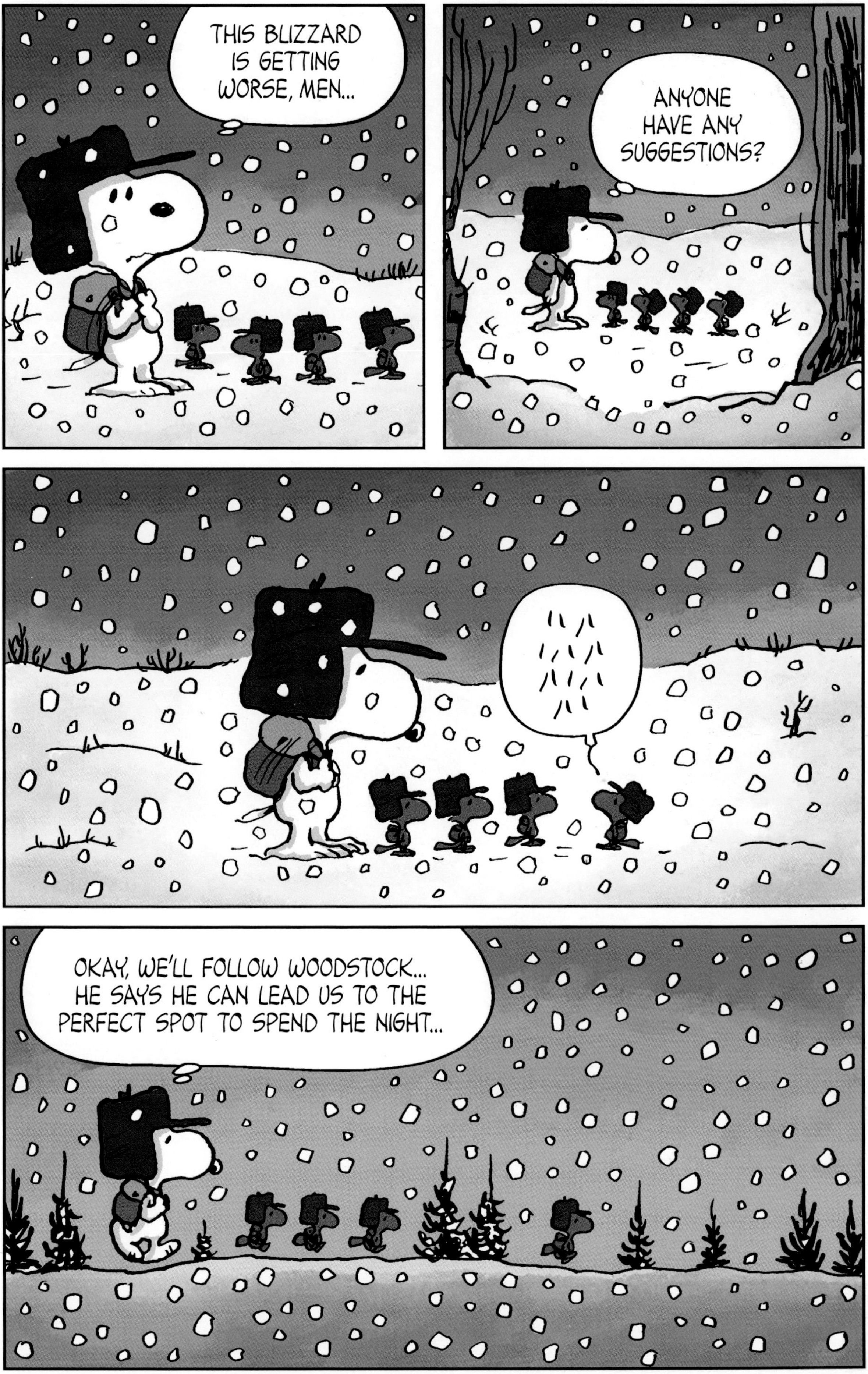
THIS BLIZZARD IS GETTING WORSE, MEN...
ANYONE HAVE ANY SUGGESTIONS?
OKAY, WE'LL FOLLOW WOODSTOCK... HE SAYS HE CAN LEAD US TO THE PERFECT SPOT TO SPEND THE NIGHT...

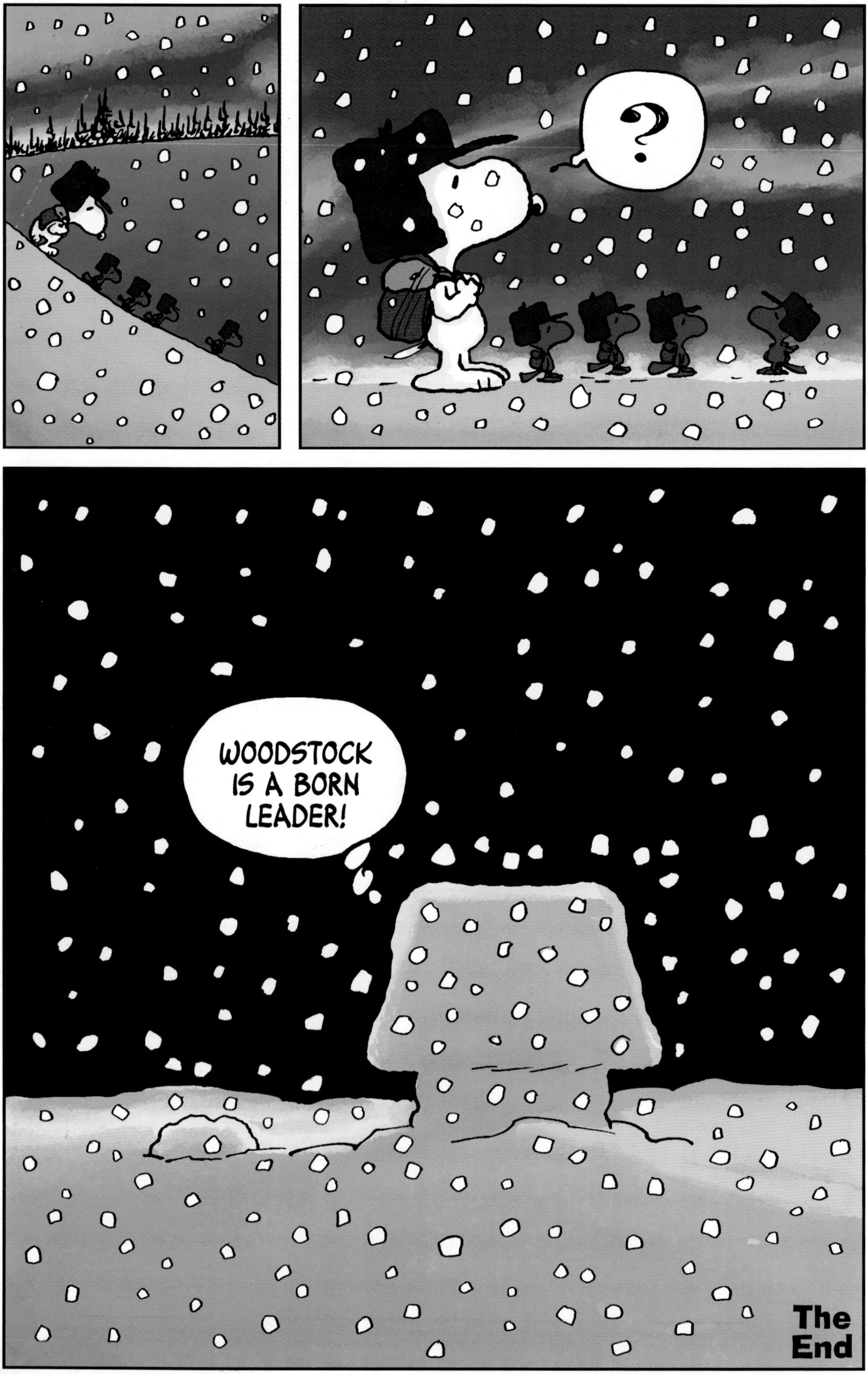
?
WOODSTOCK IS A BORN LEADER!
The End

FROM THE DRAWING BOARD

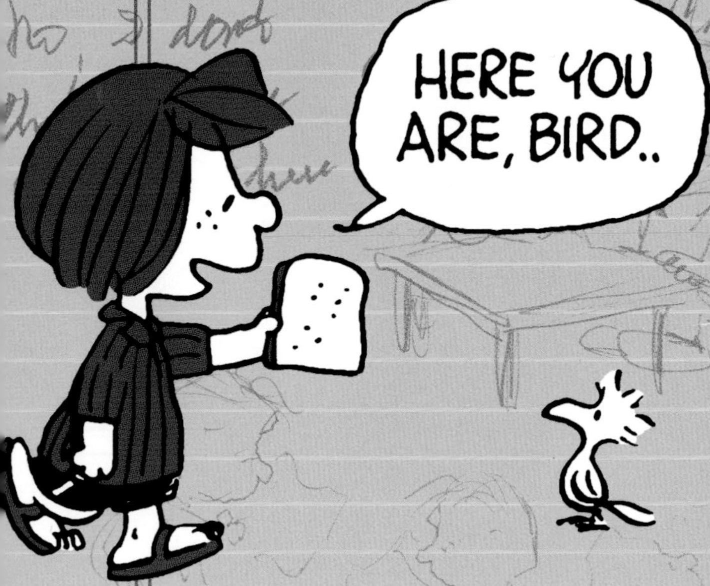
HERE YOU ARE, BIRD..

"Peppermint Patty, the tomboy, is forthright, doggedly loyal, with a devastating singleness of purpose, the part of us that goes through life with blinders on. This can be wonderful at times but also disastrous."

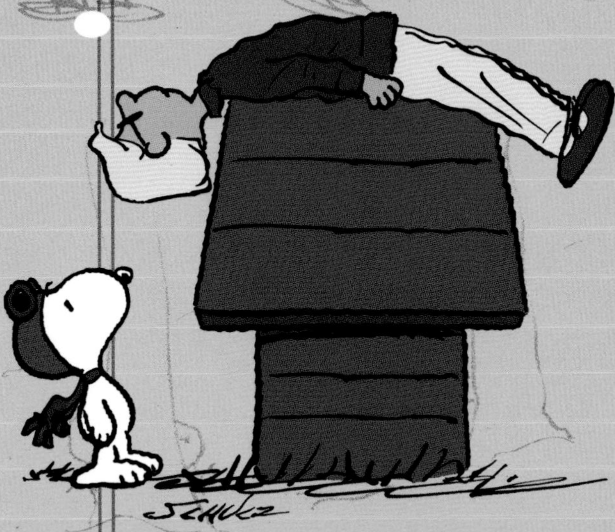

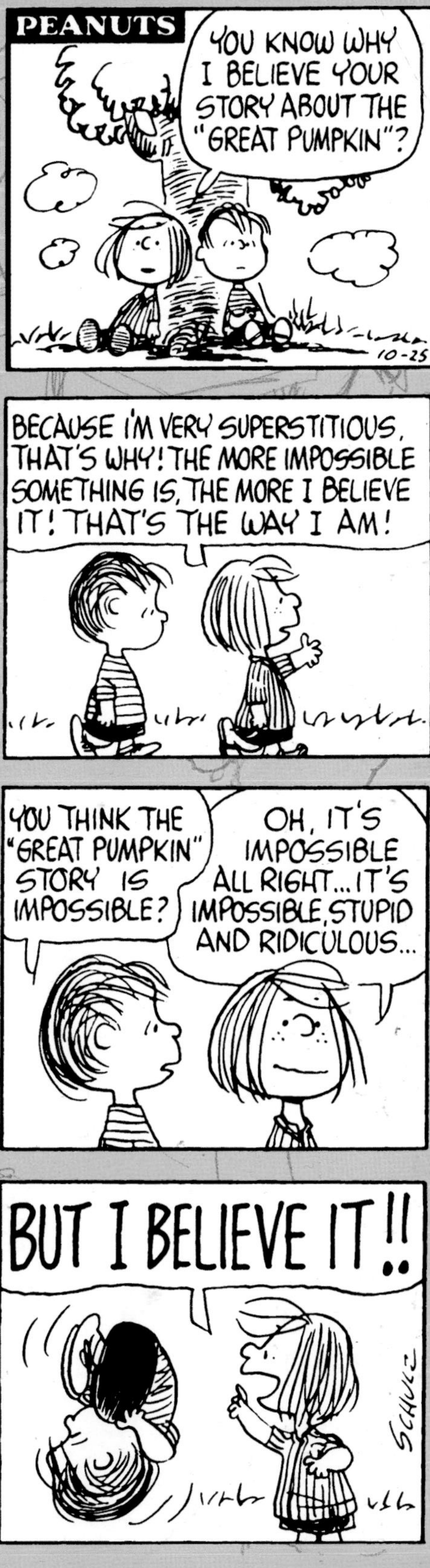
PEANUTS
YOU KNOW WHY I BELIEVE YOUR STORY ABOUT THE "GREAT PUMPKIN"?
10-25
BECAUSE I'M VERY SUPERSTITIOUS, THAT'S WHY! THE MORE IMPOSSIBLE SOMETHING IS, THE MORE I BELIEVE IT! THAT'S THE WAY I AM!
YOU THINK THE "GREAT PUMPKIN" STORY IS IMPOSSIBLE?
OH, IT'S IMPOSSIBLE ALL RIGHT... IT'S IMPOSSIBLE, STUPID AND RIDICULOUS...
BUT I BELIEVE IT!!
SCHULZ

* Sketches courtesy of the Charles M. Schulz Museum.

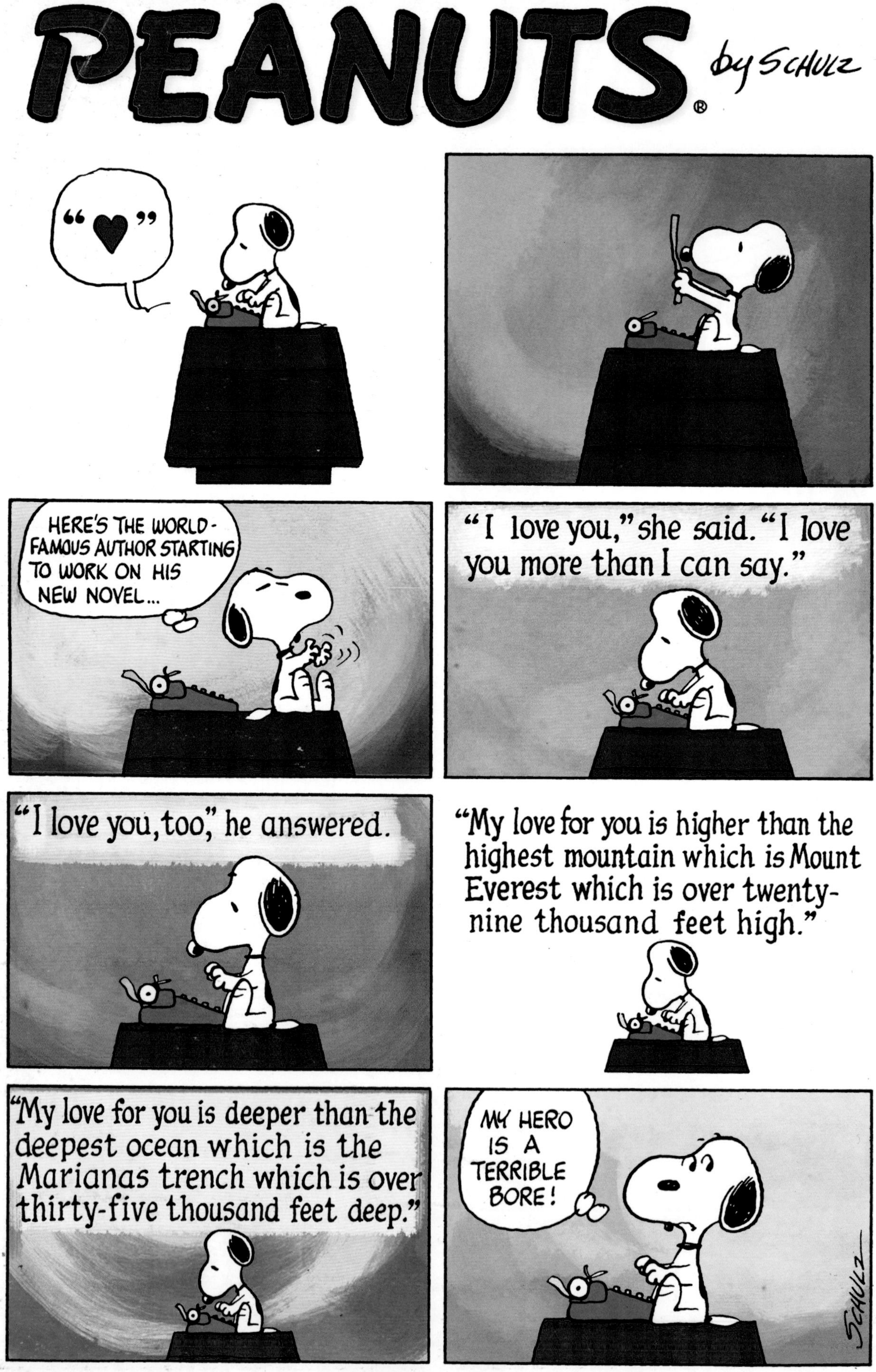
PEANUTS
by SCHULZ
"♥"
HERE'S THE WORLD-FAMOUS AUTHOR STARTING TO WORK ON HIS NEW NOVEL...
"I love you," she said. "I love you more than I can say."
"I love you, too," he answered.
"My love for you is higher than the highest mountain which is Mount Everest which is over twenty-nine thousand feet high."
"My love for you is deeper than the deepest ocean which is the Marianas trench which is over thirty-five thousand feet deep."
MY HERO IS A TERRIBLE BORE!
SCHULZ

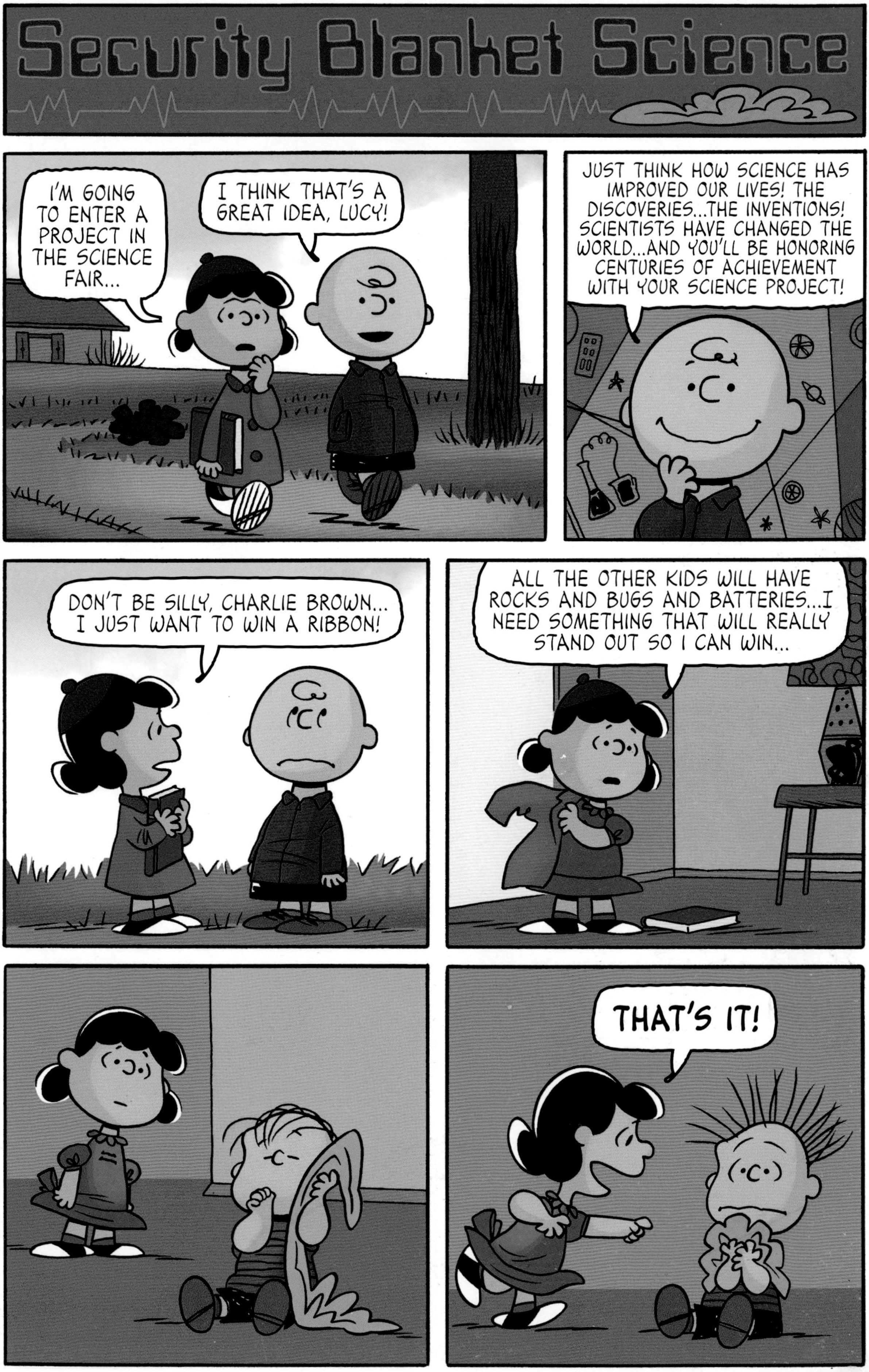

Security Blanket Science
I'M GOING TO ENTER A PROJECT IN THE SCIENCE FAIR...
I THINK THAT'S A GREAT IDEA, LUCY!
JUST THINK HOW SCIENCE HAS IMPROVED OUR LIVES! THE DISCOVERIES...THE INVENTIONS! SCIENTISTS HAVE CHANGED THE WORLD...AND YOU'LL BE HONORING CENTURIES OF ACHIEVEMENT WITH YOUR SCIENCE PROJECT!
DON'T BE SILLY, CHARLIE BROWN... I JUST WANT TO WIN A RIBBON!
ALL THE OTHER KIDS WILL HAVE ROCKS AND BUGS AND BATTERIES...I NEED SOMETHING THAT WILL REALLY STAND OUT SO I CAN WIN...
THAT'S IT!

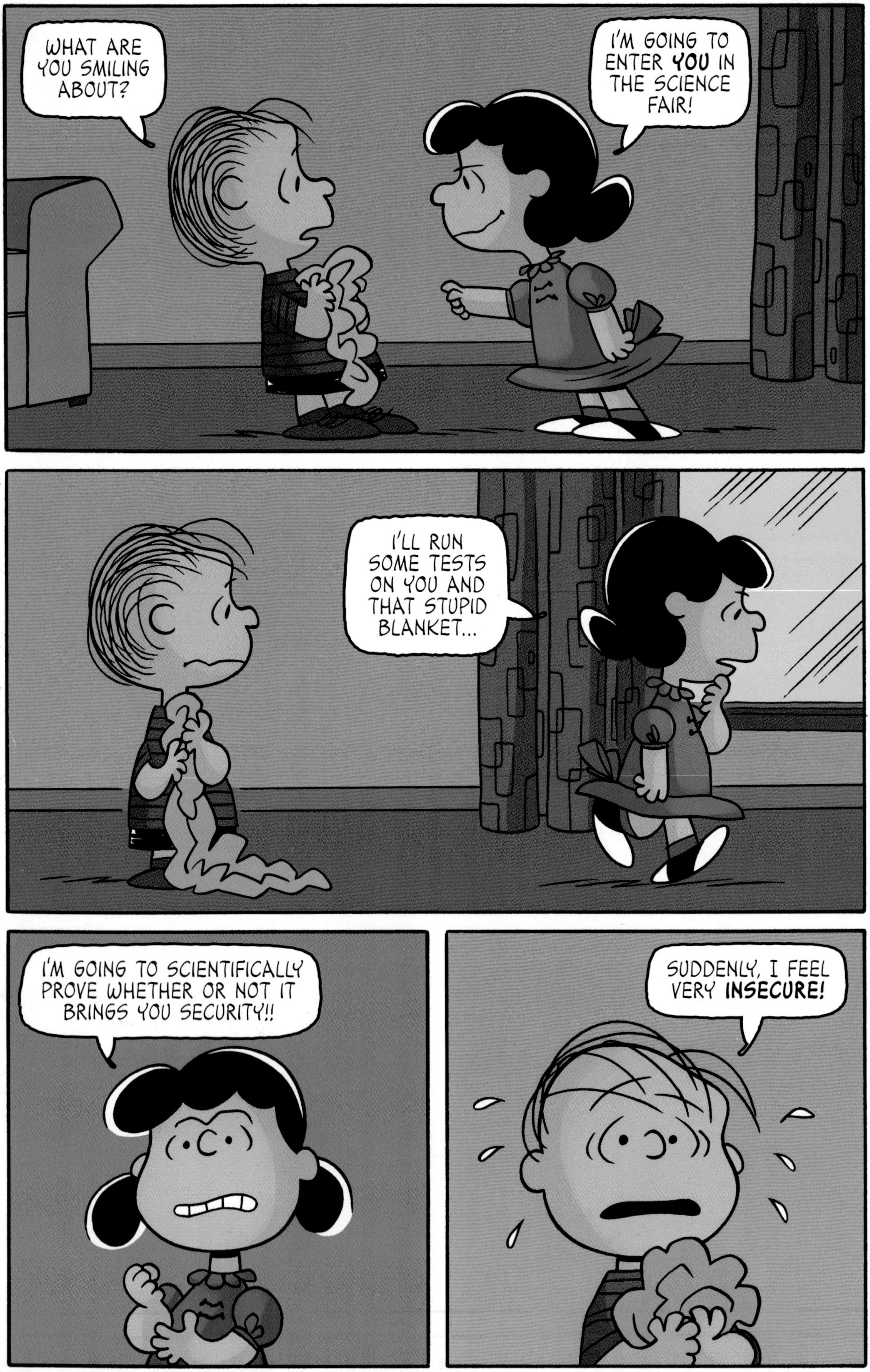
WHAT ARE YOU SMILING ABOUT?
I'M GOING TO ENTER YOU IN THE SCIENCE FAIR!
I'LL RUN SOME TESTS ON YOU AND THAT STUPID BLANKET...
I'M GOING TO SCIENTIFICALLY PROVE WHETHER OR NOT IT BRINGS YOU SECURITY!!
SUDDENLY, I FEEL VERY INSECURE!

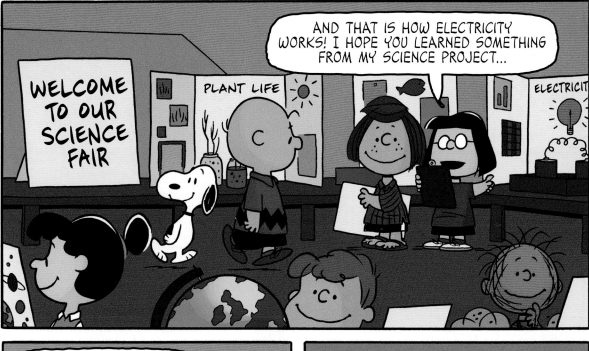

WELCOME TO OUR SCIENCE FAIR

PLANT LIFE

ELECTRICIT

AND THAT IS HOW ELECTRICITY WORKS! I HOPE YOU LEARNED SOMETHING FROM MY SCIENCE PROJECT...

OKAY, MY TURN! AT FIRST I HAD A LITTLE TROUBLE TRYING TO DECIDE WHAT TO DO, BUT HERE IT IS...

TOAST!!

WELL DONE, SIR...

SCIENCE PROJECT

BREAD UNTOASTED

BREAD TOASTED

"OUR WILDLIFE AND TREES ARE PROTECTED BY BRAVE AND DEDICATED MEN AND WOMEN...THESE PEOPLE LIVE BY THEMSELVES IN TOWERS AND ARE CALLED FOREST STRANGERS..."

I WONDER IF I SHOULD INCLUDE AN EXPLANATION OF HOW THEY GOT THAT NAME...

I WOULDN'T...

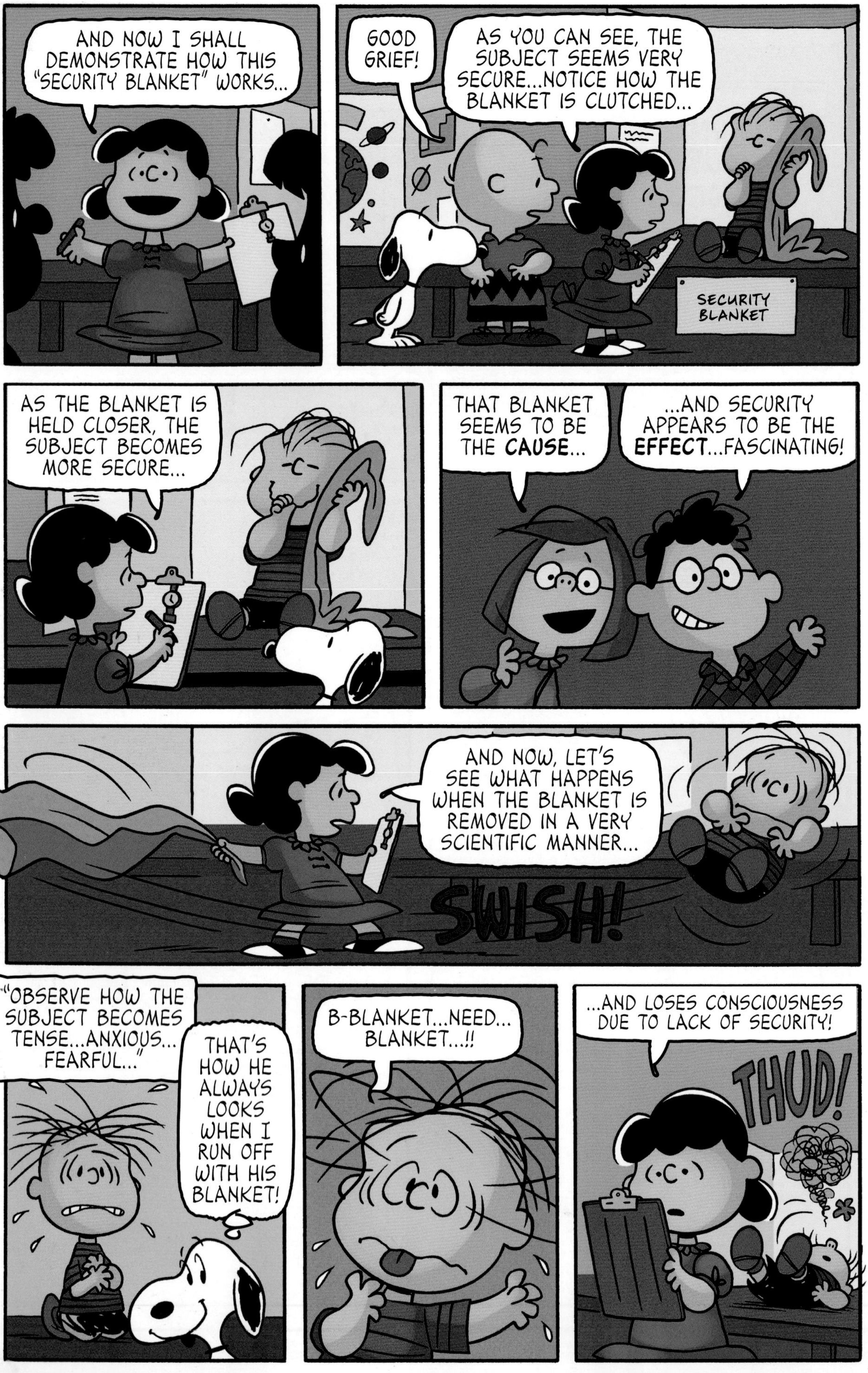
AND NOW I SHALL DEMONSTRATE HOW THIS "SECURITY BLANKET" WORKS...
GOOD GRIEF!
AS YOU CAN SEE, THE SUBJECT SEEMS VERY SECURE...NOTICE HOW THE BLANKET IS CLUTCHED...
SECURITY BLANKET
AS THE BLANKET IS HELD CLOSER, THE SUBJECT BECOMES MORE SECURE...
THAT BLANKET SEEMS TO BE THE **CAUSE**...
...AND SECURITY APPEARS TO BE THE **EFFECT**...FASCINATING!
AND NOW, LET'S SEE WHAT HAPPENS WHEN THE BLANKET IS REMOVED IN A VERY SCIENTIFIC MANNER...
SWISH!
"OBSERVE HOW THE SUBJECT BECOMES TENSE...ANXIOUS... FEARFUL..."
THAT'S HOW HE ALWAYS LOOKS WHEN I RUN OFF WITH HIS BLANKET!
B-BLANKET...NEED... BLANKET...!!
...AND LOSES CONSCIOUSNESS DUE TO LACK OF SECURITY!
THUD!

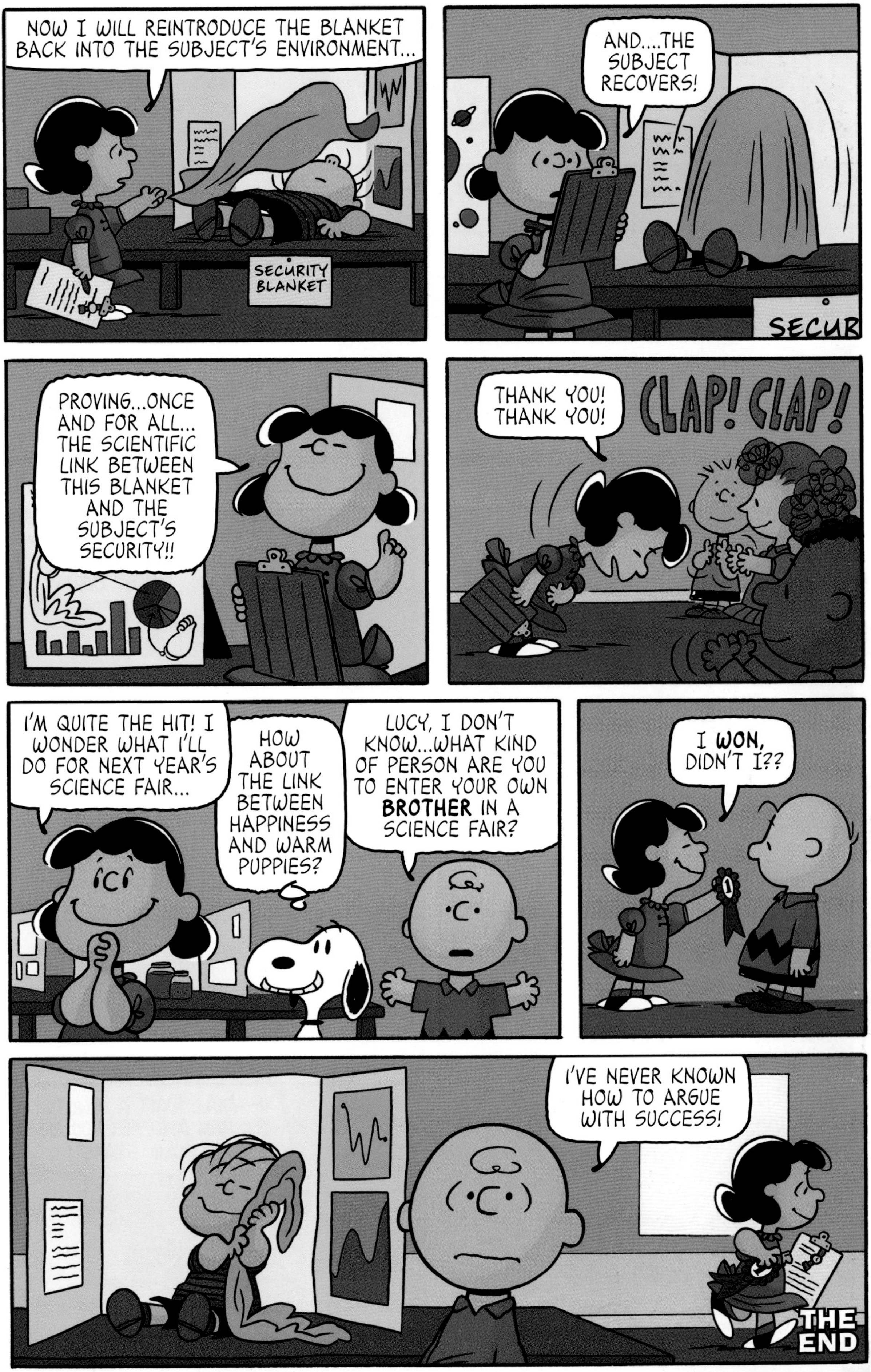
NOW I WILL REINTRODUCE THE BLANKET BACK INTO THE SUBJECT'S ENVIRONMENT...
SECURITY BLANKET
AND....THE SUBJECT RECOVERS!
SECUR
PROVING...ONCE AND FOR ALL... THE SCIENTIFIC LINK BETWEEN THIS BLANKET AND THE SUBJECT'S SECURITY!!
THANK YOU! THANK YOU!
CLAP! CLAP!
I'M QUITE THE HIT! I WONDER WHAT I'LL DO FOR NEXT YEAR'S SCIENCE FAIR...
HOW ABOUT THE LINK BETWEEN HAPPINESS AND WARM PUPPIES?
LUCY, I DON'T KNOW...WHAT KIND OF PERSON ARE YOU TO ENTER YOUR OWN **BROTHER** IN A SCIENCE FAIR?
I **WON,** DIDN'T I??
1
I'VE NEVER KNOWN HOW TO ARGUE WITH SUCCESS!
THE END

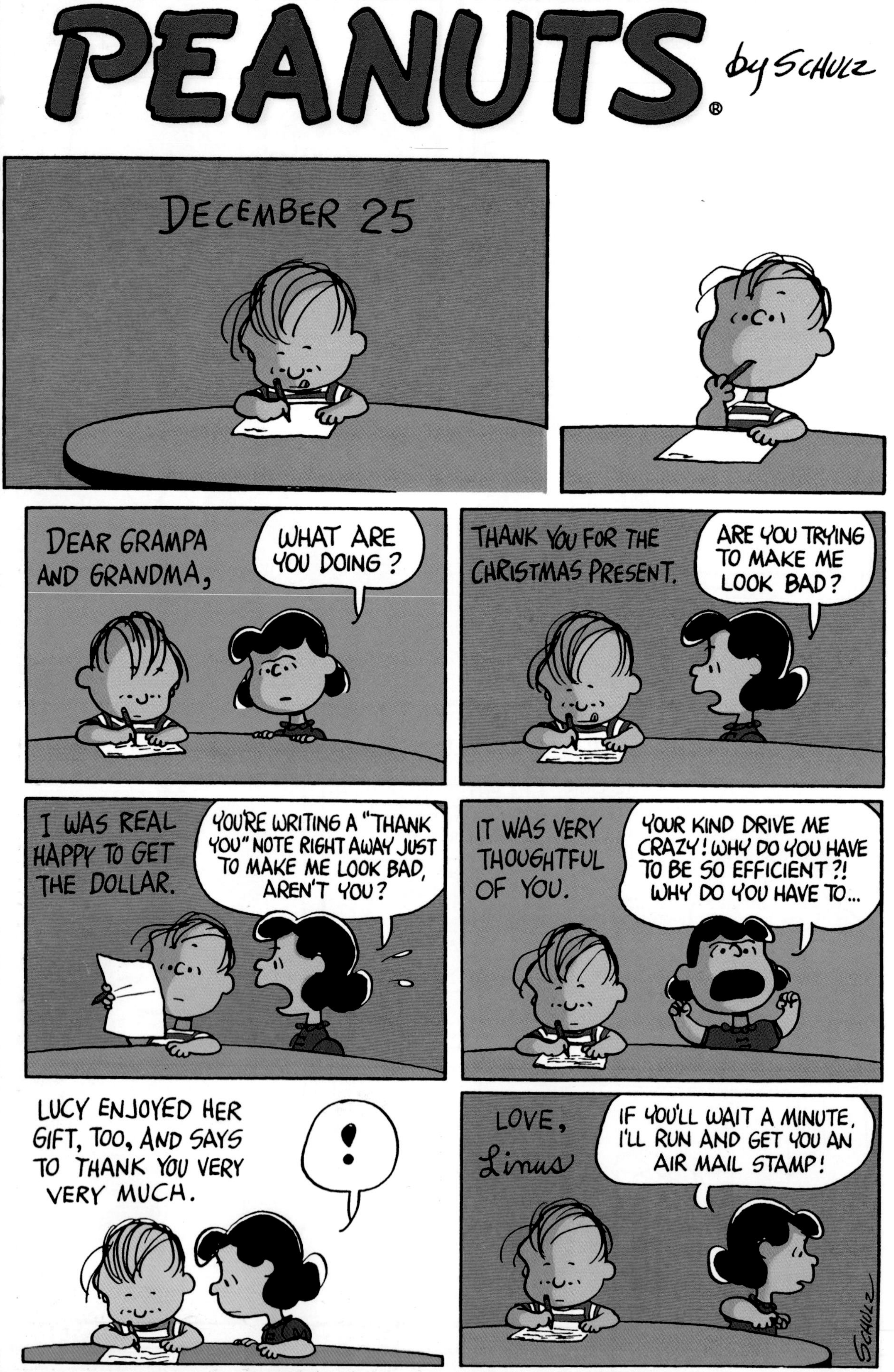
PEANUTS
by SCHULZ
DECEMBER 25
DEAR GRAMPA AND GRANDMA,
WHAT ARE YOU DOING?
THANK YOU FOR THE CHRISTMAS PRESENT.
ARE YOU TRYING TO MAKE ME LOOK BAD?
I WAS REAL HAPPY TO GET THE DOLLAR.
YOU'RE WRITING A "THANK YOU" NOTE RIGHT AWAY JUST TO MAKE ME LOOK BAD, AREN'T YOU?
IT WAS VERY THOUGHTFUL OF YOU.
YOUR KIND DRIVE ME CRAZY! WHY DO YOU HAVE TO BE SO EFFICIENT?! WHY DO YOU HAVE TO...
LUCY ENJOYED HER GIFT, TOO, AND SAYS TO THANK YOU VERY VERY MUCH.
!
LOVE,
Linus
IF YOU'LL WAIT A MINUTE, I'LL RUN AND GET YOU AN AIR MAIL STAMP!
SCHULZ

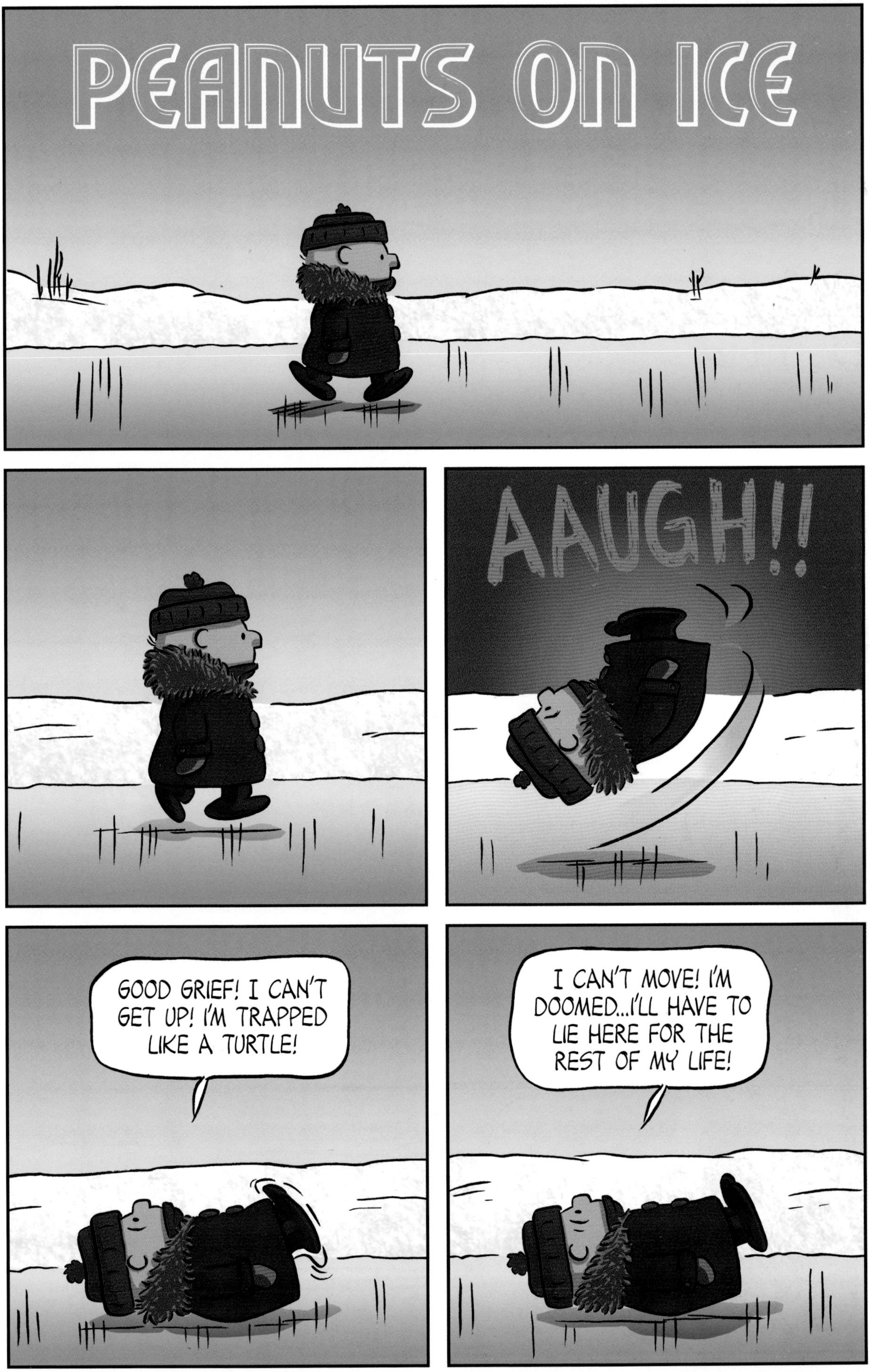
PEANUTS ON ICE
AAUGH!!
GOOD GRIEF! I CAN'T GET UP! I'M TRAPPED LIKE A TURTLE!
I CAN'T MOVE! I'M DOOMED...I'LL HAVE TO LIE HERE FOR THE REST OF MY LIFE!

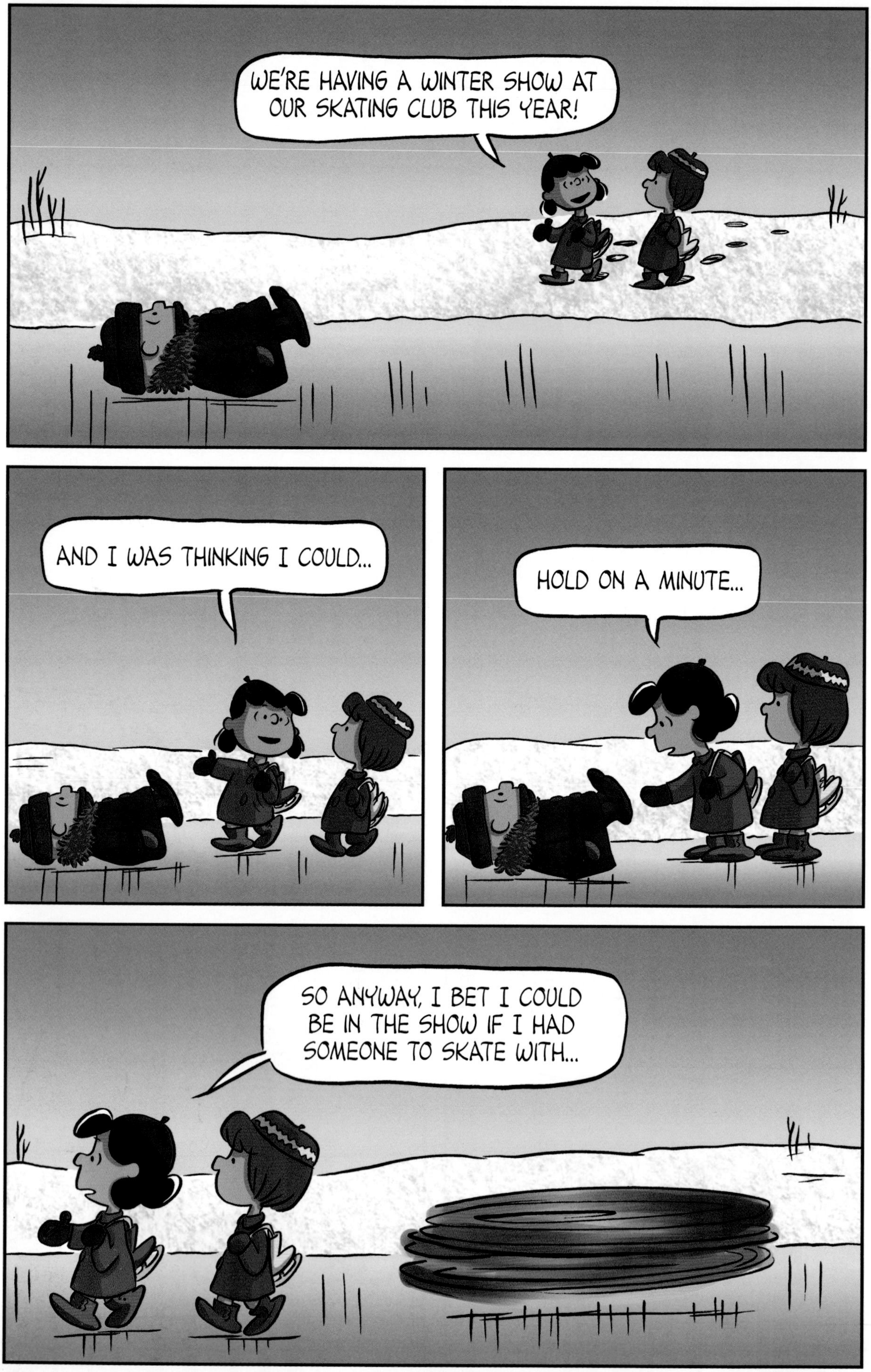
WE'RE HAVING A WINTER SHOW AT OUR SKATING CLUB THIS YEAR!
AND I WAS THINKING I COULD...
HOLD ON A MINUTE...
SO ANYWAY, I BET I COULD BE IN THE SHOW IF I HAD SOMEONE TO SKATE WITH...

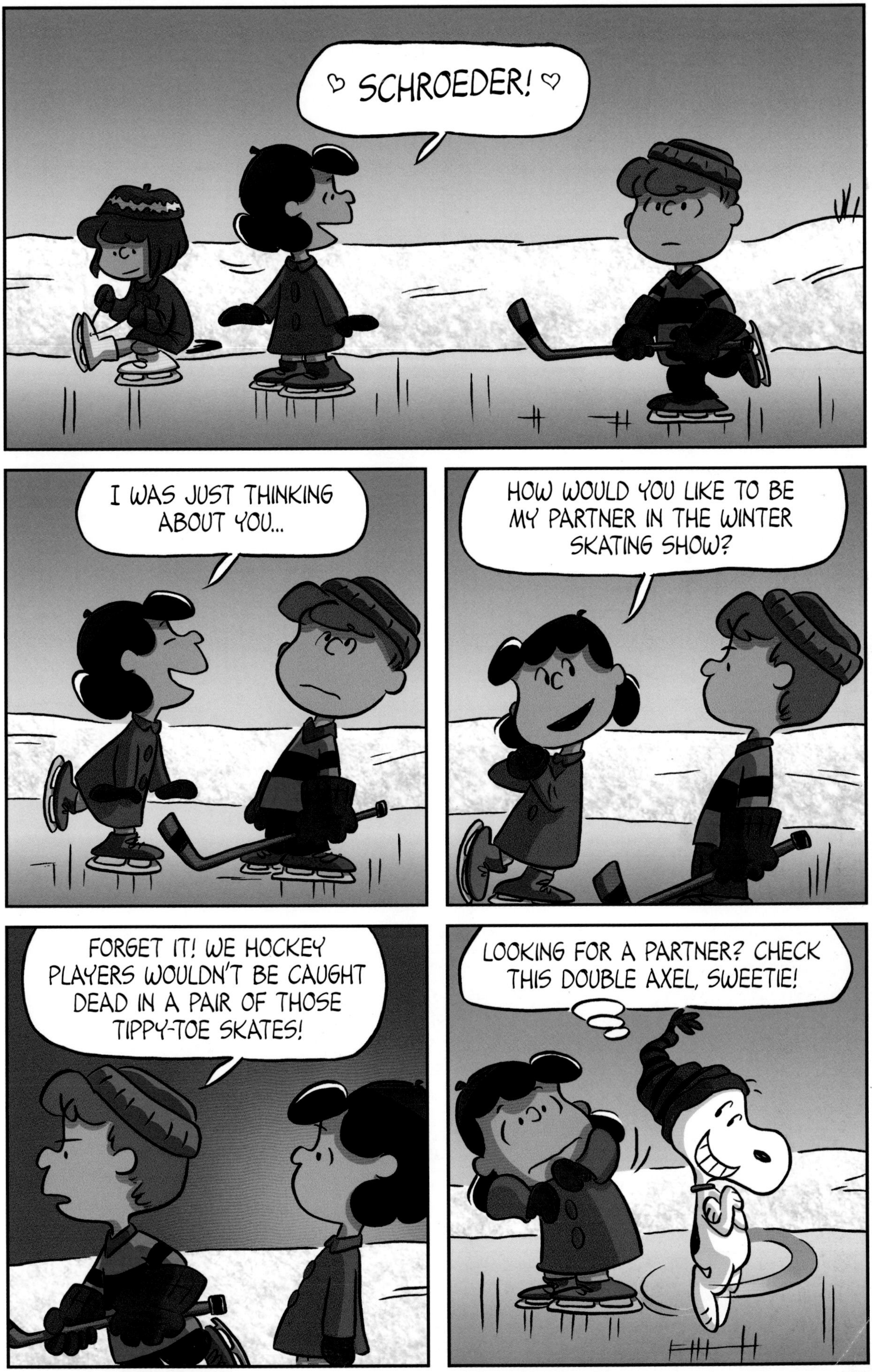
SCHROEDER!
I WAS JUST THINKING ABOUT YOU...
HOW WOULD YOU LIKE TO BE MY PARTNER IN THE WINTER SKATING SHOW?
FORGET IT! WE HOCKEY PLAYERS WOULDN'T BE CAUGHT DEAD IN A PAIR OF THOSE TIPPY-TOE SKATES!
LOOKING FOR A PARTNER? CHECK THIS DOUBLE AXEL, SWEETIE!

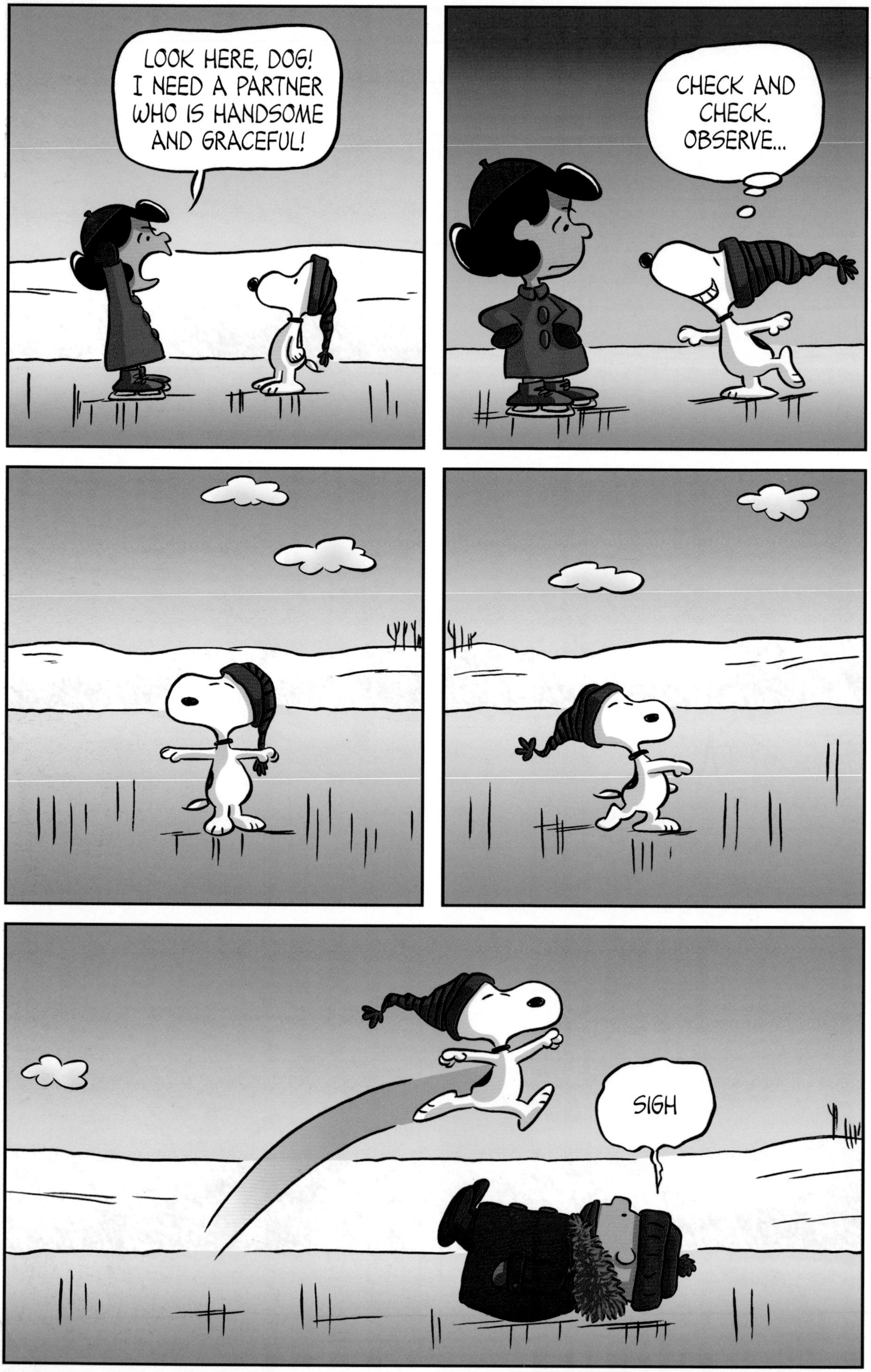
LOOK HERE, DOG! I NEED A PARTNER WHO IS HANDSOME AND GRACEFUL!
CHECK AND CHECK. OBSERVE...
SIGH

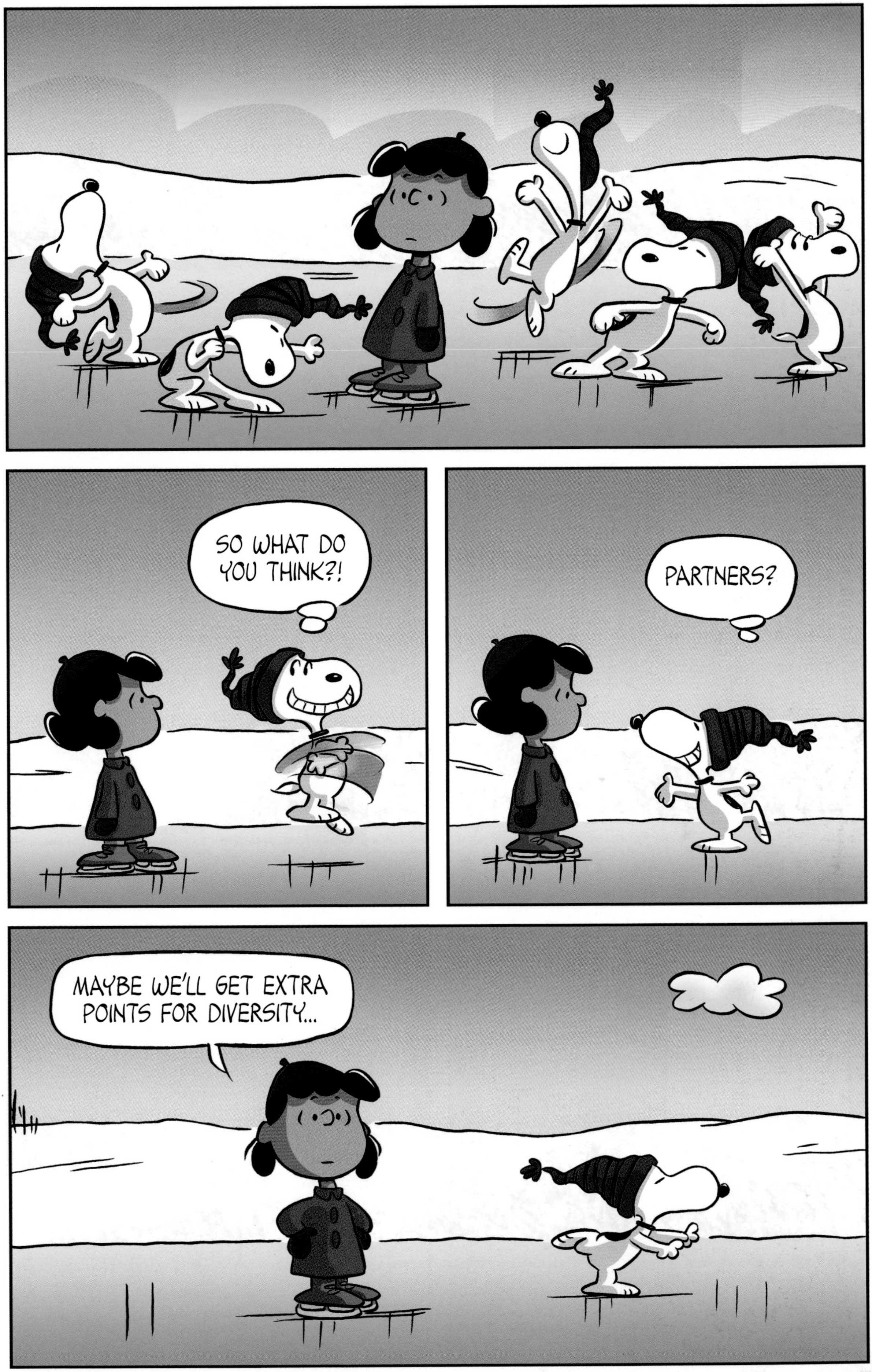
SO WHAT DO YOU THINK?!
PARTNERS?
MAYBE WE'LL GET EXTRA POINTS FOR DIVERSITY...

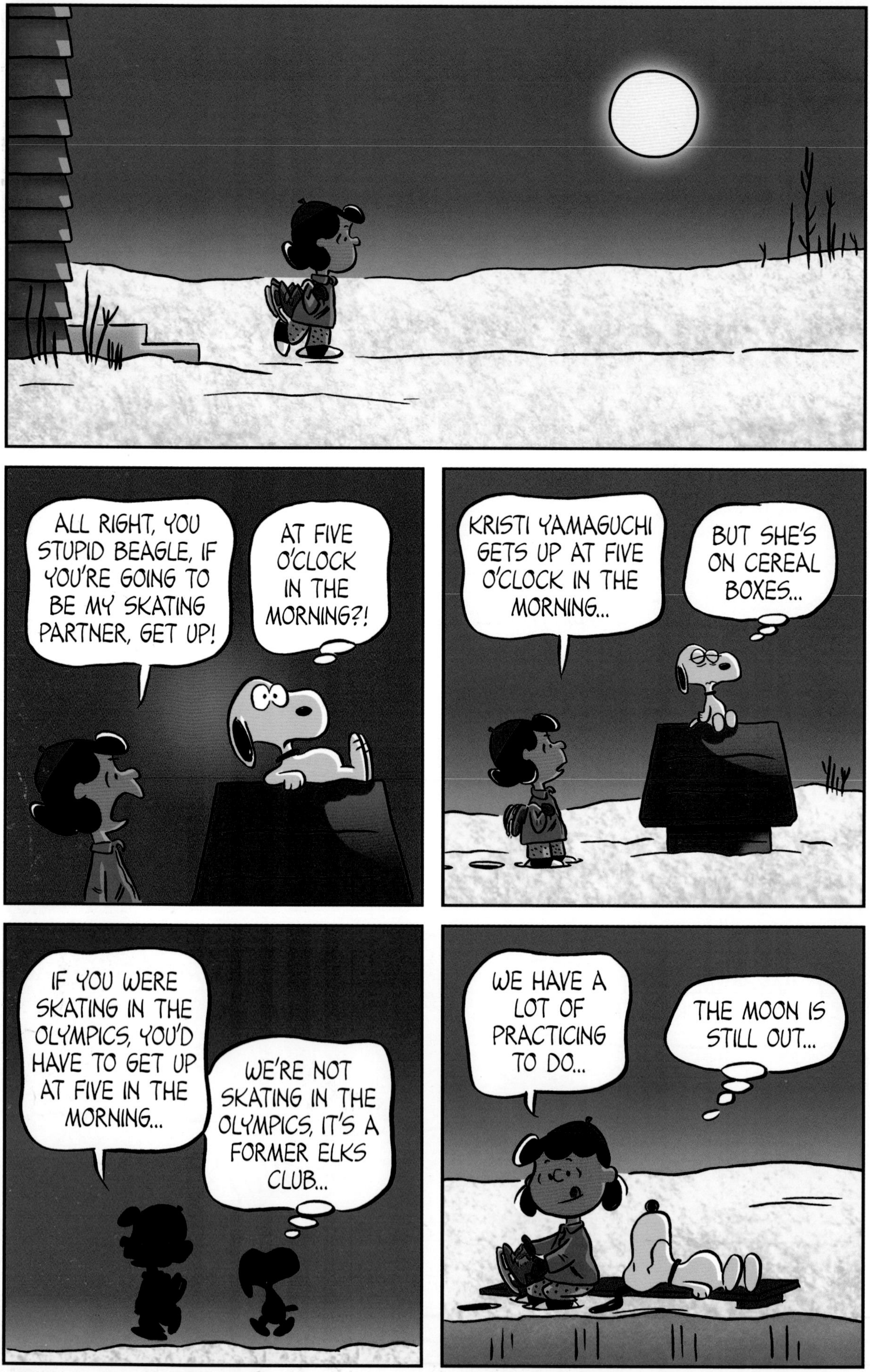
ALL RIGHT, YOU STUPID BEAGLE, IF YOU'RE GOING TO BE MY SKATING PARTNER, GET UP!
AT FIVE O'CLOCK IN THE MORNING?!
KRISTI YAMAGUCHI GETS UP AT FIVE O'CLOCK IN THE MORNING...
BUT SHE'S ON CEREAL BOXES...
IF YOU WERE SKATING IN THE OLYMPICS, YOU'D HAVE TO GET UP AT FIVE IN THE MORNING...
WE'RE NOT SKATING IN THE OLYMPICS, IT'S A FORMER ELKS CLUB...
WE HAVE A LOT OF PRACTICING TO DO...
THE MOON IS STILL OUT...

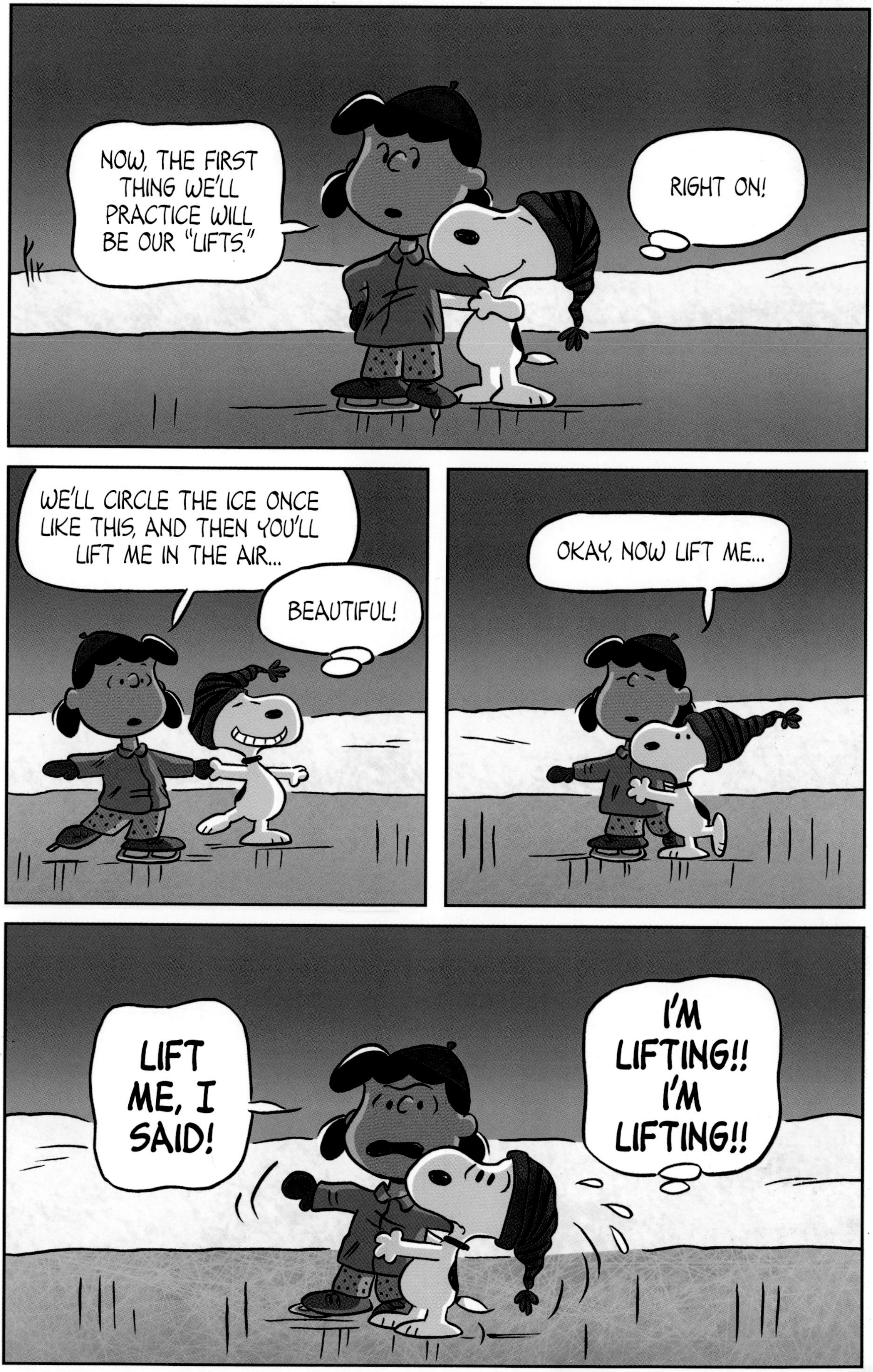
NOW, THE FIRST THING WE'LL PRACTICE WILL BE OUR "LIFTS."
RIGHT ON!
WE'LL CIRCLE THE ICE ONCE LIKE THIS, AND THEN YOU'LL LIFT ME IN THE AIR...
BEAUTIFUL!
OKAY, NOW LIFT ME...
LIFT ME, I SAID!
I'M LIFTING!! I'M LIFTING!!

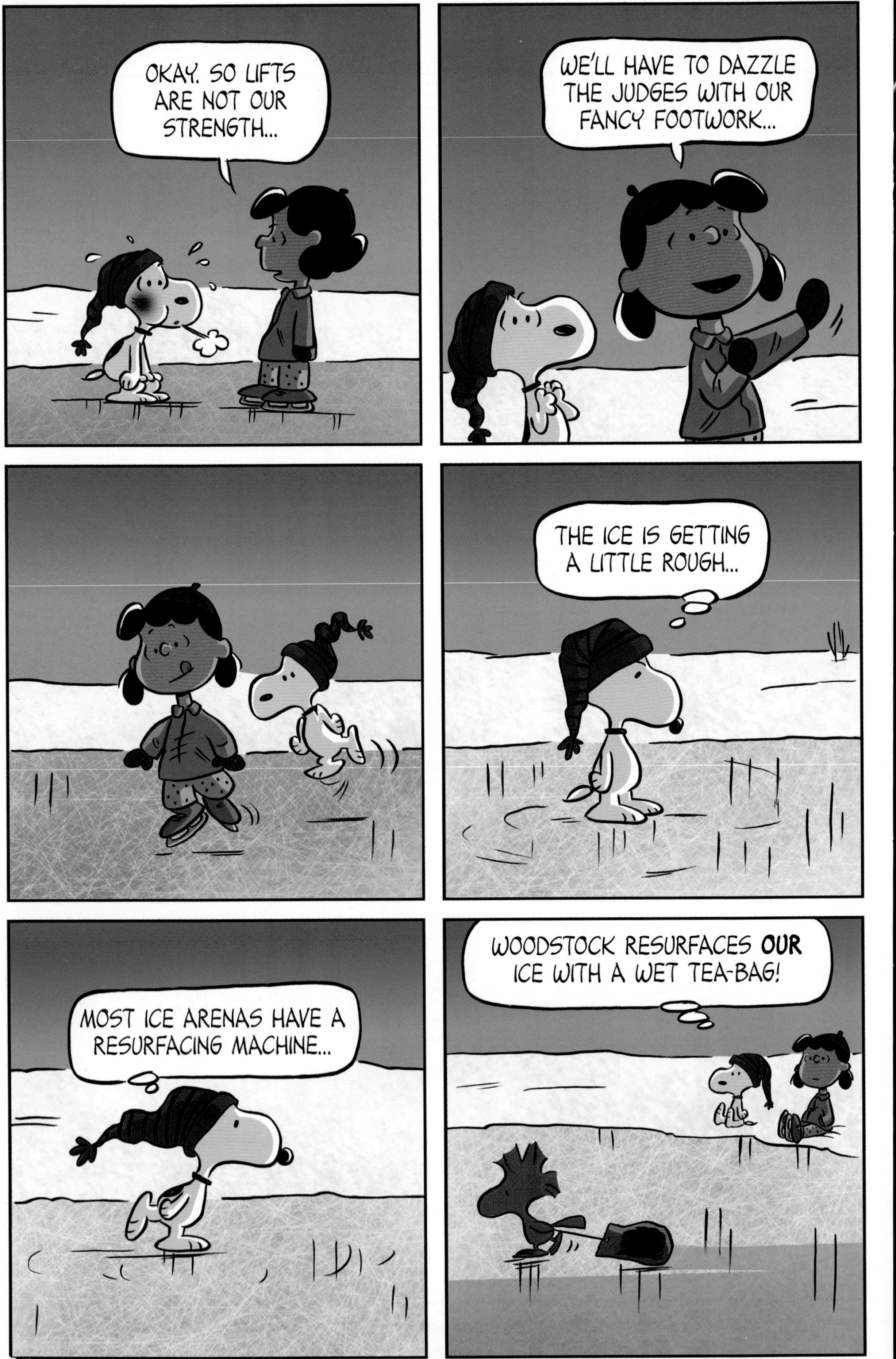
OKAY. SO LIFTS ARE NOT OUR STRENGTH...
WE'LL HAVE TO DAZZLE THE JUDGES WITH OUR FANCY FOOTWORK...
THE ICE IS GETTING A LITTLE ROUGH...
MOST ICE ARENAS HAVE A RESURFACING MACHINE...
WOODSTOCK RESURFACES **OUR** ICE WITH A WET TEA-BAG!

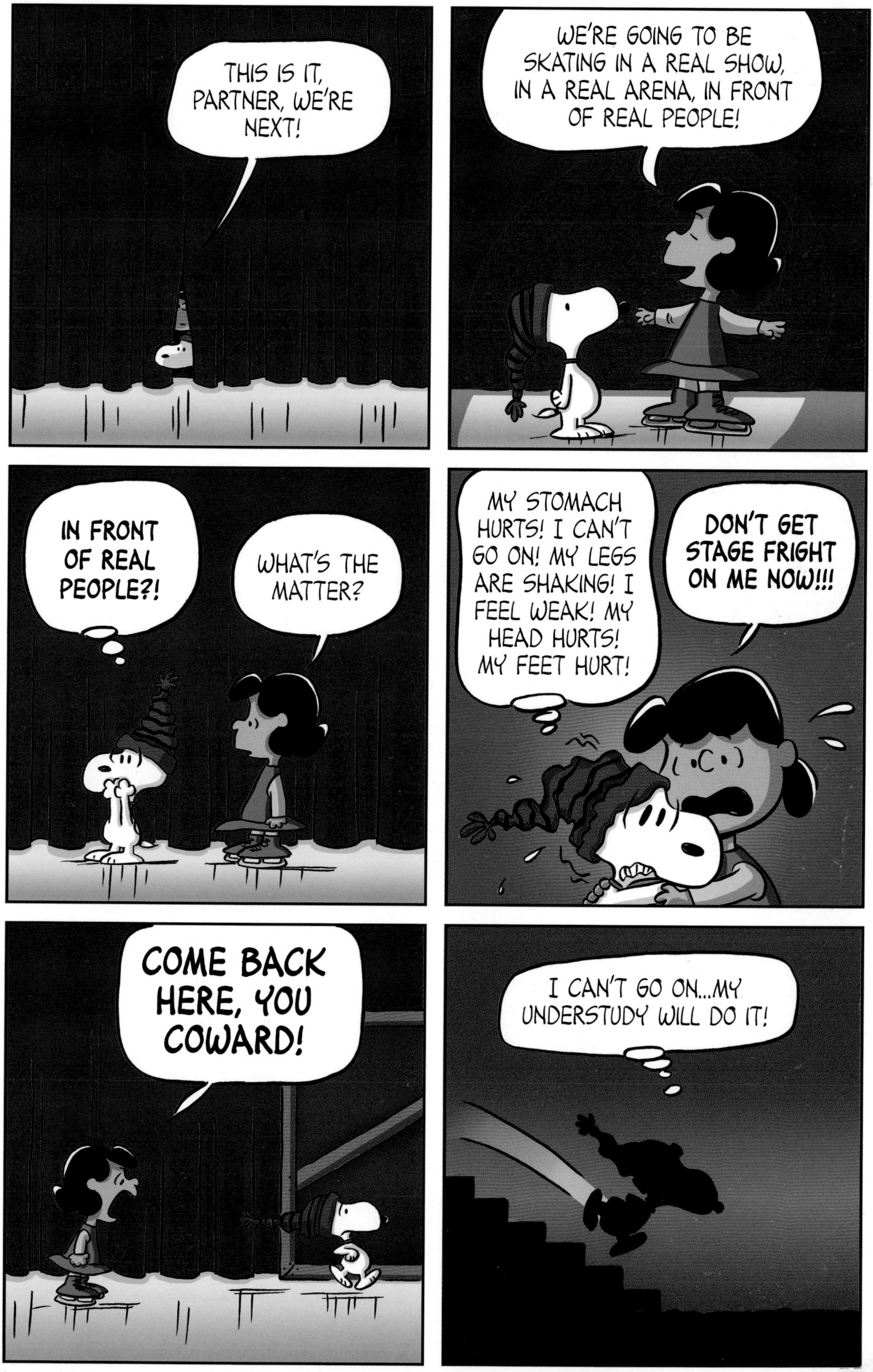
THIS IS IT, PARTNER, WE'RE NEXT!
WE'RE GOING TO BE SKATING IN A REAL SHOW, IN A REAL ARENA, IN FRONT OF REAL PEOPLE!
IN FRONT OF REAL PEOPLE?!
WHAT'S THE MATTER?
MY STOMACH HURTS! I CAN'T GO ON! MY LEGS ARE SHAKING! I FEEL WEAK! MY HEAD HURTS! MY FEET HURT!
DON'T GET STAGE FRIGHT ON ME NOW!!!
COME BACK HERE, YOU COWARD!
I CAN'T GO ON...MY UNDERSTUDY WILL DO IT!

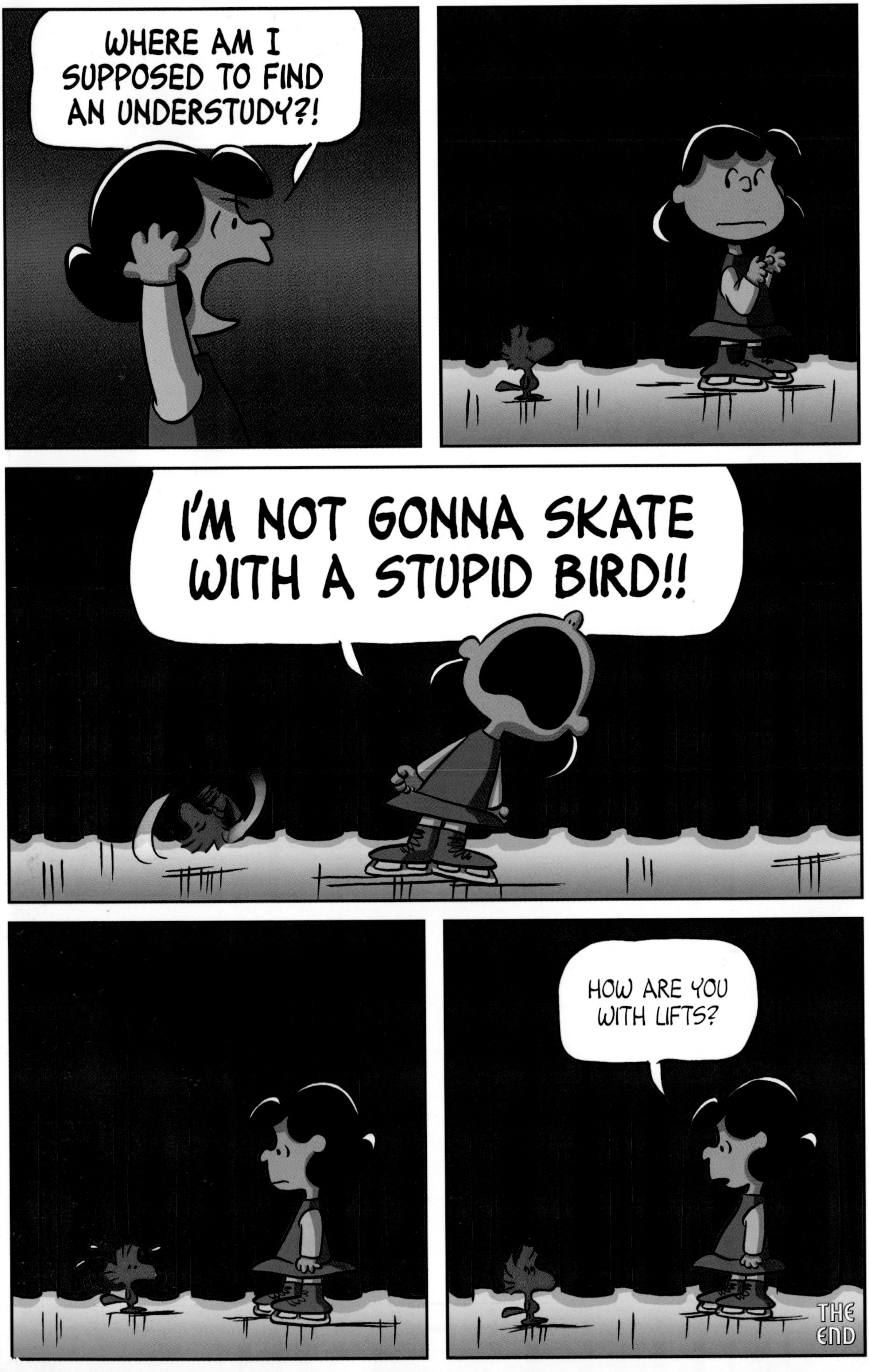
WHERE AM I SUPPOSED TO FIND AN UNDERSTUDY?!
I'M NOT GONNA SKATE WITH A STUPID BIRD!!
HOW ARE YOU WITH LIFTS?
THE END

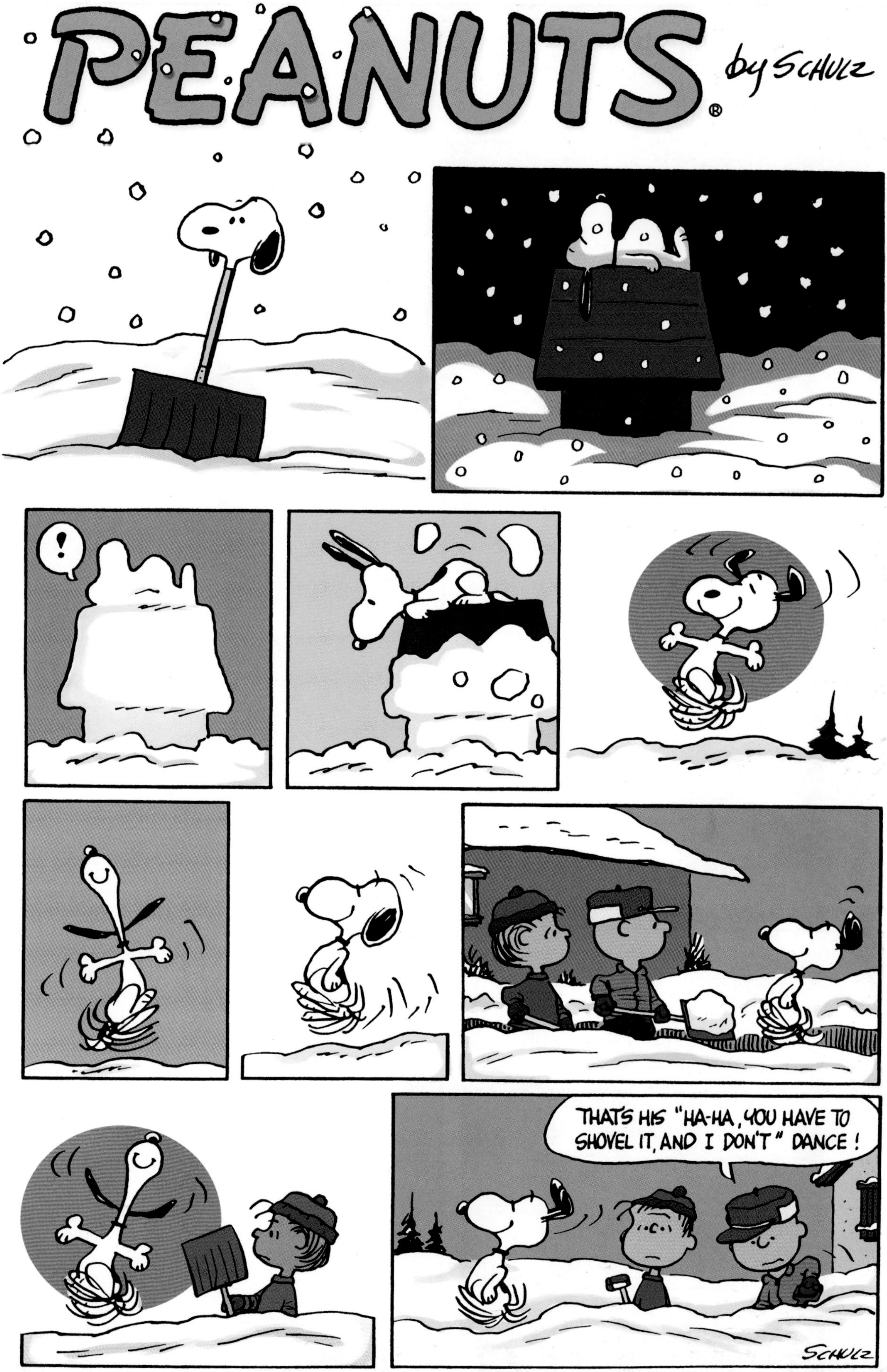
PEANUTS
by SCHULZ
!
THAT'S HIS "HA-HA, YOU HAVE TO SHOVEL IT, AND I DON'T" DANCE!
SCHULZ

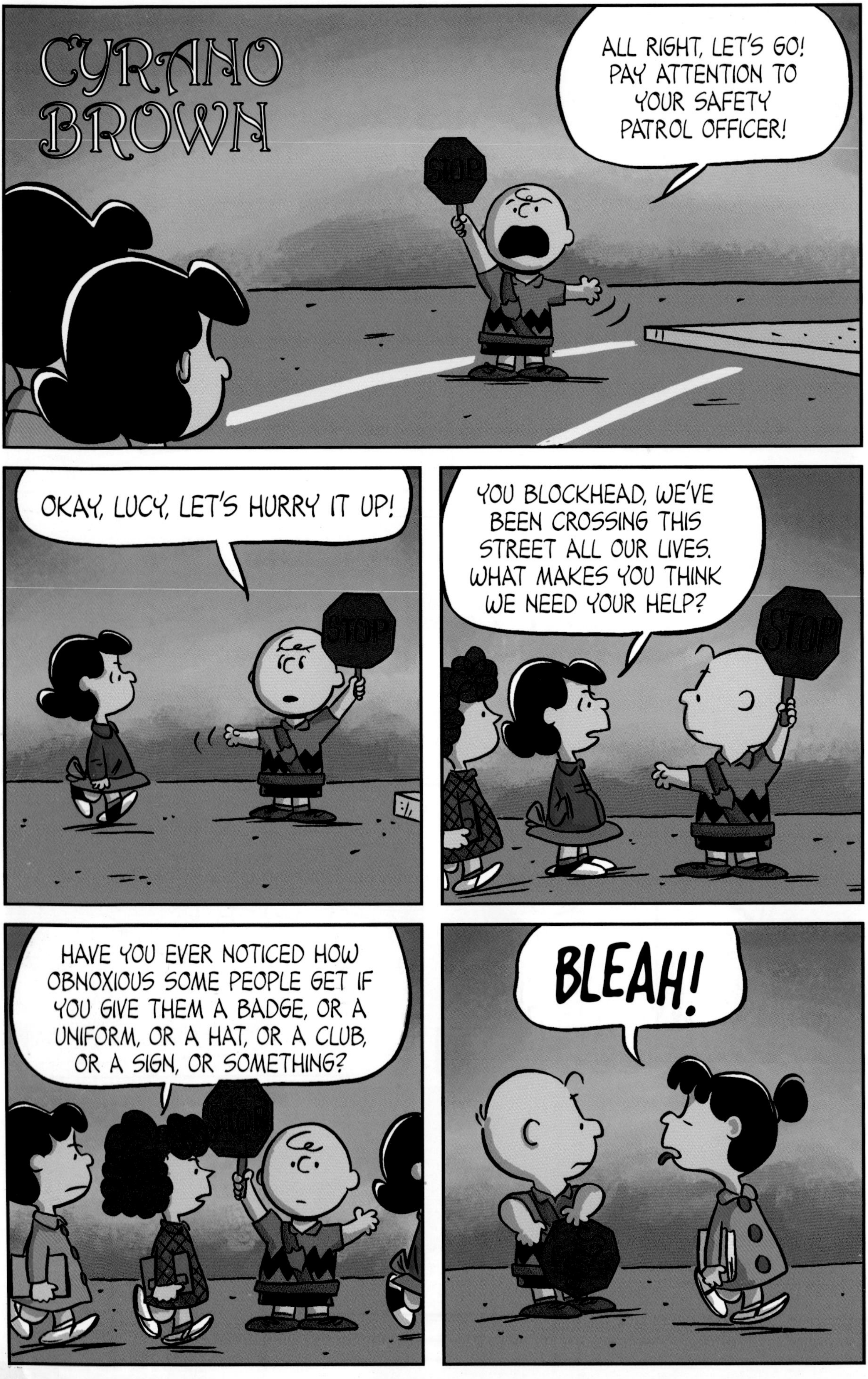
CYRANO BROWN
ALL RIGHT, LET'S GO! PAY ATTENTION TO YOUR SAFETY PATROL OFFICER!
STOP
OKAY, LUCY, LET'S HURRY IT UP!
STOP
YOU BLOCKHEAD, WE'VE BEEN CROSSING THIS STREET ALL OUR LIVES. WHAT MAKES YOU THINK WE NEED YOUR HELP?
STOP
HAVE YOU EVER NOTICED HOW OBNOXIOUS SOME PEOPLE GET IF YOU GIVE THEM A BADGE, OR A UNIFORM, OR A HAT, OR A CLUB, OR A SIGN, OR SOMETHING?
BLEAH!

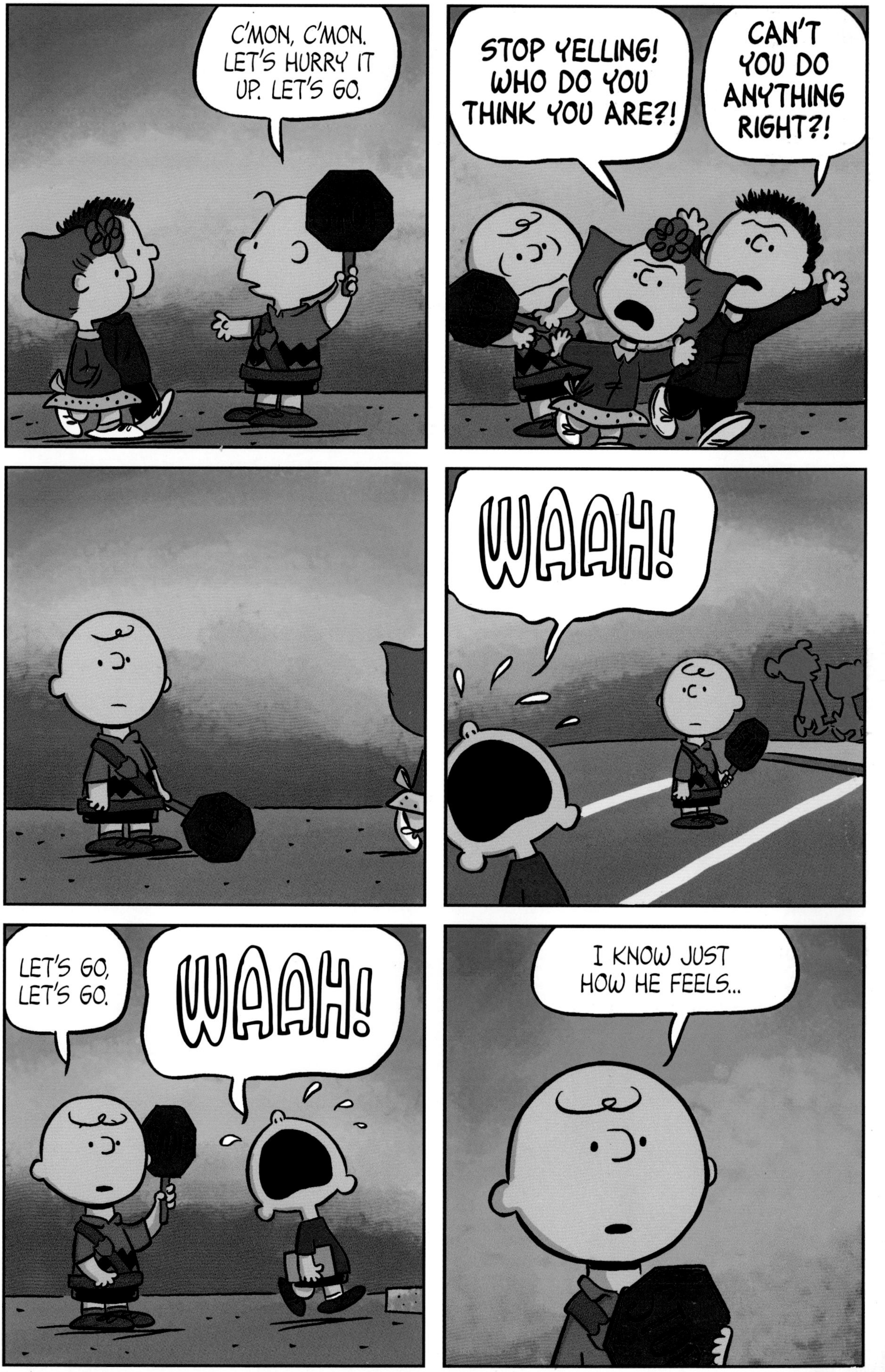
C'MON, C'MON. LET'S HURRY IT UP. LET'S GO.
STOP YELLING! WHO DO YOU THINK YOU ARE?!
CAN'T YOU DO ANYTHING RIGHT?!
WAAH!
LET'S GO, LET'S GO.
WAAH!
I KNOW JUST HOW HE FEELS...

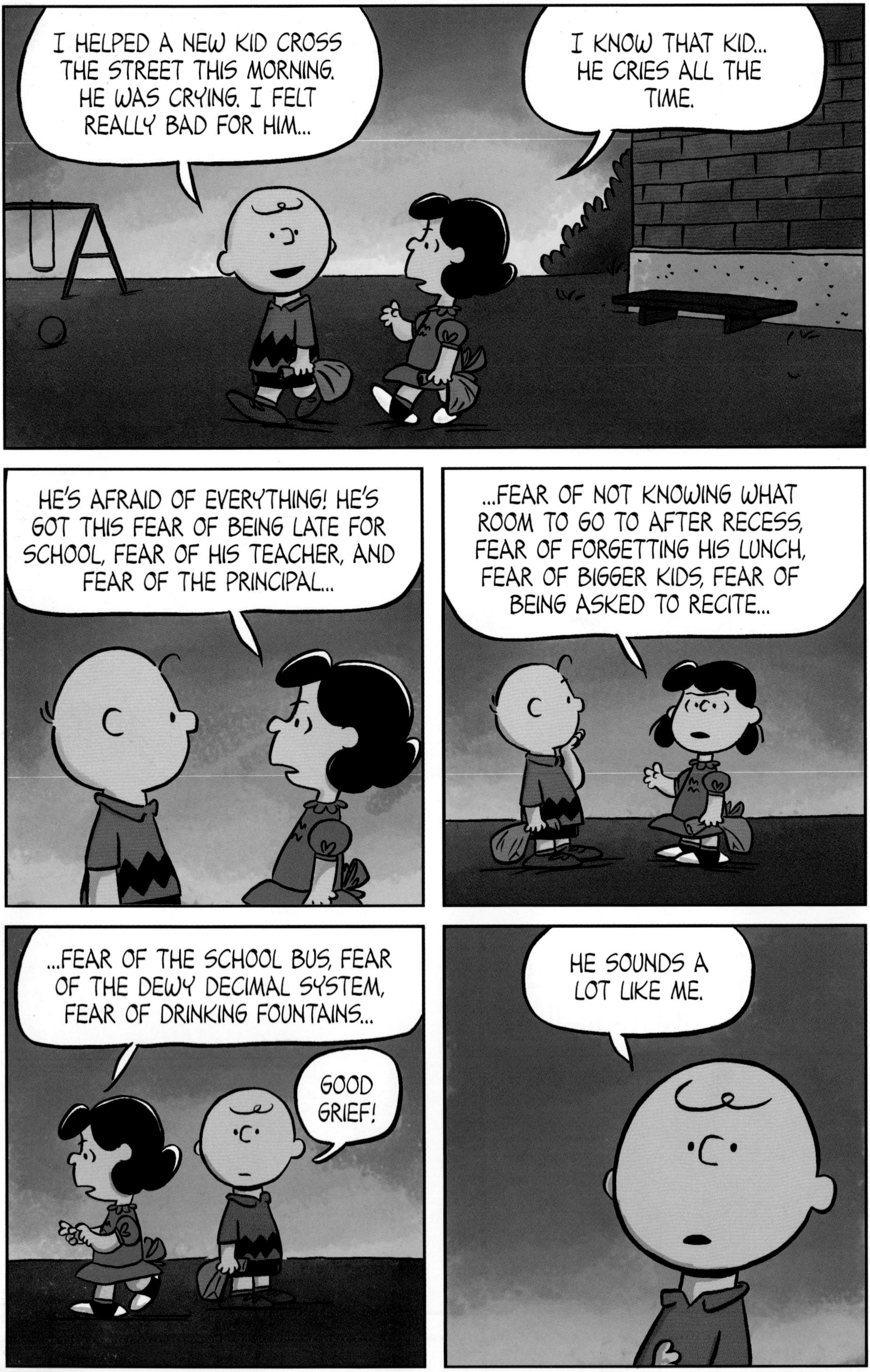
I HELPED A NEW KID CROSS THE STREET THIS MORNING. HE WAS CRYING. I FELT REALLY BAD FOR HIM...
I KNOW THAT KID... HE CRIES ALL THE TIME.
HE'S AFRAID OF EVERYTHING! HE'S GOT THIS FEAR OF BEING LATE FOR SCHOOL, FEAR OF HIS TEACHER, AND FEAR OF THE PRINCIPAL...
...FEAR OF NOT KNOWING WHAT ROOM TO GO TO AFTER RECESS, FEAR OF FORGETTING HIS LUNCH, FEAR OF BIGGER KIDS, FEAR OF BEING ASKED TO RECITE...
...FEAR OF THE SCHOOL BUS, FEAR OF THE DEWY DECIMAL SYSTEM, FEAR OF DRINKING FOUNTAINS...
GOOD GRIEF!
HE SOUNDS A LOT LIKE ME.

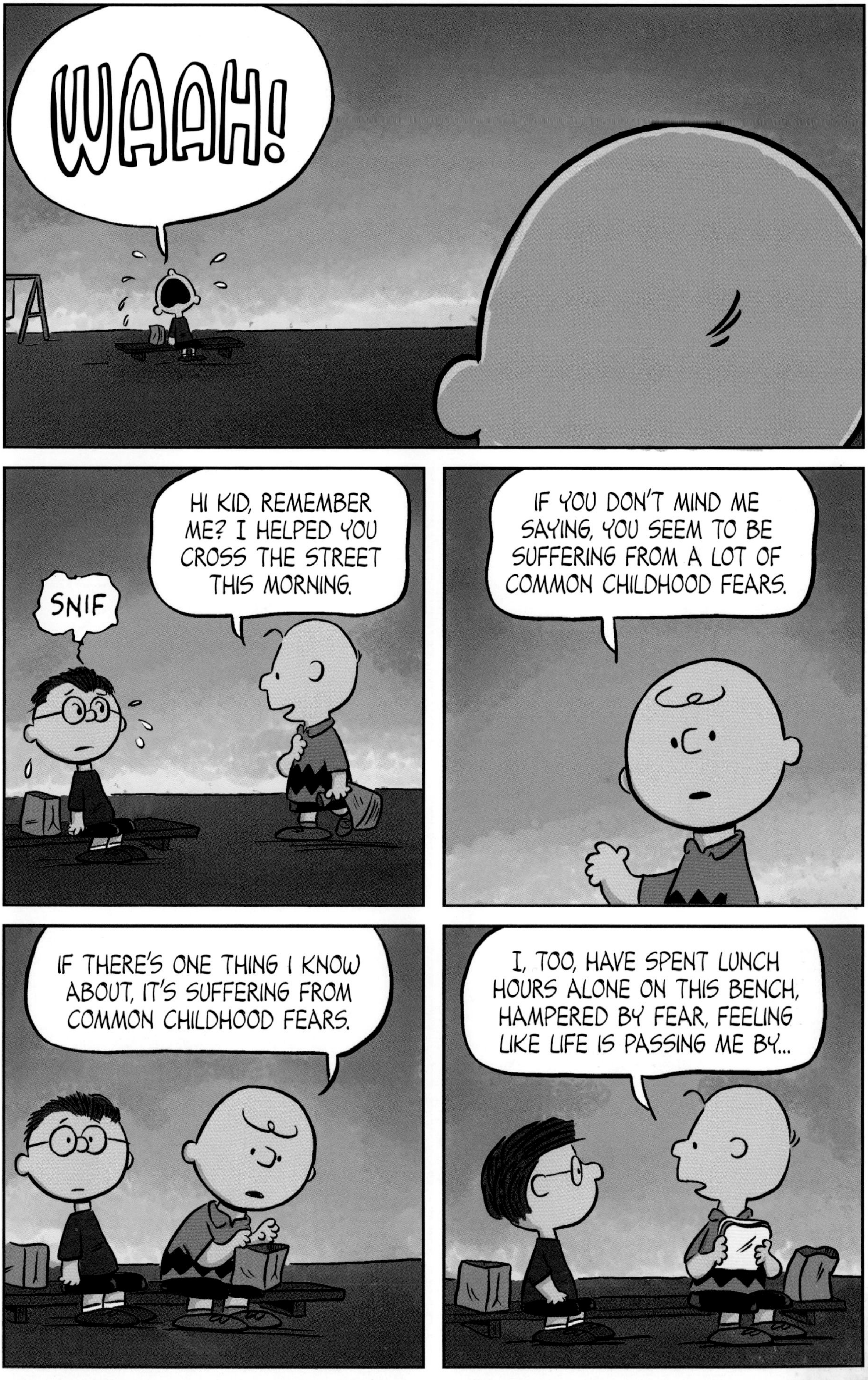
WAAH!
HI KID, REMEMBER ME? I HELPED YOU CROSS THE STREET THIS MORNING.
SNIF
IF YOU DON'T MIND ME SAYING, YOU SEEM TO BE SUFFERING FROM A LOT OF COMMON CHILDHOOD FEARS.
IF THERE'S ONE THING I KNOW ABOUT, IT'S SUFFERING FROM COMMON CHILDHOOD FEARS.
I, TOO, HAVE SPENT LUNCH HOURS ALONE ON THIS BENCH, HAMPERED BY FEAR, FEELING LIKE LIFE IS PASSING ME BY...

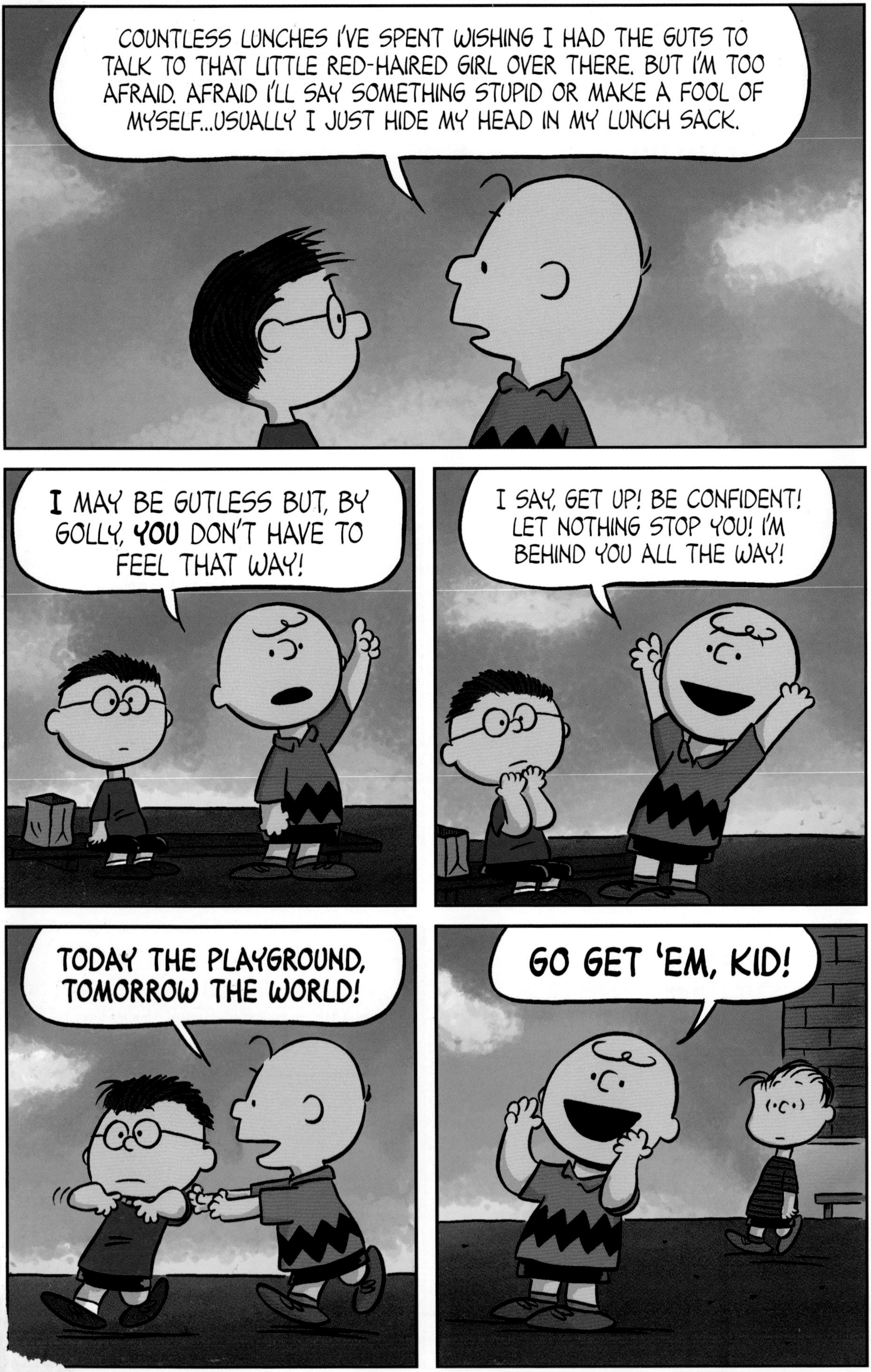
COUNTLESS LUNCHES I'VE SPENT WISHING I HAD THE GUTS TO TALK TO THAT LITTLE RED-HAIRED GIRL OVER THERE. BUT I'M TOO AFRAID. AFRAID I'LL SAY SOMETHING STUPID OR MAKE A FOOL OF MYSELF...USUALLY I JUST HIDE MY HEAD IN MY LUNCH SACK.
I MAY BE GUTLESS BUT, BY GOLLY, YOU DON'T HAVE TO FEEL THAT WAY!
I SAY, GET UP! BE CONFIDENT! LET NOTHING STOP YOU! I'M BEHIND YOU ALL THE WAY!
TODAY THE PLAYGROUND, TOMORROW THE WORLD!
GO GET 'EM, KID!

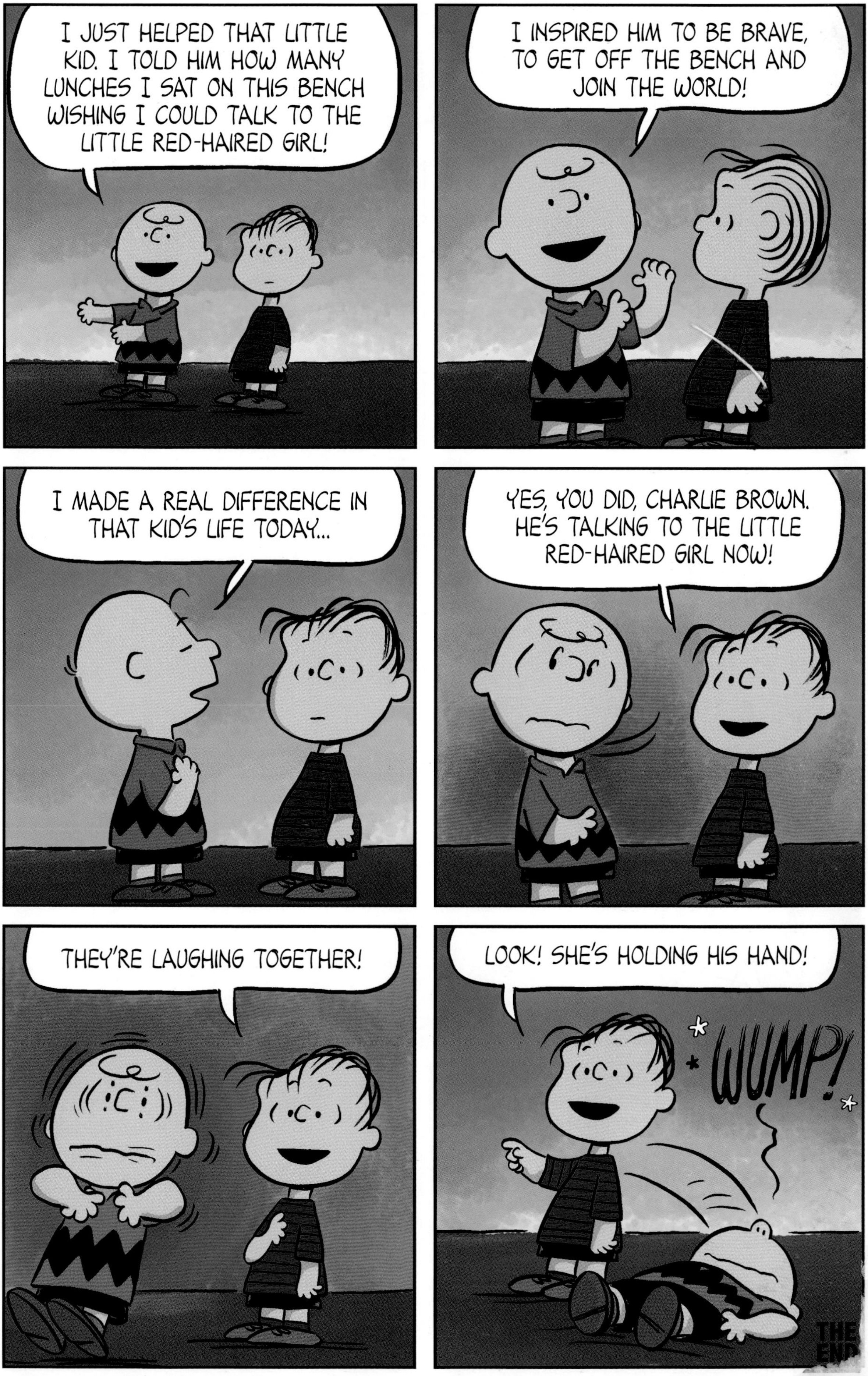
I JUST HELPED THAT LITTLE KID. I TOLD HIM HOW MANY LUNCHES I SAT ON THIS BENCH WISHING I COULD TALK TO THE LITTLE RED-HAIRED GIRL!
I INSPIRED HIM TO BE BRAVE, TO GET OFF THE BENCH AND JOIN THE WORLD!
I MADE A REAL DIFFERENCE IN THAT KID'S LIFE TODAY...
YES, YOU DID, CHARLIE BROWN. HE'S TALKING TO THE LITTLE RED-HAIRED GIRL NOW!
THEY'RE LAUGHING TOGETHER!
LOOK! SHE'S HOLDING HIS HAND!
WUMP!
THE END

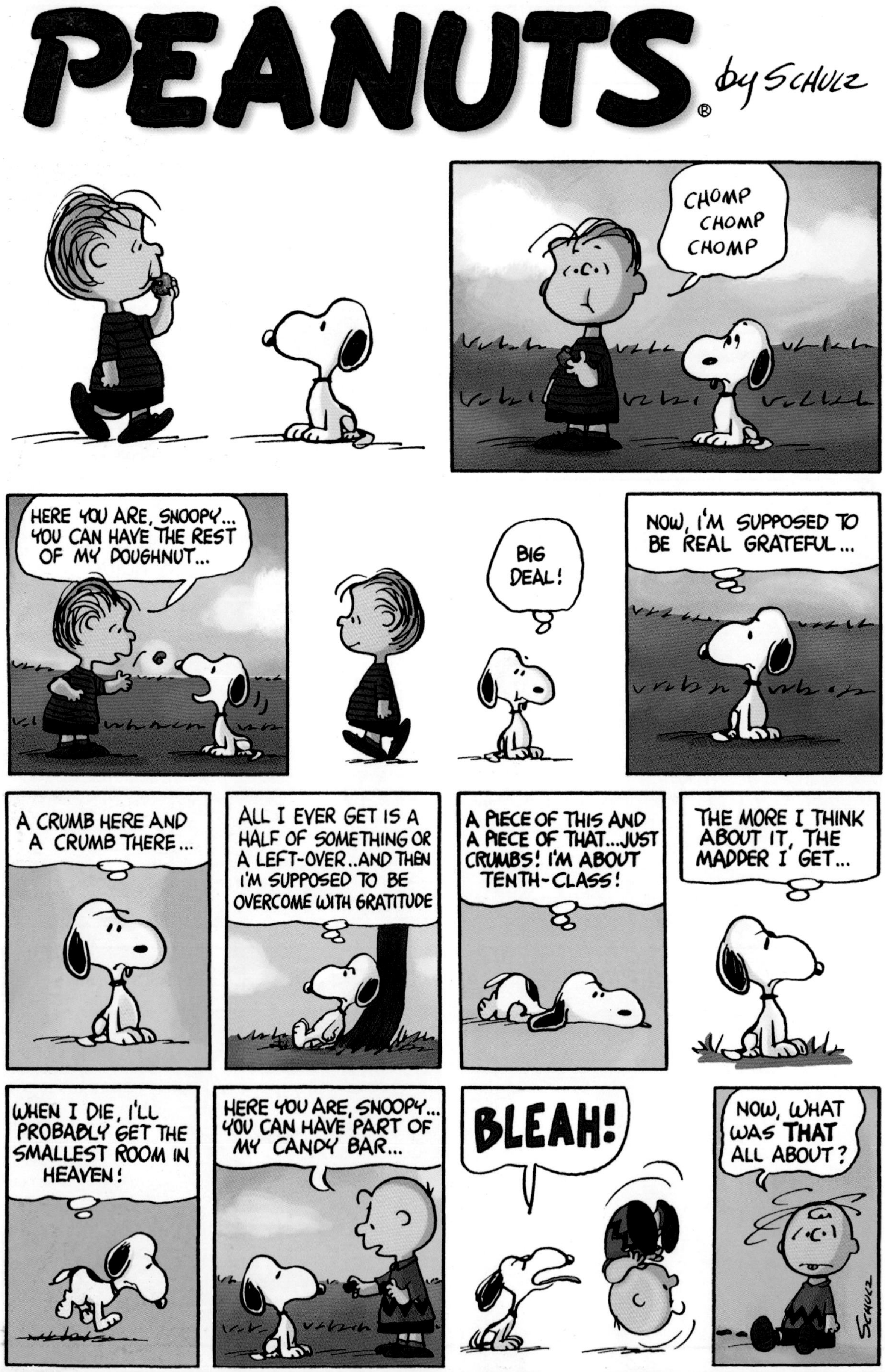
PEANUTS® by SCHULZ
CHOMP CHOMP CHOMP
HERE YOU ARE, SNOOPY... YOU CAN HAVE THE REST OF MY DOUGHNUT...
BIG DEAL!
NOW, I'M SUPPOSED TO BE REAL GRATEFUL...
A CRUMB HERE AND A CRUMB THERE...
ALL I EVER GET IS A HALF OF SOMETHING OR A LEFT-OVER..AND THEN I'M SUPPOSED TO BE OVERCOME WITH GRATITUDE
A PIECE OF THIS AND A PIECE OF THAT...JUST CRUMBS! I'M ABOUT TENTH-CLASS!
THE MORE I THINK ABOUT IT, THE MADDER I GET...
WHEN I DIE, I'LL PROBABLY GET THE SMALLEST ROOM IN HEAVEN!
HERE YOU ARE, SNOOPY... YOU CAN HAVE PART OF MY CANDY BAR...
BLEAH!
NOW, WHAT WAS THAT ALL ABOUT?
SCHULZ

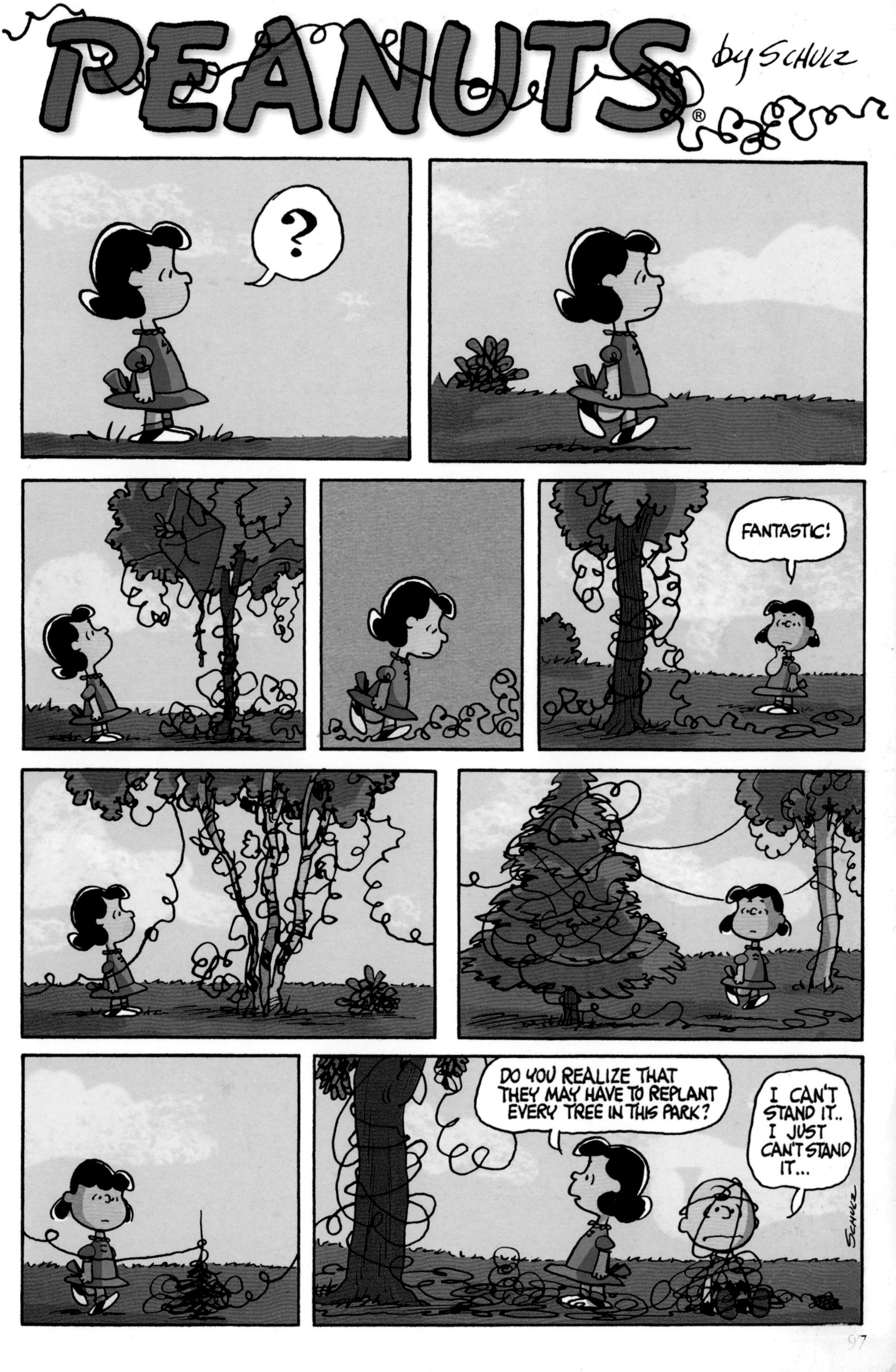
PEANUTS
by SCHULZ
?
FANTASTIC!
DO YOU REALIZE THAT THEY MAY HAVE TO REPLANT EVERY TREE IN THIS PARK?
I CAN'T STAND IT.. I JUST CAN'T STAND IT...
SCHULZ

Cover Gallery

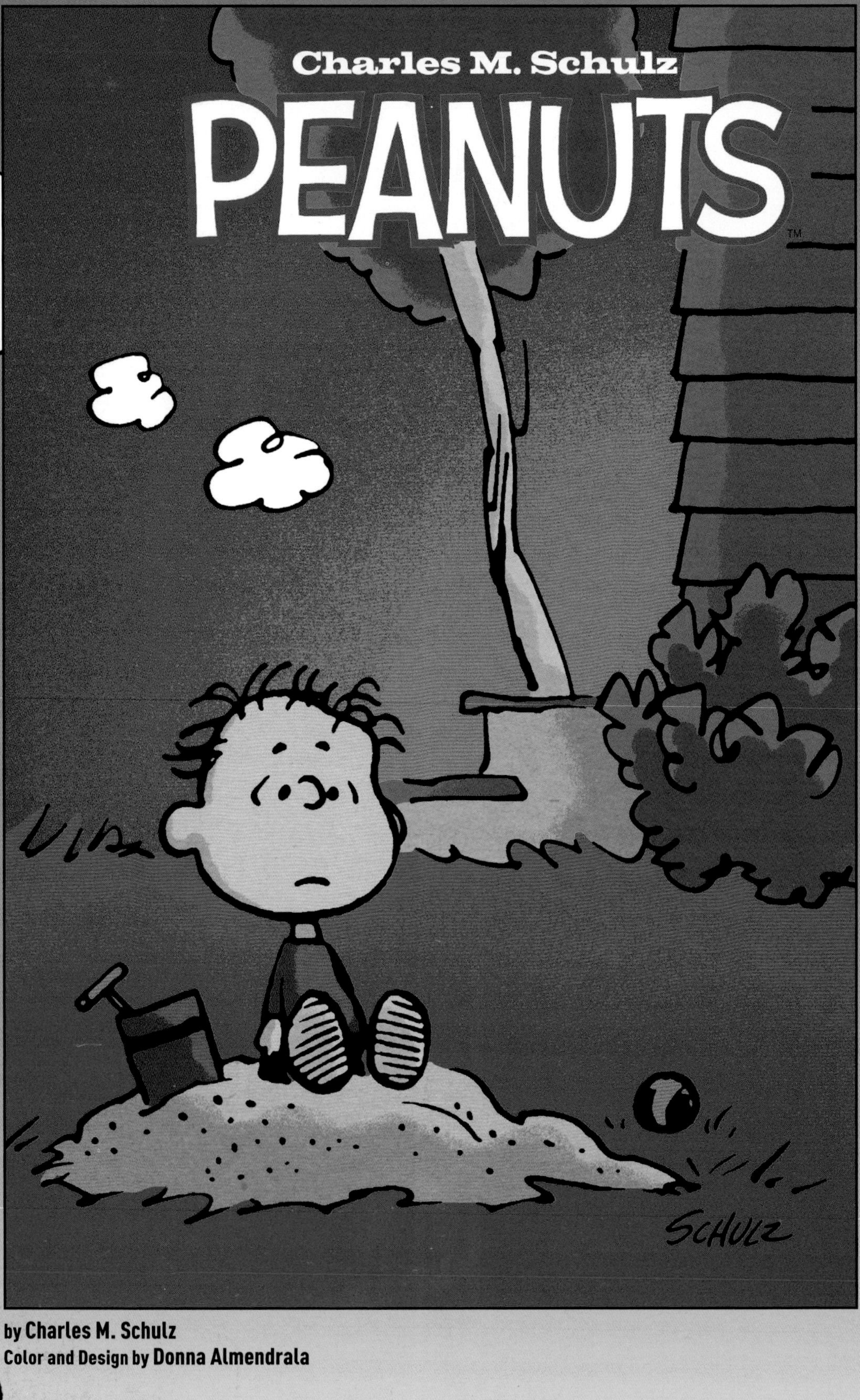
Charles M. Schulz
PEANUTS
TM
SCHULZ

by Charles M. Schulz
Color and Design by Donna Almendrala

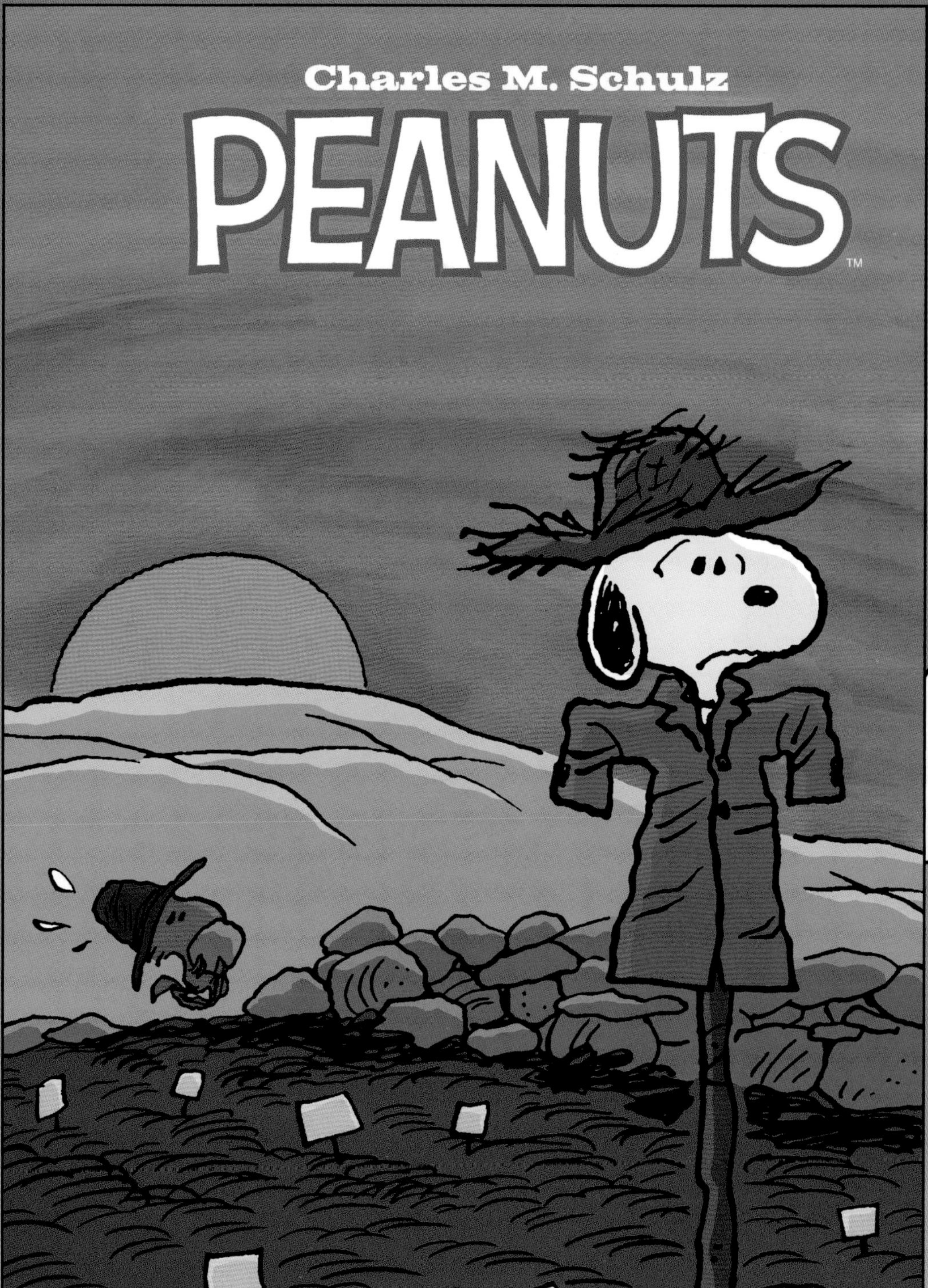
Charles M. Schulz
PEANUTS
SCHULZ

by Charles M. Schulz
Color and Design by Donna Almendrala

by **Charles M. Schulz**
Color and Design by **Donna Almendrala**

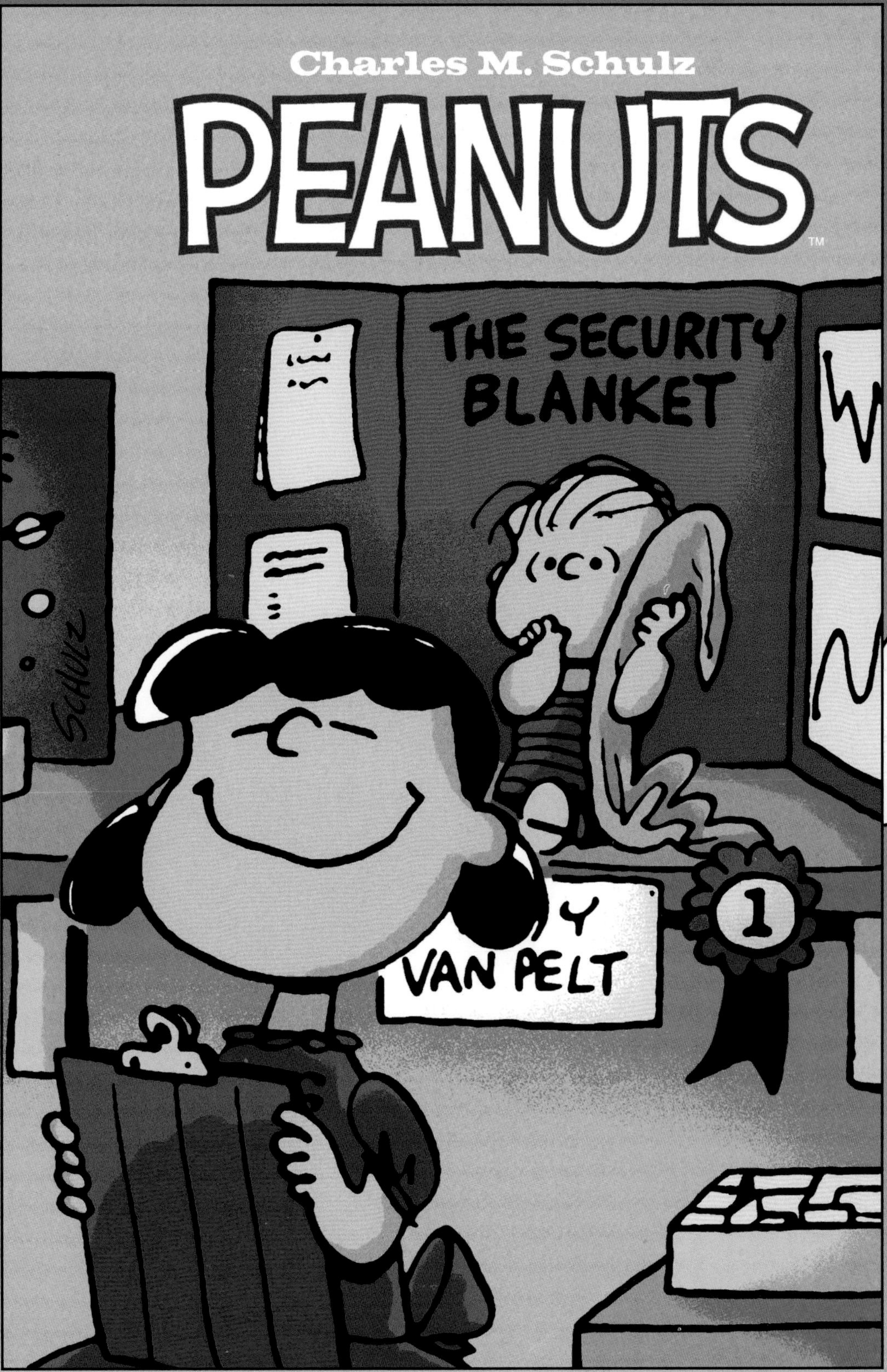
Charles M. Schulz
PEANUTS
THE SECURITY BLANKET
VAN PELT
SCHULZ

by Charles M. Schulz
Color and Design by Donna Almendrala

Peanuts #21
"THE KITE-EATING TREE" First Appearance

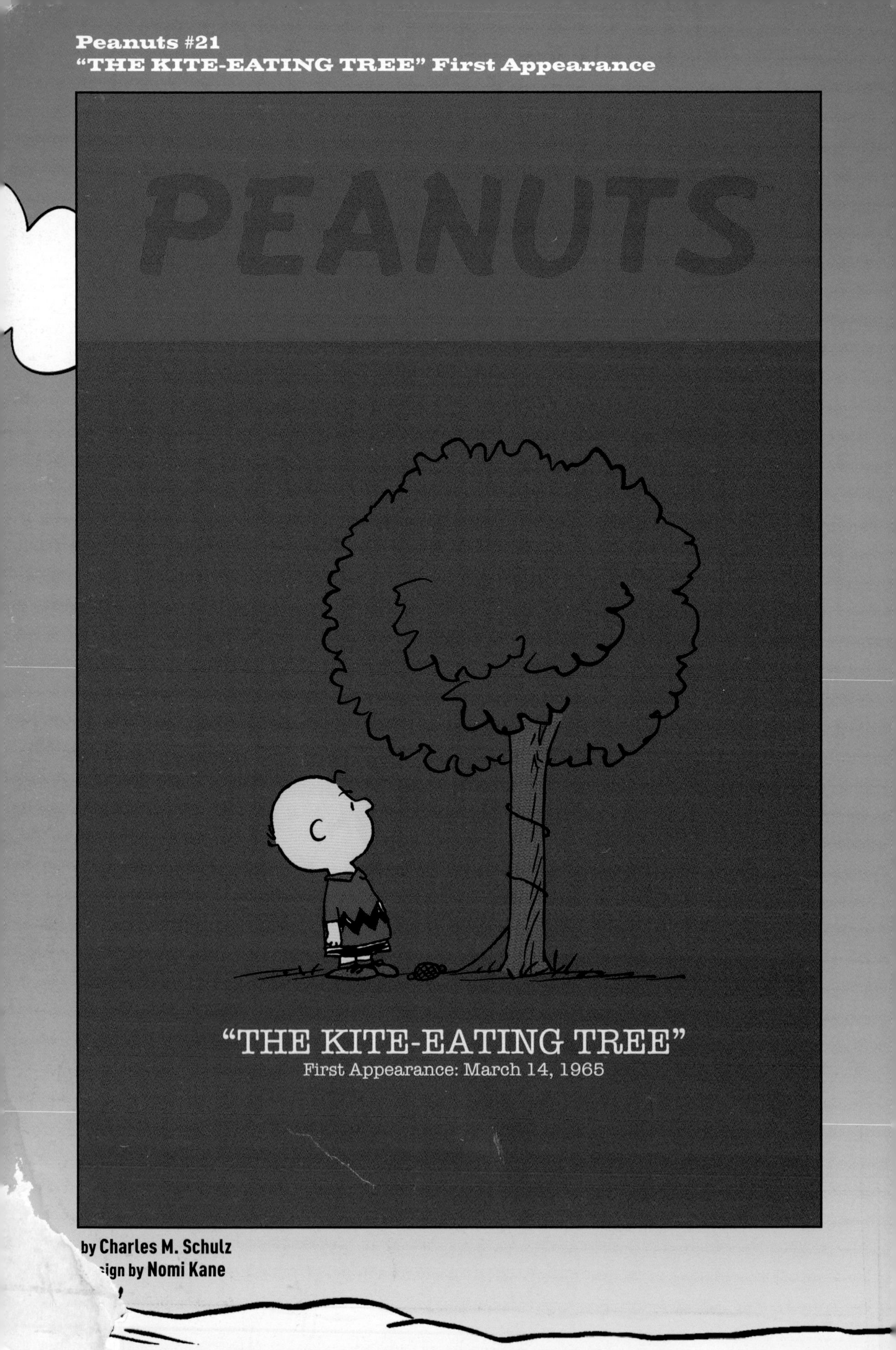
PEANUTS
"THE KITE-EATING TREE"
First Appearance: March 14, 1965

by Charles M. Schulz
...sign by Nomi Kane

PEANUTS
by
SCHULZ
NOW, LOOK, TREE!
THAT'S MY KITE YOU'VE GOT UP THERE, AND I WANT IT BACK!
I PAID SEVENTY-NINE CENTS FOR THAT KITE.. YOU HAVE NO RIGHT TO TAKE IT!
YOU CAN'T GO GRABBING EVERY KITE THAT FLIES BY, YOU KNOW! NOW, GIVE IT BACK, DO YOU HEAR ME?
SIGH
YOU CAN'T ARGUE WITH A KITE-EATING TREE!

"THE KITE-EATING TREE"
First Appearance: March 14, 1965

kaboom!™

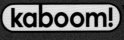

BOOM! STUDIOS EXCLUSIVE #21

Peanuts #22
"THE GREAT PUMPKIN" First Appearance

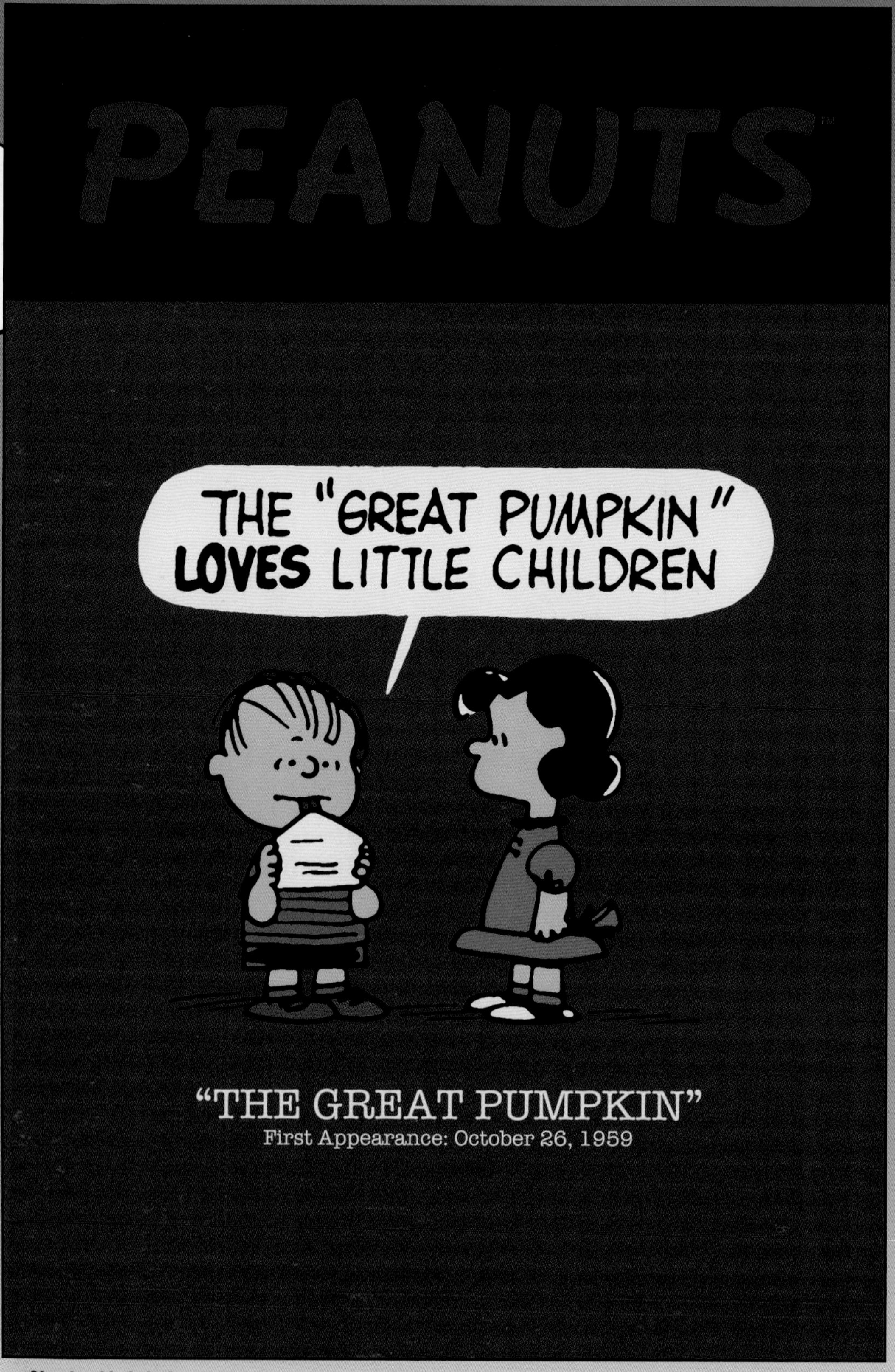
PEANUTS™
THE "GREAT PUMPKIN" LOVES LITTLE CHILDREN
"THE GREAT PUMPKIN"
First Appearance: October 26, 1959

by Charles M. Schulz
Design by Nomi Kane

PEANUTS
10-26
WHAT IN THE WORLD ARE YOU DOING?
DON'T YOU KNOW?
THIS IS THE TIME OF YEAR WHEN WE ALL WRITE TO THE "GREAT PUMPKIN," AND TELL HIM WHAT WE WANT FOR HALLOWEEN
THE "GREAT PUMPKIN" LOVES LITTLE CHILDREN
I CAN SEE HIM NOW RISING UP OUT OF THE PUMPKIN PATCH WITH HIS BIG BAG OF TOYS!

"THE GREAT PUMPKIN"
First Appearance: October 26, 1959

kaboom!™

BOOM! STUDIOS
EXCLUSIVE
#22

Peanuts #23
"SNOOPY'S PERCH" First Appearance

PEANUTS™

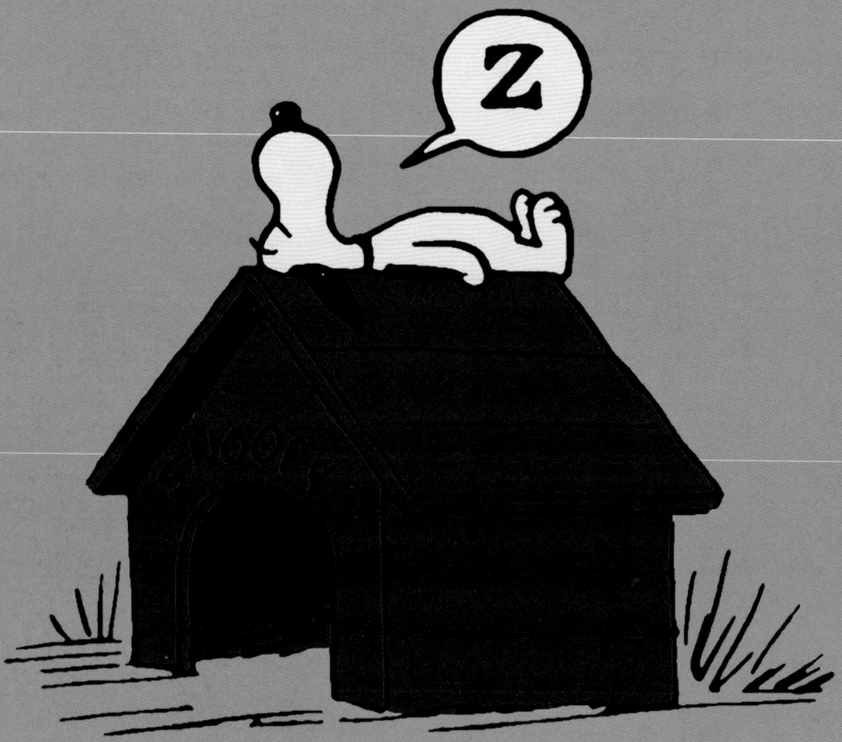
Z

"SNOOPY'S PERCH"
First Appearance: December 12, 1958

by Charles M. Schulz
Design by Nomi Kane

12-12
Z
SNOOPY
?!
SNOOPY
WHAM!
LIFE IS FULL OF RUDE AWAKENINGS..
SCHULZ

"SNOOPY'S PERCH"
First Appearance: December 12, 1958

kaboom!™

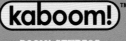

BOOM! STUDIOS
EXCLUSIVE
#23

Peanuts #24
"LUCY'S PSYCHIATRIC BOOTH" First Appearance

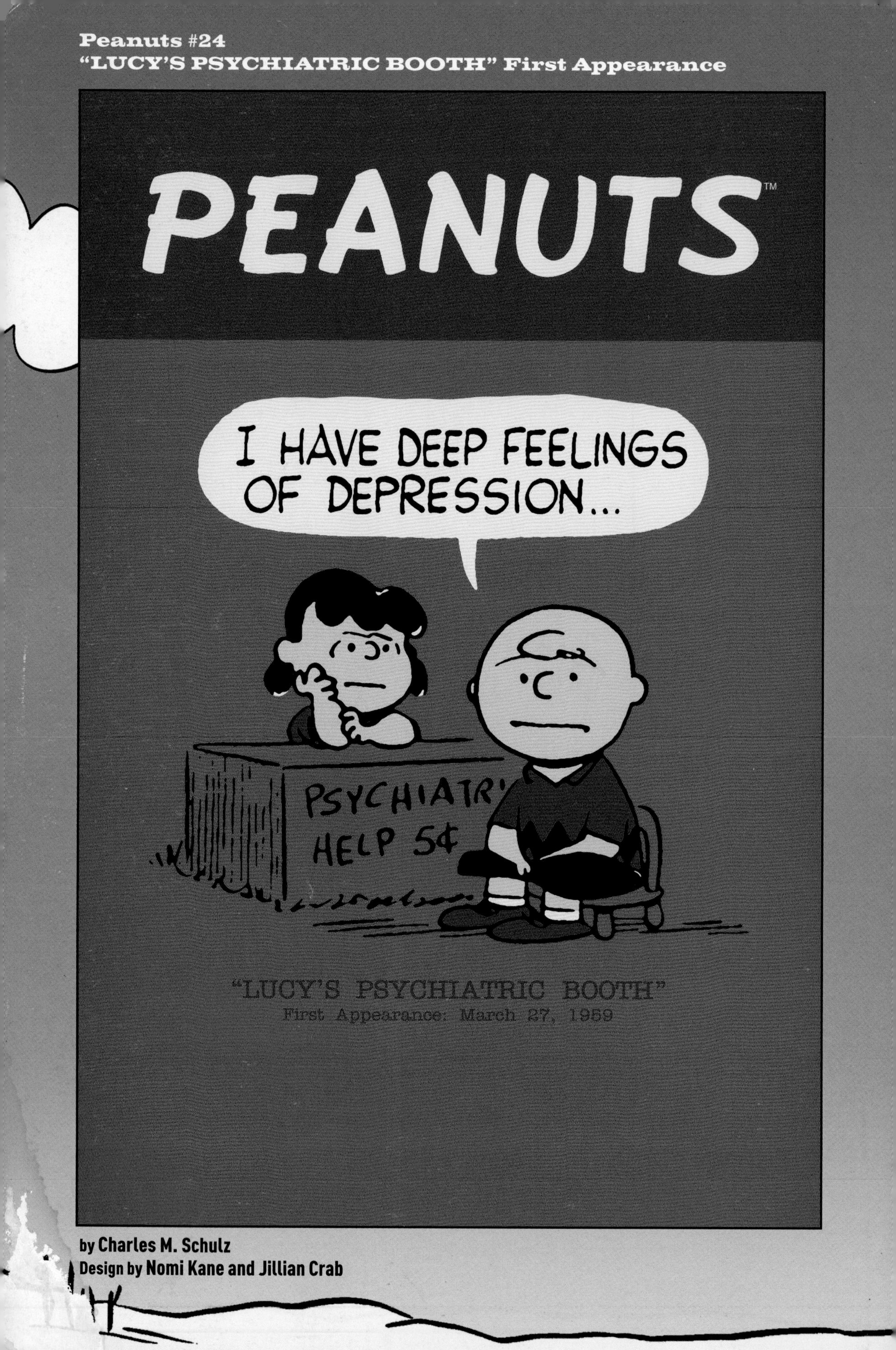
PEANUTS™
I HAVE DEEP FEELINGS OF DEPRESSION...
PSYCHIATRI HELP 5¢

"LUCY'S PSYCHIATRIC BOOTH"
First Appearance: March 27, 1959

by Charles M. Schulz
Design by Nomi Kane and Jillian Crab

PEANUTS
PSYCHIATRIC HELP 5¢
I HAVE DEEP FEELINGS OF DEPRESSION...
WHAT CAN I DO ABOUT THIS?
SNAP OUT OF IT! FIVE CENTS, PLEASE.
SCHULZ

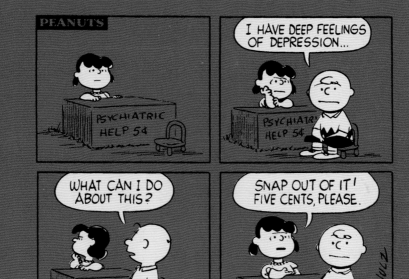

"LUCY'S PSYCHIATRIC BOOTH"
First Appearance: March 27, 1959

kaboom!™

BOOM! STUDIOS
EXCLUSIVE
#24

Charles M. Schulz once described himself as "born to draw comic strips." Born in Minneapolis, at just two days old, an uncle nicknamed him "Sparky" after the horse Spark Plug from the "Barney Google" comic strip, and throughout his youth, he and his father shared a Sunday morning ritual reading the funnies. After serving in the Army during World War II, Schulz's first big break came in 1947 when he sold a cartoon feature called "Li'l Folks" to the St. Paul Pioneer Press. In 1950, Schulz met with United Feature Syndicate, and on October 2 of that year, PEANUTS, named by the syndicate, debuted in seven newspapers. Charles Schulz died in Santa Rosa, California, in February 2000—just hours before his last original strip was to appear in Sunday papers.